THE FRUITFUL VINE

*The third volume in the enthralling Leicester-
shire chronicle*
After nine years in America, Adam has
come home, bringing with him his wife,
Isabelle. His mother's initial surprise turns
to joy as she realises she will be spared
the unsuitable Emily as a daughter-in-
law. Emily copes with Adam's betrayal
by flinging herself into various causes,
including the Chartist Movement, where
she meets radical Irishman Rory Aherne,
who is determined to make her his mistress.
But when Adam comes back into her life
they are both aware that the old attraction
is far from dead ...

For John, with all my love

THE FRUITFUL VINE

by
Audrey Willsher

Magna Large Print Books
Long Preston, North Yorkshire,
England.

British Library Cataloguing in Publication Data.

Willsher, Audrey
  The fruitful vine.

  A catalogue record for this book is
  available from the British Library

  ISBN 0-7505-1429-9

First published in Great Britain by Severn House Publishers
Ltd., 1998

Published in Large Print 1999 by arrangement with Severn
House Publishers Ltd.

Magna Large Print is an imprint of
Library Magna Books Ltd.
Printed and bound in Great Britain by
T.J. International Ltd., Cornwall, PL28 8RW.

Chapter One

'A letter, from Adam,' said Clare, scrutinising the handwriting and the American stamp before she handed the envelope to her aunt.

'Thank you, dear.' News from her son, always brightened Matilda's day and she quickly broke the seal.

'Is something wrong, Aunt Tilda?' asked Clare in concern, for as her aunt read down the page a variety of emotions flitted across her face and there was a noticeable tremor in her fingers.

'Just the opposite, but I think I'll sit down just the same, my legs feel all peculiar,' answered Matilda, and sank down onto the sofa.

'But what, tell me?'

Matilda pressed the letter to her breast and her face was iridescent with happiness. 'He's coming home! After nine years my son is at last coming back to me.'

'I can't believe it! When?' In a fever of excitement, Clare threw herself down next to her aunt and, peering over her shoulder, tried to read the letter. Adam's decision to go to America and the painful circumstances that had brought about his departure, had left his mother mourning him as if her son were dead. And even though she had Christopher, because there had always been a closeness between her and Adam that went beyond kinship, the separation had been hardly less painful for Clare.

'Here, read it to me, just to make sure I'm not imagining it all.' Struggling with her emotions, Matilda pushed the letter into Clare's hand and dabbed her eyes with a small lace handkerchief.

'"*The ship docks in Liverpool on September fifth*",' Clare read. '"*I shall travel by train to Leicester, so expect me about two days after that, and be prepared for a surprise*".'

Matilda stood up and flicked over the leaves of the calendar. 'Why, that's only a week away.' Becoming practical again, she tapped her index finger against her lips and thought hard for a moment. 'I must talk to the servants, have his room made ready, see that Mrs White prepares all his favourite dishes. And we'll have a grand party, invite the whole county, kill the fatted calf.' She hugged her niece. 'Oh, isn't it wonderful, Clare? To tell the truth, he's been away so long, in my darkest moments I've often wondered if I'd ever see my son again.'

'I always knew he'd come back. He loves

6

this place too much, and you, and don't forget there is Emily.'

'Ah yes, Emily.' Matilda sighed. 'She hasn't found herself another young man, then?' she asked without much hope.

'Of course not. She promised to wait for Adam, you know that.'

'She promised to wait for two or three years, not nine. She's a young woman and life is passing her by. I wouldn't have blamed her if she'd looked elsewhere.'

'Emily is very loyal.'

More's the pity, Matilda brooded. It would have solved so many problems if the girl had married before Adam returned. That way she'd be spared the socially demeaning experience of having her ex-maid's child as a daughter-in-law.

'I wonder what Adam's surprise is,' Clare mused. 'Perhaps he's lost all his hair, put on ten pounds and is preparing us for the worst,' she giggled.

'I should imagine that's most unlikely, my dear,' Matilda answered a trifle coolly.

'Of course it is, I was only joking. Adam will still be handsome when he's eighty. But I'd better be getting back. It's nearly dinnertime, the children will be coming out of school, and I'm dying to tell Christopher the news, although how I'm going to concentrate on teaching this afternoon, I don't know.'

7

Walking down to the village a short while later, Clare wondered if Adam would notice the many changes in Leicester. He was coming by train for a start, to a modern new railway station that hadn't been built when he left. The old lathe and plaster buildings were giving way to brick, omnibuses conveyed people to and from the station and the town was well served with hackney carriages and flys. In fact, local dignitaries, ignoring the dire poverty, were inclined to boast that Leicester was fast becoming as modern as London. Halby, on the other hand, remained much the same, except that the school had expanded into the cottage next door and was full of other people's children, but sadly not their own.

Although this was a great sorrow to her and Christopher, Clare tried hard not to let their childless state get her down, reasoning with herself that although they hadn't yet been blessed, she and Christopher were both still young and there was heaps of time for babies. Meanwhile there was Freddie, the sad, slow-witted little boy she'd come to the conclusion was unteachable in her early days at the school.

What neither she nor Christopher had known at the time was that Freddie's mother, a widow, was slowly dying and it was her young son who looked after her, carefully tending to all her needs; cooking, washing her and seeing she was comfortable before he left for school each day. Then she died and the boy's dumb grief tore at Clare's heart. Then she discovered there wasn't even money enough for a coffin. Taking charge, she paid the local carpenter to make one, and began making enquiries around the village, trying to find out if there were any relatives who might be prepared to give Freddie a home. But his mother, it seemed, had come from Yorkshire and never spoke of any family. The only definite information about his father was that he was dead.

But Freddie was another mouth to feed and it soon became apparent that, no matter how many hints Clare dropped, no hard stretched villager was going to take him in. Eventually Clare saw that there was only one other alternative. 'A seven-year-old boy can't stay on in the cottage on his own, and my conscience wouldn't allow him to go to the workhouse,' she said to Christopher one evening as he sat preparing the next day's school work.

'Well, I don't know what the alternative is,' Christopher answered absent-mindedly.

Clare went and removed the pen from his hand, sat down on his lap and kissed him on the forehead. 'I do. We could have him here, there's plenty of room.'

'Dearest, he's a rough country child, barely house-trained,' Christopher protested.

'We can give it a try. What's the harm in showing some kindness to him? He's had little enough of it.'

Christopher thought of his own lonely childhood. 'You're quite right, darling, what is the harm?' And so Freddie came to live with them at Thatchers Mount, which Clare had inherited when her grandparents died.

The early days hadn't been without their problems, but he was a gentle, compassionate boy who loved animals and nature, hated the cruel snares put down by farmers—injured birds and small animals were regularly carried home and carefully nursed back to health. Many didn't survive, of course, then Freddie would weep buckets over the small corpses. A shady corner in one of the fields was reserved as a burial ground, each grave marked with a tiny cross. He was so sensitive to the suffering of others, Clare sometimes worried about how he would fare in the adult, uncaring outside world.

As she reached the Green, Christopher and Freddie came out of one of the cottages that housed the school. Freddie was nearly sixteen now, a tall, gangly boy with large feet and hands and an awkward manner. Once he'd come to live with them they'd quickly realised he wasn't a dullard after all, just a child suffering from exhaustion. After some extra tuition from Christopher, he caught up with the other children and it quickly became apparent that he had a natural aptitude for figures, in fact, was something of a mathematical genius. Now Christopher had his hopes set on Oxford for him.

Clare stopped and waited for them. They were both smiling at her as they approached and in that split second, aware of their love for her, Clare knew she was extremely fortunate, in spite of having no children of her own.

'How are my two boys?' she asked, kissing them both on the cheek then, linking arms, they walked back up Blackthorn Lane together.

'Come on, what's the gossip?' asked Christopher, who knew from his wife's expression that she was bursting to tell him something.

'You'll never guess, Adam's coming home.'

Christopher stopped and stared at his wife. 'Good Lord! Frankly I never thought we'd see that young man back in this country.'

'Who's Adam?' asked Freddie.

'My cousin.'

'Oh,' answered Freddie, without much interest then, seeing his pet dog, Jelly, small, spherical and hairy, bouncing down the lane to meet them, he ran on, calling, 'Here boy, here.' Freddie paused, held out his arms and with one bound Jelly was in them covering the boy in lavish doggy kisses.

'Why are you so surprised Adam's coming home?' Clare asked her husband, slightly put out that he'd never once confided his doubts to her.

'Don't get me wrong, I'll be as delighted as anyone to see him again, but he has been gone rather a long time and the New World has many opportunities—and temptations.'

'But he wouldn't desert us permanently, not his family. And there's Emily. They have an understanding.'

'He can't be held to that after all this time.'

'Adam nearly ruined Emily's reputation, remember?'

'Indeed I do.'

'Well, take my word for it, Adam will honour his pledge.'

Christopher stroked his wife's hand placatingly for he could see she was becoming agitated. 'I'm sure he will, my dear.'

'And I shall ask you to drive me into Leicester to see Emily on Saturday. I know she will have heard from Adam and be as excited as we are.'

'More factories, more smoke,' Clare fretted as she and Christopher drove into Leicester a day or two later. The speed of change alarmed her and it seemed to have accelerated since young Queen Victoria came on the throne.

'And more slum dwellings and more beggars, too, by the look of it,' answered Christopher, as ragged urchins ran along beside the trap with outstretched hands. Clare tossed them some coppers and while the children scrambled to pick up the coins, Christopher turned the horse into High Cross Street and stopped outside the bookshop.

'Now,' said Christopher, helping his wife down, 'if you want to speak to Emily on your own I can easily make myself scarce for an hour.'

'No, it's all right. We need some new readers anyway. You can order some while you're waiting.' Clare had seen little of Emily of late and after Adam's departure she'd only once visited Trent Hall with her parents. This had proved such an uncomfortable experience for everyone, the invitation had never been repeated.

13

Her own life was busy with the school occupying most of her time and Clare realised with a jolt of guilt that it was nearly two years since she'd last seen any member of the Fairfax family. But news trickled through. Villagers had seen Emily at Chartist meetings with her father. In fact, it was said that she'd become a she-Chartist, which was another black mark against her in Matilda's book, and when it originally came to her aunt's ears, her comments had been scathing: 'What can you expect, with a father who's nothing more than a rabble-rousing rick burner?' she'd spat out. Adam wouldn't approve of any wife of his traipsing around the country waving banners and having pitched battles with the police, either. He'd expect her to be in her rightful place at home bringing up his children, Clare decided, as she pushed open the shop door.

With its slightly musty smell of old books, in a constantly changing world, the shop remained much as it had always done. However, the two people behind the counter had changed. Rachel was still handsome, but she was plumper and her once black hair was now liberally streaked with grey, while Jed's had definitely thinned. There were no recriminations, though, and they both embraced her with genuine affection, while Jed shook

14

Christopher's hand as if he were pumping water.

'Where's Emily?' asked Clare, looking about her.

Jed laughed tolerantly. 'Upstairs preparing a speech. She and me are going to Manchester next week to a big Chartist gathering.'

Rachel rolled her eyes to heaven and sighed. 'You can see what I have to put up with. A chip off the old block, I'm afraid.'

'In other words our lass is concerned about the world and the many inequalities in it, Clare.' Jed answered tersely.

'I'm sure she is, Jed.' Not anxious to start a domestic dispute, Clare gave him a placatory smile then asked, 'Can I go up and see her?'

'Of course.'

'And while I'm gone, Christopher wants to order some books for school, don't you, dear?'

Clare exchanged a smile with her husband then climbed the stairs to the rooms above the shop. She reached the top, saw the door was ajar so after a quick tap she poked her head round it and called, 'It's me, can I come in?'

Emily, who was surrounded by pamphlets and newspaper cuttings, and scribbling away industriously, paused and looked up.

15

'My, you're a stranger.'

It was a definite rebuke. Neither did Emily rise to embrace Clare as, being kin, she would have expected. 'Are you busy? Shall I go?' Clare went to back out of the door.

Relenting, Emily patted a chair. 'Of course not, come and sit down. I'll make us some tea.' She rose to put the kettle on the fire and laid out cups and saucers. 'Is the school going well?'

'By leaps and bounds, and so are the children.' Clare leaned forward in her chair. 'Emily, have you heard from Adam?'

Emily poured milk into the cups with intense concentration. 'Not for over a year. Even before that the letters had become pretty spasmodic. But I understand Adam leads a different life now, and nine years is a long time.'

'So you don't know then?' Clare wriggled excitedly.

'Know what?'

'That he's coming home.'

Apparently unaffected by this news, Emily went on pouring milk, although Clare noticed that most of it now slopped into the saucers. She was also aware of a glint of gold at Emily's neck as she leaned forward, and realised it was the locket Adam had given to her before he left.

'Well, say something.'

16

'What, for instance?'

'Oh, come on, Emily, you must be pleased.'

'Of course I am, for you and your aunt.' Emily spooned tea from the caddy into the teapot, filled it with boiling water, stirred it, then asked casually, 'When are you expecting him?'

'In about a week. There's to be a grand celebration. You will come, won't you?'

'I doubt if I'd be made very welcome by your aunt.'

'You and Adam have an understanding, you have every right to be there.'

'Not any longer. I'd feel like the spectre at the feast. Anyway, I shall probably be in Manchester with Papa.'

'You won't be in Manchester forever. Tell me when you are back and I'll bring Adam here.'

Emily's head came up and she spoke in a clear, unemotional voice. 'I'm sorry, Clare, but there really isn't much point. You see, Adam means absolutely nothing to me now.'

In that case, why are you wearing his locket? Clare almost blurted out, but she knew it would be an intrusion on Emily's feelings so, curbing her tongue, she took the cup Emily handed her and silently sipped her tea.

Chapter Two

Emily wasn't exactly lying when she said she no longer loved Adam, but then neither was she telling the truth. In fact, the only thing she was certain of was her confusion. After Clare left, she paced the room, sat down, wrote some notes, read them through then tossed them aside in disgust. Twisting the locket at her throat with restless fingers, Emily finally opened it, studied Adam's likeness, then moved to the looking glass over the fireplace. 'Which of us will have changed the most?' she asked her reflection, 'Me or Adam?' She had a centre parting now, with ringlets bunched on either side and the hair at the back drawn up from the nape of her neck into a chignon. It was a style similar to the young queen's and had been copied slavishly by most Leicester girls after their sovereign's visit to the town.

Emily wasn't in the least vain, but today she leaned forward and paid close attention to her features, acknowledging her likeness to her mother. But it was her father's character she'd inherited, she knew that, the good bits along with the bad; his honesty, his intransigence, as well as his desire to change the world. She also had his strong sense of loyalty and this extended to Adam, even if he no longer deserved it.

He'd been her sun, her moon, her stars but no love could be sustained at such youthful intensity and these days she often had to struggle to remember what it was about Adam that had made her cast caution to the winds, run away with him and put her good name in jeopardy.

When Adam first arrived in America, obviously homesick and missing her, his letters were full passionate avowals of undying love, of how he couldn't wait to return to England, and how, as soon as he did, he would make her his wife.

She'd marked off the days, then the years: two, three, four with diminishing hope as the tone of his letters changed. First came the excuses; how he needed to stay on in America a bit longer to get some money together. Then the letters became less frequent, and less loving, until finally they ceased altogether.

Wisely, neither of her parents made any comment, but Emily could sense their relief. For many reasons, a marital union between the two families was the last thing either of them wanted.

So Emily hid her pain as best she

could, decided men weren't worth the heartache, and coldly rejected any other young man's advances. Gradually her bruised soul healed, she came to terms with being discarded and funnelled her energy into Chartism. Her interest had developed slowly, for in the past she'd sided with her mother over her father's politics, considering that the time he gave to them was at the expense of his family. Until that night when, for the first time in her life, she'd seen her father weeping openly after troops in Newport had turned their muskets on a crowd of Chartists, slaughtering twenty-two. The fire of radicalism entered Emily's soul that day. She had found a new purpose in life. No longer did she feel like the faithful Penelope, waiting for Odysseus to return.

And having come to assume Adam had settled permanently in America, Clare's news that he was on his way home had shaken her. How should she react if they came face to face? What would they say to each other? Emily wondered. Perhaps there would be nothing left but a slight embarrassment. On the other hand, there might be enough left of their once intense love for it to spark into life again. A small charge of hope shot through Emily, but then common sense, like a dash of cold water in the face, told her she was too old for such girlish dreams.

Emily sighed. What she needed right now was a willing ear, not her mother or father, but someone who'd taken enormous risks for her and Adam; someone who'd shared her early happiness and comforted her later in her misery.

Her mind made up, Emily took a light shawl and her bonnet from a peg behind the door and hurried down the stairs.

'Where are you off to then at this time of day?' asked her mother.

'I won't be long. I'm just popping out to see Lily.'

'Can't it wait? You know how busy we get in the afternoon and your father's going out as well.'

'I'll be back within the hour, Mama, I promise.' Emily was almost out the door now.

Rachel clicked her tongue reprovingly against the roof of her mouth but said no more and Emily escaped with relief. As she cut through the back streets it occurred to her that Clare couldn't have mentioned Adam's return to her parents and she wondered why.

Rather than plough through the bustle of the main thoroughfare, Emily took the pleasanter route up New Walk, recalling how every time her parents came this way her mother would say in wistful tones, 'Oh,

21

Jed I'd love one of these new houses, and imagine having a garden!'

Without fail her father would reply, 'Just wait until my ship comes in and I will buy you one, my dear'. Then, knowing they were indulging in pipe dreams, they would both laugh and kiss, and Emily would think to herself: *I want a marriage like theirs, or nothing.*

Remembering her promise not to be long, Emily walked at a brisk pace down Wellington Street and out on to London Road. From here it was a short walk to Lily's house, now not far from the new railway station in Campbell Street. Lily complained bitterly about this blot on her landscape, claiming that the locomotives spouting out their soot and noise were spoiling the children's health and her tranquillity. For some time she'd been badgering Septimus to move out to Stoneygate, a desirable residential area where some very large houses were being erected. And knowing Lily, she would probably get her way for Septimus, who liked a quiet life, was inclined to give in to most of his wife's demands.

Emily reached the house in Orchard Street, pulled the bell and Bertha, wide of girth and smile, opened the door. 'Good afternoon, Miss. Come through, Madam is in the garden wi' the little 'uns.'

As well as Peter, Lily now had a five-year-old daughter called Helen. Coincidently, Helen had been born just nine months after a young man had been employed by Septimus to wallpaper the parlour.

While Peter bore a strong resemblance to the ex-gardener, it had been his sister's misfortune to inherit the Brewin looks and they were not a family noted for their physical beauty.

His thoughts elsewhere, Peter stood pushing his sister backwards and forwards on the garden swing.

'Higher, Peter, higher,' the small girl demanded.

'That is quite high enough, young lady,' answered Lily, who was sitting under a tree trying to read a novel and at the same time keeping an eye on her children. 'If you were to fall, you could hurt yourself.'

Helen stuck out her bottom lip obstinately and hauled herself upright on the swing.

'Down, this minute!' Lily ordered. Seeing Emily approach she forgot her disobedient daughter and laid her book aside. 'Adult company. What a blessing! Why did no one warn me how trying small children could be?' Lily laughed as she spoke, just to make sure Emily didn't take her complaint too seriously.

'But what brought you here at this time of ...?' She didn't finish, and they both turned as a wail of pain rent the air. Helen lay sprawled on the ground, plainly not hurt, but pounding the grass in fury with her small fists.

Peter was a dear, but in Emily's opinion Helen was spoilt and wilful, given to tantrums and, hard as she tried, she couldn't take to the child.

Distracted, Lily rushed and scooped her daughter up in her arms. 'What did Mama tell you?' Lily gently scolded, hugging her shrieking daughter close to her breast.

'Perhaps this isn't a good time,' Emily suggested, when Helen showed no sign of lowering the level of her screams.

Immediately the crying stopped and, her small face red and angry, Helen glowered at Emily. 'Yeth, go away,' she lisped.

'Darling!' Lily reprimanded her, 'You mustn't talk to grown-ups like that.'

'Will, tho there!' Helen wriggled out of her mother's arms and ran to where Peter was sitting. There, she thrust her thumb into her mouth and glared at her mother and Emily from a safe distance.

'Phew.' Lily collapsed onto the circular tree seat Pierre had made for her. 'I do love my daughter, but she is a handful at times.'

Watching all this, Emily began to

wonder if motherhood was all it was made out to be. She even dared to wonder if it was necessary for a woman to marry.

'Well, to what do I owe the pleasure of your company at this time of day?' asked Lily.

'Something pretty important.'

Lily, who loved a gossip, patted the seat beside her. 'Sounds interesting, come and tell me all about it. Bertha,' she called to the maid, 'bring some tea out for Miss Emily and myself and lemonade for the children.'

Emily waited while Bertha laid cups and saucers out on a small wicker table and Lily poured the tea.

'Well?' Lily asked, handing her a cup.

Delaying the moment, Emily bit through a piece of shortbread and took a sip of tea. Then, turning, she looked straight at Lily so that she could enjoy her friend's reaction. 'Adam's coming home from America.'

'Good heavens!' Lily slammed her cup down so violently the tea shot into the saucer.

'I thought you'd be surprised.'

'I certainly am.' Lily had never said so to her friend, but privately she had come to believe that Adam, would never set foot on English soil again. 'But when?'

'Sometime next week.'

'As soon as that? I can't believe it.' Lily studied Emily's face. 'You don't seemed very excited.'

'To tell the truth, I don't know what I feel. It still hasn't sunk in really.'

'You'll be seeing him, of course.'

Emily shrugged. 'That will be up to Adam.'

'It was an exciting time, wasn't it, when you and Adam used to meet here?'

Emily nodded.

'Then the elopement. How I envied you. It was all so romantic.' Lily gave a wistful sigh.

'It sometimes feels as if it wasn't me, but another girl who took all those risks.'

'Well, Adam can't have forgotten that he has certain obligations towards you. And do you know what I think?'

'Go on, tell me.'

Lily smiled at Emily. 'It's my belief that Adam has finally come to his senses, remembered the sacrifices you made, and has decided to come home and marry you at last.'

Chapter Three

'I wish we'd gone to the station to meet Adam,' said Matilda for what Clare calculated must have been the twentieth time that day.

'But we don't know what time he's leaving Liverpool, Mrs Bennett, and we might have waited there for hours,' Christopher pointed out. 'And remember, he has to change trains at Birmingham and Rugby, then wait for connections. I can't see him arriving before early evening.'

Matilda stared at the small carriage clock over the fireplace then, convinced the hands had stuck at two, she went over and shook it, and under this onslaught it chimed disapprovingly. From there she moved to the window, craning her neck and willing horses to pound up the drive, a carriage slide to a halt with gravel spitting from under its wheels, and her son jump out. But the drive remained empty. There were no rattling harnesses, no steaming horses. 'I can't bear this waiting,' Matilda muttered fretfully, 'I'm going to see Cook.'

Clare, suspecting there might be an

exchange of views if Mrs White received one more instruction that day, put out an arm to delay her. 'Aunt Tilda, why don't we go out for a walk? Perhaps down to the stables to see Jane. It will make the time pass more quickly.'

Matilda paused, thinking about it. 'But imagine how hurt Adam will feel if he turns up and finds none of his family here to welcome him after all his years away.'

'I promise you, he won't,' said Christopher, 'and even if he does, one of the servants can soon run down and tell us.'

Matilda was hovering, still undecided. 'I suppose time does hang heavy while you're waiting.' Finally making a decision, she added, 'You two walk on, I'll get my cloak and catch you up.'

Jane was in the yard with her son when they arrived at the stables, examining the shoe on a horse. Reuben, her husband, had left some years ago, disappearing just as mysteriously as he'd arrived. Matilda had been surprised at Jane's almost unstoppable grief, at her oft-repeated avowal that she'd truly loved her husband and he her. Although she'd commiserated with her friend, in Matilda's opinion his departure was a blessing. Reuben had had no idea how to conduct himself in company and social occasions had been

28

an embarrassment. Gradually, as with all things, Jane's grief had abated and now she never mentioned her husband. But then, thought Matilda, she only had to look at Gabriel to be reminded of him, for her son had inherited his father's fairground looks, the high cheekbones and black eyes. And like his father, Gabriel never spoke unless absolutely obliged to. With horses, though, he was quite the opposite and Matilda had watched in wonder as he calmed nervous fillies with soft, loving words. It went without saying that he could ride like a dream and she often saw him riding bareback over the fields, boy and horse fused like a centaur. Give him another six years and he'll be wreaking havoc amongst the village maidens, thought Matilda, as, at his mother's command, he greeted her politely then sloped off. Gabriel attended the village school but Matilda knew from Christopher that he was restless and inattentive. In the optimistic hope that it might turn him into a young gentleman, Jane was planning to send him away to Rugby. Gabriel, unusually voluble on the subject, protested that he would hate it there, but Jane refused to listen. She saw the barely reined-in wildness inherited from his father and wanted it tamed.

When Jane saw the party arrive in the yard, she eased herself upright, called,

'Hello there, prodigal son not back yet?' then tucked strands of her greying frizzy hair back into a coil at the nape of her neck. Although she refused to acknowledge it, after too many falls on the hunting field, Jane's bones had stiffened and her rheumaticky joints often made it difficult to mount a horse.

'No, and the waiting is driving me mad.'

'We keep trying to explain to Aunt Tilda that it will probably be quite late before Adam arrives,' said Clare, 'so we've brought her down here to take her mind off things.'

'Is everything ready for the party? It's ages since anything exciting happened in this village, it's being talked about as quite an event.'

'It's nothing terribly grand, but everyone I've invited has accepted, including Harry's daughter, Olivia and her husband, Max.' Matilda was hopeful that Olivia would soon return the invitation for she was now Lady Collins and mistress of Lindfield Hall, a magnificent place in Derbyshire. Olivia's weekend parties were much talked about and invitations keenly sought. It would be the ideal place for Adam to meet suitable young women now that, thank heaven, the unfortunate affair with the Fairfax girl appeared to have died a natural death. Although it had broken her heart to see Adam go off to America like that, it seemed to have been for the best in the end. Theirs would have been a most unsuitable match, with Adam throwing himself away on a girl of little quality.

'You are coming, aren't you, Jane?'

'Now be honest, do you really want me there, Matilda?'

'Of course I do. You've known Adam all his life.'

'What ti—'

'Missus, Missus ...' Dick, a young gardener, came stumbling into the yard. ''E's back! Mr Adam is back!' he shouted ecstatically.

'Oh, no!' Matilda pressed her hand to her heart. 'What did I tell you?' She turned accusingly to Clare and Christopher. 'He's come home to an empty house, what will he think?' Bundling her skirts and petticoats up in front of her, Matilda hurried out of the yard, and for someone not in the first flush of youth, she moved with remarkable speed. When a carriage passed them on its way back to Leicester, Matilda almost galloped up the drive. A mountain of luggage was piled in front of the house, and two servants were struggling up the steps with a large trunk.

Pushing past them, Matilda ran into the

house calling, 'Adam! Adam!'

'Hello, Mother.' Adam came out into the hall and Matilda ran to her son, flung herself against him and burst into tears. 'Oh, my dear boy,' she sobbed. 'It's wonderful to see you.'

'With all these tears it doesn't sound like it,' said Adam with a laugh, patting his mother's back a trifle awkwardly.

Matilda stood away from Adam and blew her nose. 'I'm sorry, dear, if I embarrass you. But you must make allowances for a mother who hasn't seen her only son for nine years.'

Clare, not wanting to intrude, had hung back while mother and son were reunited, but Matilda now beckoned her forward. 'Come and say hello to your cousin, dear.'

Feeling a little shy, Clare stepped forward and Adam bent and kissed her affectionately. 'Hello, cousin,' he said, ruffling her hair in a brotherly way.

'Welcome home, Adam.' Christopher, who was standing behind Clare, shook Adam's hand while servants who had appeared from various parts of the house stood in a row smiling. Adam went over, greeting those he knew by name, then asking the younger girls theirs. They replied in turn with a curtsy and a blush, for the master was an exceedingly handsome man.

'Oh, it's lovely to be home.' Arms flung wide, Adam spun round in the hall, and everyone laughed indulgently.

'I often wondered if you were so dazzled by the New World that I'd lost you for ever.' Now, with her son standing close beside her, Matilda dared to voice her darkest fears.

'I guess I was delayed a little by its excitements and opportunities, but it has always been my intention to return home. Halby is where my roots are, Mother.'

'Even if you now sound more like a Yankee, and dress like one,' laughed Matilda, noticing that his accent and mode of dress were no longer that of an English country gentleman.

'Hush, don't use the word "Yankee",' Adam replied, and taking her arm, drew her through to the drawing room, where Matilda was taken aback to find a strange young woman rising from a chair. Wondering what she could possibly be doing in her house, Matilda turned to Adam for an explanation.

'Mother, I'd like you to meet Isabelle, my wife.'

It was like being struck by a cannon-ball. Stunned, Matilda blinked, rocked back on her heels, regained some of her self-possession and gasped, 'Your ... *wife?*'

Clare and Christopher, equally flabbergasted, stared at the girl as she glided forward as if on wheels. Her hand was outstretched in greeting and she smiled, showing very becoming dimples. 'Ah've heard so much about y'all from Adam, Mrs Bennett, why ah feel ah know you already.'

The girl, who spoke with an unfamiliar accent, had light brown hair and slender bones, but the most striking thing about her was her eyes, which were a strange, almost transparent grey. Aware of the girl's cool hand in hers, Matilda recovered sufficiently to take stock of the situation. There was no escaping it, she had been totally unprepared for this 'surprise' of Adam's. Nonetheless, her son had made his choice, and he now had a wife, which put the lid firmly on any relationship starting up again with that Fairfax girl. Well, it's an ill wind ... thought Matilda, and smiled at Isabelle. 'Welcome to England, my dear and Trent Hall, I hope you'll be very happy amongst us,' she said, then leaning forward, Matilda embraced her new daughter-in-law with genuine warmth.

After this there had been some quick reorganising to do. Matilda ordered a servant to move her personal belongings and clothes from her bedroom into a

34

smaller one so that Adam and his wife could have hers. A young kitchen maid called Hattie Bonner suddenly found herself promoted to Isabelle's personal maid and a short while later she was unpacking the large trunks as they were brought up to the bedroom.

However, that evening Adam came down to dinner on his own. 'Isabelle sends her apologies, Mother. It has been a long tiring day and the excitement has given her a headache, so she has gone to bed.'

'I understand, darling. Shall I have something sent up on a tray?'

'Don't worry, she eats very little and she's probably already asleep.'

'It will be nice just the two of us, and there's so much news to catch up on. And you can tell me all about Isabelle. I must say she's delightful,' *particularly compared with Emily,* was Matilda's silent addendum, as she took her son's arm and drew him into the dining room.

Although Adam drank more than his fair share of wine, Matilda noticed that he pushed his food around his plate. 'Isn't the beef to your liking, dear?' she asked, anxious that everything should be just right. 'Shall I get you something else from the kitchen?' Matilda half rose from her chair.

'No, no, this is fine. Delicious, in fact.

I'm like Isabelle, tired, that's all. A good night's sleep and I'll be fit as a fiddle tomorrow.' To reassure his mother, Adam straightened and smiled. 'I want to ride round the estate, see everything. Meet the tenants.'

Matilda covered Adam's hand with hers, gazed at him tenderly and thought, he's almost too handsome for his own good. When he'd left England, his had been a boy's face, beautiful in its way but lacking in maturity. The years had taken care of that though, toughened his features and hardened his body, and it became him. 'You won't want to talk, then? I'm so dying to hear how you met Isabelle and where her family are from. You dark horse,' she joked, 'never mentioning her in your letters.'

Adam stood up. 'I'll have a brandy and coffee with you in the drawing room, tell you all you want to know and try not to fall asleep.'

Although the weather hardly warranted the fire in the drawing room, Adam collapsed into a chair and stretched his legs towards it. 'My, it's good to be back.'

'You are definitely planning to stay? You won't get itchy feet and want to wander off to somewhere exotic again?' Matilda waited tensely for his answer.

'I can't pretend I didn't enjoy my years in America, it broadened my outlook on life. I learnt a great deal about business and I made myself some money, but there is only one place I'd settle and that is here, in Halby.'

'Then as soon as it can be arranged, I think you should take over the running of the estate. Managing it on my own for all these years has been hard work, but it is in good order and there are no debts. I haven't the energy I once had so I shall be glad to hand over the responsibilities to you, which has always been my intention. Then I shall have a small house built for myself, and leave you and Isabelle to fill this one with children. It will give me a great deal of pleasure to sit back and watch the next generation grow.'

'Well, one thing at a time, Mother,' Adam laughed. 'We both need time to settle in.'

'You were going to tell me how you met, and about her family.'

Adam stirred his coffee and took a sip. 'She has no family. Her father was a wastrel, who gambled away his plantation and broke her mother's heart. They are both dead and she has no brothers or sisters.' This was what Isabelle had told him anyway, although he was beginning to suspect that she had tampered with the truth a little.

'I must say she's charming; I took to her instantly.' She was about to add, *and I bet you're thanking me now that you didn't tie yourself to that Emily Fairfax,* then decided her son might not welcome such a blunt opinion.

'I'm glad she's to your liking, Mother,' answered Adam, also thinking of Emily and imagining her reaction to his gross betrayal with a sick heart.

'Don't you think she'll pine for home, though?' Matilda asked. 'After all, she's in a new country, with different customs and it's bound to feel strange for a while.'

'No, I doubt if Isabelle has any reason for wanting to return to America,' answered Adam. He'd decided to let his mother assume that they'd met in the normal way, at a ball or through friends, whereas it had, in fact, been in rather strange circumstances in New Orleans.

Although he loved the rough vigour of America, Adam had come to detest slavery and when his friend, James McBride—with whom he'd caroused many a night away—married, he'd felt a sudden homesickness. With a fat roll of bank notes in his pocket, Adam made a detour to New Orleans, looking for a final fling and a woman. After a night in a whorehouse in the arms of a honey-toned girl, he'd staggered out the following morning with a hangover and post-coital guilt. He'd found a park bench where he sat nursing a sore head and a deep sense of shame, and forcing himself to remember his promises to Emily, all now broken.

His thoughts were so focused on Emily, and a need to return and be forgiven by her, that Adam was unaware of the shadow of the young woman falling across his path until she paused and gave a small moan. Hardly awake himself, he'd watched her press her hand to her forehead, then crumple at his feet in a dead faint.

Adam blinked, stared at the unconscious girl then, feeling ineffectual, he knelt, took her hand and rubbed it between his. To his relief her eyelids began to flutter. He eased her to a sitting position then, when she was fully conscious, he helped her onto the bench.

As they sat there she had haltingly told him of the circumstances which had brought her there. Her name was Isabelle Dubois and until recently, she'd been governess in a wealthy family to four children whom, she emphasised, she'd loved dearly. However her employer's persistent overtures had culminated one night in him coming to her bedroom and trying to force himself upon her. With no one to protect her, Isabelle had been forced to flee to save her good name. Soon what little money she'd had was spent and she was now penniless. As this heart-wrenching story unfolded it had become apparent to Adam that the poor creature had fainted from hunger. Anxious to make amends for the brutality of his own sex, he'd asked if she would permit him to buy her a meal.

At first, Isabelle had protested that she couldn't accept charity from a stranger, but he'd persisted and eventually she was persuaded to go with him to a restaurant.

And so it had gone on from there. Somehow, he'd felt unable to abandon Isabelle, and that night he'd paid for a room for her in the hotel where he was staying. Before long she was sharing his bed. Adam had hidden his surprise when he'd discovered that she wasn't a virgin, and he'd found himself wondering where a well brought up southern belle could have learnt such lovemaking skills. Then he would check these thoughts by reminding himself that it was none of his business, since theirs was only a temporary arrangement anyway. Soon, he would be taking the train to New York, then booking a berth on a ship home. In the meantime, he'd decided, he would enjoy the pleasures she nightly offered. He'd met some hot young women during his years in Louisiana, but they only went so far, making it clear that their virginity was available only in exchange for a wedding ring. Adam had fallen sufficiently enough in love with a couple of girls to be tempted to grant them their wish, but then in time he would remember Emily, his commitment to her, and the great sacrifice she'd made for him.

Adam wasn't the slightest bit in love with Isabelle and he had been honest with her right from the beginning about the nature of their relationship. He'd told her he was planning to return to England, and made it clear that their liaison could last only until then. Isabelle had appeared to accept this, but asked if she could travel as far as New York with him where, she said, she had more chance of obtaining employment. Having made use of her body, and burdened by a sense of responsibility, Adam had felt unable to refuse. A woman alone in the world and without protection of any kind, was extremely vulnerable and could quickly fall into a life of prostitution. And he'd made a sizeable amount of money while he was in America, so he could afford to be generous, settle a sum of money on her which, if Isabelle invested it wisely, would free her of worry for a number of years.

However, his plans didn't work out quite as neatly as he'd imagined. On the morning of the day he'd intended to present her with this evidence of his generosity, she was sick into the wash basin. Wan and tearful, Isabelle dropped her own bombshell: she was with child. His.

Adam had reeled back at the news and, because he'd always been careful, his instinct was to deny it. In the end common sense told him he had to be the father. Then, because only an utter cad would desert a woman in such circumstances, he'd done the decent thing and married Isabelle in New York, but with a heart heavy with betrayal.

In the end it had turned out to be an unnecessary sacrifice, for halfway across the Atlantic, Isabelle woke him one night in considerable distress to tell him she was bleeding heavily. Adam summoned the ship's doctor, Isabelle was rushed off to the sickbay but unfortunately the doctor couldn't save the baby.

Isabelle bore the loss surprisingly well, but Adam was surprised at the strength of his own grief.

In spite of this, however, he didn't consider it necessary, on his first night home, to burden his mother with any of these sad details.

Chapter Four

'Pleased with the evening?' Harry, standing with his shoulder pressed against Matilda's, turned and smiled at her.

'Yes, considering the short time I had to get it all organised, I would say it's going extremely well. The young soprano I managed to hire sang like a nightingale, Cook surpassed herself with the supper buffet and Isabelle is making a most favourable impression with my friends. Several people have already come over to congratulate me on my charming daughter-in-law.'

'I must say I agree, for what she lacks in beauty, she certainly makes up for in vivacity. And she's bewitching everyone with that delightful southern accent. But I hope Adam has done the decent thing and written to Emily to explain that he's married. After all, he does have certain obligations towards the girl.'

'Adam has only been home a few days, give him a chance, Harry.'

'The news will spread quickly, particularly after tonight. It would be awful if she heard about it through idle gossip.

She deserves better treatment than that.'

'They weren't betrothed, you know. And they'd stopped writing to each other.'

'You mean, Adam stopped writing to Emily.'

Matilda shrugged. 'If you like.' She paused for a moment, then went on, 'Look, I'll make no bones about it, I'm glad he won't be marrying into the Fairfax family. Ecstatic, in fact. It would have been a disastrous union. Isabelle is a much more suitable match in every possible way. You only have to watch her for a few minutes with people. She's from one of the best families in Louisiana, and it shows. Breeding oozes out of her and she has perfect manners. Look how well she and Olivia are getting on.'

'Yes, they do seem to have hit it off,' Harry agreed, gazing across at the girls, heads fused and giggling conspiratorially. In spite of two sons, a daughter and a title, Olivia was still a child herself in many ways and very flirtatious. Harry suspected liaisons, although of course that wasn't his business but Max's. What are the two of them plotting? he wondered indulgently. Mischief, if he knew his daughter. Almost as if she could read his thoughts, Olivia looked up, smiled, linked arms with Isabelle and guided her to where he and Matilda were standing.

'Papa, I've invited Adam and Isabelle to spend a weekend with us at Lindfield Hall in two weeks' time. Would you come, Mrs Bennett, and Clare and Christopher, too?'

'Why, I'd be delighted,' answered Matilda, whose ambition it had been for some time to see the inside of one of the grandest houses in Derbyshire. 'I'm not so sure about Clare and Christopher, though.' In fact Clare hadn't taken the news of the marriage at all well and although she maintained a distant courtesy towards Isabelle, she more or less ignored Adam. Matilda knew why, of course. Her loyalties lay, rather misguidedly in Matilda's opinion, with Emily. Adam had been branded a bounder. 'But ask them. I think they are outside on the terrace, shall we go and look for them?'

Adam, who'd been discussing the Corn Laws and whether it was about time they were repealed with a group of local landowners, now moved away from a situation he could see was about to become heated. Immediately, Isabelle ran to him, took his hand, kissed it, then drew him out through the French windows.

Touched by this display of affection, Matilda followed Harry and Olivia out onto the terrace. Allowing the others to walk on, she leaned against the balustrade, surveyed the scene in front of her and

45

gave herself a mental pat on the back. She was a good organiser, there was no doubt about it. The evening air was mild, the trees were hung with Chinese lanterns, and some of the best families in the county strolled about on *her* lawn. The murmur of conversation and an occasional burst of laughter told that her guests were relaxed and enjoying their evening. *Yes,* Matilda decided, *I've got every right to feel pleased with what I've achieved.* Then her thoughts drifted back to that very unpromising start, the day she'd driven up to Trent Hall as the young unhappy bride of Francis Bennett, carrying Harry's child. She remembered the neglected house and land, the pile of debts she'd inherited when Francis died; but more importantly she could recall, word for word, the promise she'd made to her son when he was barely six weeks old, and she recited it quietly to herself now. 'One day this will be all yours, Adam. You'll be squire here, honoured by the village, and a man of substance.'

Well, that pledge would soon be accomplished. Adam was home and he had sensibly chosen the right sort of girl to go with him through life. She could slacken the reins and look forward to some well-earned leisure. Now, there would be time to read, sew and visit friends, maybe take an occasional trip to London. Then, when the grandchildren came along, spoil them disgracefully.

'Mother, what are you doing standing there on your own?' Adam called to her.

'Just coming, dear.' Moving across the lawn to join her family, Matilda allowed herself to feel optimistic about the future. *Yes,* she thought, *the worrying times are definitely behind me.* From now on life should be plain sailing.

'Have you seen this, Rachel?' asked Jed from behind the newspaper.

Engrossed in a novel, Rachel glanced up vaguely. 'Seen what, dear?'

Jed rustled the paper angrily, folded it at the appropriate column and handed it to her. 'Read it, out loud.'

When a newspaper article particularly angered him, or parted company with him on some political opinion or other, Jed always demanded that Rachel read it out to him so that he could take verbal side-swipes at the piece. So, accommodating wife that she was, Rachel pushed her spectacles up her nose, cleared her throat and began. '"*Mrs Matilda Bennett*",' she read, "*widow of the late Francis Bennett Esq, was hostess on Wednesday night to a distinguished gathering at Trent Hall to celebrate the homecoming and marriage*" ...' Rachel's voice faltered then she lowered the paper and stared at Jed with shocked eyes.

'Go on.' The set of Jed's jaw was grim indeed.

'... *"of their son, Adam, to the former Miss Isabelle Dubois, of Louisiana, in the United States".*' Rachel managed to continue to the end, then in a voice cracked with anguish, she demanded, 'How could he! How could he do such a thing to our lovely girl?'

'It's no more than I might have expected from any offspring of Matilda Pedley, although if you want my honest opinion, I'm glad she isn't marrying one of that rabble.'

'But how are we going to break this dreadful news to Em ...?'

'Do I hear my name being taken in vain?'

As Emily's bright face appeared round the door, Rachel hastily stuffed the newspaper behind a cushion, picked up her book and held it high in front of her. 'No, dear,' she lied.

'Mama!' Emily reprimanded her, walked over to her mother's chair and pulled the newspaper out from behind her back.

Tense with anxiety, Rachel watched her daughter skim the page then the colour leeched out of her face, leaving it a sickly green.

'Dearest, we're both so sorry.' Rachel rose to her feet but as she approached her daughter, Emily raised her hand to ward her off.

'Don't fuss please, Mama.' She sat down heavily. 'Just give me a second and I'll be perfectly all right.'

'I'll make tea then,' said Rachel, which was her palliative for all ills.

Jed, who'd held his tongue in case it got the better of him and he said more than he intended, studied Emily with a grave, loving concern. Since their elopement, Adam had always hung like a shadow between them and there was no point in adding to the weight of her misery today. Although Emily appeared to have her emotions under control, he knew it was a brave front for their benefit. But to him, this was one more crime to add to the already long list committed by *that* family against his. Their misdeeds ran like an infecting slime through each generation: first his own father, then Rachel and now his daughter. The desire to reap some damage on them for a change, to find a pistol and go and murder the boy, almost swamped common sense, and Jed had to fight to remind himself that they weren't worth swinging for.

Above him, Jed heard Natalie moving about, then the thump of his adopted daughter's feet on the stairs. A moment later she hurled herself into the room, hair glowing like amber in the dim light. Staring at each member of her family in turn, she asked with the tact typical of a ten-year-old, 'Why does everyone look so gloomy?'

Emily, who was a question away from complete collapse, stood up. 'I think I'll go for a walk.'

'Have a cup of tea first, dear,' pleaded Rachel, who was now pouring water into the pot.

'I don't want tea, *I want Adam,*' Emily wailed, threw herself against the door then, leaving it swinging, stumbled down the stairs while her parents stared at each other with bleak expressions and despair in their hearts.

'Hey, what's this? Our Emily in tears. Somethin' must be very wrong to bring them on.' Mr Birt the greengrocer, whose shop was two doors down from theirs, watched with a sympathetic expression as Emily fled past him.

'Nothing's wrong,' Emily mumbled then, turning her head away, she rubbed her hands across her wet cheeks in shame.

But the greengrocer was more perceptive than Emily could have imagined and he called after her, 'Some bounder let you down, 'as 'e? Forget 'im, he's not worth the salt of yer tears, me dook.'

It was advice which Emily wished she had the guts to take, particularly since in the last few months she'd imagined herself almost free of Adam. She could even accept that he no longer loved her, but what stuck in her gullet was the callous way in which he'd finally abandoned her, without so much as a letter of explanation, leaving her instead to read of his marriage in *The Leicester Journal.* It showed an utter contempt for her feelings and was quite unlike the Adam she'd loved so desperately, and taken all those risks for. But then of course, people changed, grew older and sadly, harder.

Emily's emotions were in such turmoil she hadn't given any thought to where she might be going, but somehow she found herself outside All Saints' Church, where she worshipped each Sunday. Sensing a destructive bitterness creeping into her soul, Emily decided to go in, sit quietly and try to empty her mind of anger. Pushing open the door, she stepped into the dim interior and collided violently with a dark-garbed figure on its way out.

'Steady on,' said a man's voice and Emily was about to mumble an apology at his chest, when he went on, 'Miss Fairfax, isn't it?'

Recognising the voice of the new curate, the Reverend William Jackson, Emily stared at the ground. Even in the depths of misery she had time to be struck by the high polish of his boots before a shower of tears splashed onto them, dulling their shine.

'Why, you are crying!' exclaimed the young man. 'Come, let's go and sit down.' Taking her arm, he led her to a pew.

Ashamed to be caught betraying all the weaknesses she so despised in women, and to a comparative stranger at that, Emily struggled to compose herself. And gradually, in the sanctuary of the church, with its gloom and silence and familiar religious artifacts, a calming hand was laid on her and she was able to wipe her eyes and blow her nose.

'Would you like to talk about it?' William Jackson asked, with a sidelong glance at her. It was all part of his pastoral duties, to minister to his parishioners, he knew that, but finding himself alone in the company of a distraught but extremely attractive young woman wasn't something he'd bargained for so early on in his career.

Emily stared straight ahead at the altar. 'No, thank you,' she answered, not having the slightest desire to see the situation lapse into a confessional.

'I don't want to intrude, but are you sure?'

Emily nodded.

Coming to the conclusion that the girl was squandering her tears on some undeserving young man, William Jackson stood up. He'd done his duty by her. 'Well, if you'll excuse me then, I must be going. I have a visit to make. I'm trying to persuade a girl called Mary Todd to attend our Sunday School. She promised me faithfully she'd come, but she hasn't been near and I want to find out why.'

Somewhat surprised to be so abruptly abandoned, Emily stood up too and followed the curate out of the church. Outside, he raised his hat. 'Good-day to you, Miss Fairfax, I trust we will see you in church on Sunday?'

'May I come with you ... on your visit, I mean?'

It was now William Jackson's turn to show surprise. 'Why, of course. But it's Sanvey Gate way and a rather rough area.'

Emily knew he was trying to put her off, but she couldn't face returning home to her family just now. Their anxious sympathy would make her tearful again, and at least she would be spared that with William Jackson. 'I've lived here all my life, I do know that,' she answered.

'Shall we go then?'

Halfway down Sanvey Gate the curate turned into a street which led to the canal. It wasn't a street that any respectable woman would dare walk down on her own, and when they passed several young men lounging outside a public house, clearly drunk, their bold stares made Emily feel distinctly uneasy. But worse was to come and when one shouted after them, 'Brought a bit o' tottie wi' you, 'ave you, yer 'oliness?' she turned brick red.

'Take no notice,' said William Jackson. He took her arm protectively and guided her down an entry that brought them out into a grim, squalid court. A stomach-turning odour rose from an open cesspit and they had to pick their way round stagnant pools of filthy water. Several anaemic-looking women, with equally sickly children playing at their feet, stood gossiping on their steps, obviously inured to the smells. When Emily and William appeared in their midst, like apparitions from another universe, the conversation stopped in mid-sentence and the women stared at them with open hostility.

William couldn't help it, he lowered his glance, noticing as he did, that his boots were now smeared with something quite unmentionable. Deeply conscious of his lack of experience, he knew it was imperative that he take control of the situation or forever be the laughing stock of these women and, heaven forbid, Miss Fairfax. 'Can you help me, please? I'm looking for the Todd household,' he managed at last in what he hoped was an authoritative tone.

'Just there, Reverend, sir,' replied one of the children, pointing to several hovels, each identical in squalor.

'Now, ladies, why do I never see you in our church on Sunday?' Gaining courage, William moved closer to the women, but their expressions told him he was an intruder, a do-gooder poking his nose in where it wasn't wanted.

Then to his surprise, one of the women spoke. 'How can we sing the praises of God wi' 'ungry bellies?' she demanded, not unreasonably, Emily considered.

Another woman, whose baby was sucking a dirty rag dummy, also found her voice. 'There in't no God, Reverend. If there wa' we shouldn't be livin' like pigs and last night I wouldn't have had to suckle my little 'un on cold water. I tell 'e, such things drive out Christian thoughts.'

Her opinion wasn't delivered aggressively but as a matter of fact. Listening, Emily silently praised the women. *Good for you for speaking your minds.* What could the Reverend Jackson know about poverty? She bet he didn't have parents who spent their own wages, and their children's, getting drunk every Saturday night. Neither was it likely he'd ever come close to starvation, nor pledged his clothes to the pawnbroker on the Monday and been unable to afford to redeem them on the Friday night.

'Well, if you can't come to church why don't you try our sewing circle?' William suggested. Although this was another situation his theological college hadn't prepared him for, he was anxious to bring these women to God.

But they turned their back on His mercy. 'No thankee.'

William looked at Emily, gave a defeated shrug, then walked over to a door hanging half off its hinges and banged on it, vaguely hopeful of a more positive response here.

Emily watched him with a growing sympathy as a listless looking girl, arms and face blotchy with bug bites, came to the door. 'What d'ya want?' she demanded and glared at them both with a malevolent expression.

'Mary, do you remember me? I'm the curate at All Saints'.' Accepting that she did, Mary nodded. 'I was wondering why you haven't come along to Sunday School like you promised me you would. You would find it of great benefit. Just think, you'd get the chance to learn to read and write.'

Mary shrugged. 'What's the point in learnin'? It won't never do me no good.'

'Yes, it will.' Bending so that her eyes were level with the girl's, Emily took her hand. 'Education is never wasted.'

Although Mary's ignorance was almost total, she was a skilful pickpocket. In her short life she'd also acquired a certain low cunning on the streets of Leicester and could recognise a gullible fool a mile off. 'I can't come, miss, ye see, I ain't got no shoes.'

Mary's voice had taken on a pathetic whine which immediately aroused Emily's crusading spirit. Staring down at the girl's filthy feet and jagged, uncut toenails, she thought, what are my misfortunes compared with this lost soul's? My heart will mend. If Mary isn't helped she will quickly go to perdition. 'If I got hold of a pair for you, would you come then?' she asked.

'Oh, yeah.' Mary shook her head with such vigour it was in danger of falling off.

Judging the girl's feet to be about the same size as her own, Emily straightened. 'Right, we'll get you a pair and bring them to you tomorrow.'

Mary managed to squeeze a grateful tear

57

out of the corner of her eye and it slid down her cheek, cutting a clean white line through the grime. 'Oh, thankee, miss.'

'In fact we'll go up to the market first thing, won't we Mr Jackson?'

'Why certainly, Miss Fairfax.'

'We'll see you here tomorrow same time then, Mary?'

Mary nodded, and the vicar, wondering what mysterious power Emily had that he lacked, took her arm and guided her back down the entry and into the street. 'Thank you, Miss Fairfax. With your help I think we might have rescued at least one soul from the forces of darkness.'

'Yes, some seeds may fall by the wayside ...'

'But others fall into good ground, and bring forth fruit ...' William Jackson finished for her, then they looked at each other, smiled and decided to themselves that, on the whole, it had been an hour well spent.

Mary, who had heard the tail end of the conversation, clawed at the red weals on her face and thought, *daft buggers,* then turned and peered into the dim interior of the room. Her mam lay dead drunk on the bed and her little brother, Joe, sat bare-arsed, squashing bugs against the wall for entertainment. Joe had never learnt to get his tongue round words and the only sounds he made were strange quacking noises. With the natural cruelty of children this had earned him the nickname 'Quacky', but not when Mary was around. She was fiercely protective of her brother, had the temper of an alley cat and the other kids were inclined to be wary of her.

'Trying to save yer soul, were they, Mary?' one of the women called to her, and her cronies cackled with delight at such a preposterous idea. With two of the boys transported, her old man topped, of all the families in the area the Todds were accepted as being real scum whom everyone else could safely look down on.

'None of yer soddin' business,' the girl retorted then padded down the entry to check that the do-gooders had gone. Extending her head a fraction she saw they were some way up the road. 'Bye-bye.' She waggled her hand at their backs then pulled an embroidered ladies' handkerchief from her apron pocket. It felt slightly damp but she studied the neat handrolled border and embroidered roses in one corner with an expert eye, and felt well pleased with her acquisition. Nice piece of stitchin', fine linen, too. Mary usually made do with her sleeve, but for a second she was tempted to indulge herself and use the handkerchief to blow her nose. Better not, she decided, and stuffed it back in her pocket.

There wa' a few coppers to be made if she could lift a couple more, but it wouldn't do to 'ave snot on 'em. There were shoes comin' her way as well, although she'd have to make sure her mam didn't get her thieving paws on 'em. She aimed to pop 'em, not wear 'em, then come Saturday night she'd have a tanner or more. Anyways, enough to buy her and Joe somethin' really tasty to eat, plus a few tots of gin to drown her sorrows and bugger Sunday school, God and learnin', Mary sniffed.

Chapter Five

'Ma word!' Isabelle exclaimed, leaning out of the carriage window to get her first glimpse of Lindfield Hall through the half-mile avenue of lime trees the horses were now trotting along. Matilda was determined not to appear as openly impressed as her daughter-in-law, but the great house they were now approaching, with its classical frontage and curving flight of steps, was certainly living up to her expectations. 'What a shame Clare and Christopher couldn't come,' said Isabelle, falling back into her seat.

'It was the school,' Matilda lied. In fact Clare, who remained obstinately immune to Isabelle's charm, had refused point-blank to accompany them, making it clear she considered that Adam had behaved like a despicable rat who didn't deserve Emily anyway.

Matilda glanced at her son, sitting next to Harry. Well, he no doubt had a lot of his father in him, and by golly, Harry had certainly treated her badly in his time. He came begging to her in the end, though, and she couldn't pretend that it hadn't afforded her a great deal of satisfaction. But he had been long forgiven and since the death of his wife, Charlotte, in the winter of 1840, she and Harry had maintained a discreet relationship, although it was a more or less an open secret in the County.

The carriage was now drawing up in front of Lindfield Hall and even before it had stopped, liveried footmen were waiting to let down the steps and help them from the coach. Then, while the luggage was being dealt with, Irish wolfhounds, retrievers and various other breeds of dog came pounding boisterously out of the house followed by Olivia, Max, three young children and their nurse.

'Dearest, it's wonderful to see you

again.' Olivia embraced Isabelle, kissed her father and greeted Adam and Matilda more formally. Finally, she introduced the children, Felicity, Henry and Bertie, then almost at once ushered them away. 'Off you go, children,' she ordered and handed them back to the care of the nurse.

'I didn't realise you lived in something quite so grand, Olivia,' said Adam rather forthrightly, standing back to admire the frontage. 'What a pity Clare is missing the chance to see it.'

'Another time, perhaps,' answered Matilda, while over Olivia's shoulder she studied with interest someone who, at first glance, she'd taken to be a young man.

Only when this apparition with cropped hair and wearing a man's riding outfit cried, 'Papa,' and flew down the steps and into Harry's arms, did Matilda realise it was Judith.

'You remember my daughter, Judith, don't you, Matilda?'

Faintly embarrassed, Matilda answered, 'Why, of course. You're over from Paris, then?'

'Yes, to see my family. I was planning to return and then I heard that Adam was home and I couldn't miss seeing an old friend. We used to have such fun, the four of us, didn't we?' said Judith a little wistfully, moving over to Adam.

'We did indeed,' Adam agreed. 'In fact, I remember them as very happy times.'

'But where is Clare?' Judith looked about her.

'She couldn't come, dear,' said Harry gently and took her hand when he saw his daughter's face fall.

'It might not be Paris, but there will be all sorts of interesting people arriving later in the day and they'll keep you amused,' Max promised his sister-in-law, as he ushered the party up the steps and into the great hall.

Light poured in from its many windows and an enormous candelabra drew Matilda's glance up to an ornate ceiling of frolicking cherubs linked together by sheaves of corn. The staircase was wide and solid and when they were shown to their rooms, Matilda saw that Olivia had thoughtfully put her and Harry in adjacent bedrooms with a connecting door.

Her bedroom was in the Chinese style with black lacquered furniture and highly decorative wallpaper depicting scenes from Chinese life. Another door opened to reveal a water-closet and huge bath with claw feet and brass taps. To Matilda's eyes this was an unbelievable luxury—at Trent Hall they still made do with hip baths and jugs of hot water carried up by the servants. With growing envy she fingered the fluffy towels, sniffed the expensive soaps and decided that, included in the plans for the dower house, there would be a bathroom and a water-closet.

Matilda was strongly tempted to disrobe and steep herself in the hot scented water right away, but then decided to wait until she'd rested. Enjoying herself, she wandered around the room picking up porcelain figurines and checking their marks, studied the silver dressing table set, then finally she went and pulled up the window and leaned out. Her gaze swept over the grounds, taking in the ornamental lake, gazebo and judiciously placed clumps of trees. As a backdrop there were the Derbyshire peaks and dales, darkening, then lightening again under the restless movement of billowing cloud. Well, there there was no denying it, Olivia had done well for herself, a title, plus all this.

While Matilda was standing pondering on whether Olivia loved her husband, her hostess came out of the house and sauntered across the lawn with Isabelle and Judith. Strolling a short way behind the girls were Adam, Max and a gentleman she didn't recognise. She was trying to work out who he might be when a tap on the door forced Matilda to turn her attention from the outside scene. 'Come in,' she called.

A maid entered, gave a small curtsy and said, 'I've come to unpack for you, Madam.'

'I'd like to take a rest. Do it while I'm at tea. You can help me out of my dress and corset, though.' The girl moved forward and obediently unhooked the dress then, as it fell to the ground, she unlaced the corset. Matilda gave a small sigh of relief as her flesh was released from the restricting stays. 'There is a wrap in that small case, hand it to me, please.' The girl brought the robe and while she was slipping it on Matilda said, 'Call me at half past three, then you can help me dress and do my hair.'

'Certainly, Madam.' The girl bobbed. 'Will that be all, Madam?'

'For the time being, yes.' Matilda waited until she'd gone then lay down on the bed and thought of the coming weekend, and the connecting door between hers and Harry's bedroom, with an enjoyable sense of anticipation. From there, somehow, her thoughts drifted to Judith. Of course she'd heard about mannish women who only enjoyed making love to their own sex, and Harry's daughter must be one of that sort. One of the great pleasures in life, as far as she was concerned, was the fusing of the male and female body in the act of love, and it puzzled Matilda what two women could *actually do* together that would bring them fulfilment. The expert on such matters was Harry, and he'd told her some of the incredible things that people got up to in order to obtain sexual satisfaction. However, she could hardly question him about Judith's sexual preferences, which meant it was likely to remain one of life's great mysteries ... Thinking this, Matilda drifted off into a pleasant sleep.

In between tea and assembling for dinner, several more of the guests who would make up the weekend party had arrived and been introduced. As well as Max's brother, Gregory and his wife, Daisy, there were a Mr and Mrs David Warren and Mr Theodore Bartlett and his sister, Dorothy, who appeared to be connected to the family in some way. The last person down was Sir Austin Beauchamp, a near neighbour of Olivia and Max.

'And how far is it from here to your residence, Sir Austin?' Isabelle smiled, and Matilda noticed how those strange grey eyes, with their almost hypnotic quality, fixed themselves upon the gentleman.

'I'd say it's no more than five miles distant,' he answered.

'Yes, and the lucky beggar has found coal on his land and they've just sunk the

66

first shaft. Black gold will make Beauchamp wealthy as a Rothschild before long,' Max predicted.

'Well, I don't know about that, it depends how much there is,' answered Sir Austin. 'Anyway, Chalcombe will probably eat up any money the mine makes and the roof is in such a dire state, I was considering selling it not long ago.'

'But you couldn't!' exclaimed Max. 'Chalcombe has been in your family for how many generations?'

'Since Henry's time. The Eighth, that is. But I've no longer any feeling for the place, it holds too many sad memories for me now.' Saying no more, he moved away and stood gazing out of the window at the darkening sky.

He looked a sad, lonely figure and Isabelle, who'd followed this conversation with intense interest, turned back to her host. 'Sir Austin looks rather unhappy, has he had some tragedy in his life?' she asked.

'A double tragedy, I'm afraid. He lost both his wife and baby in childbirth last year. They'd been married ten years and were devoted to each other. It was their first child after a long wait and they were both looking forward to the event with such joy. Austin hasn't been the same man since and I doubt if he'll ever get over it.'

'Poor man,' Isabelle eyes dampened in sympathy. 'All the money in the world is no recompense for such a loss.'

Perhaps sensing his past was being put under the microscope, Sir Austin rejoined the group and held out his arm for Isabelle to take. 'I believe I am to have the honour of escorting you in to dinner, Mrs Bennett.'

'Why, thank you, Sir Austin.' Isabelle placed a small gloved hand on his arm and allowed herself to be led in and helped to her seat. To begin with, seated amidst the silver and crystal and with stern forbears gazing down at them, the guests were rather reserved with each other. But the food and fine wine quickly oiled tongues and turning to Sir Austin, Isabelle smiled at him. 'I'd be most interested to see this mine of yours, Sir Austin.'

Sir Austin, a shy, slightly awkward man in his early forties, felt deeply flattered. He considered himself a dry old stick, not likely to be of much interest to any member of the opposite sex and yet here was this charming young woman expressing a wish to spend time in his company. 'Would you really Mrs Bennett? Then I should be delighted to take you, the question is when?'

'Would tomorrow be possible?'

'I'm afraid not. I hear our host has arranged a trip to Matlock Bath for us all. How would Sunday suit you? Perhaps after church?'

Isabelle clasped her hands together in delight. 'That sounds a splendid idea.'

'What's a splendid idea?' asked Olivia turning her attention from Theo Bartlett, who was seated opposite Isabelle.

'Sir Austin has offered to show me the mine. You must come, too.'

Olivia gave Isabelle a strange look. 'I'm not sure that it is something that interests me a great deal, dearest.'

'I should like to be included,' said Theo.

'Perhaps we'll all go then,' said the hostess and stood up. 'Shall we withdraw, ladies, and leave the gentlemen to their port and politics?'

The women rose and and followed Olivia into the drawing room. Having over-indulged, everyone, apart from Judith who refused to wear corsets, now regretted the tight lacing they'd earlier insisted upon to their maidservants. So, behind politely raised hands the ladies burped and wondered when they could safely retire to their rooms.

When the conversation, which had never risen above the mundane, finally petered out, Isabelle stood up and strolled over to the pianoforte. Lifting the lid, she tinkered with the keys. 'Shall I play?' she asked finally.

'Please do, dear,' answered Olivia, deeply grateful to her friend for coming to her rescue. Her reputation as a hostess was at stake here, for her weekend parties were famous, and if word got round that they were becoming dull ... Olivia shuddered ... well, it didn't bear thinking about.

However, as soon Isabelle sat down and began to play, Olivia was aware of a subtle change in the mood of the room. When she started to sing some charming French songs the men, hearing her sweet voice, left their port and cigars and drifted in to join the ladies. Olivia relaxed and smiled and secretly blessed her friend. All was right with the world after all. Her confidence in her own skills as the perfect hostess restored, Olivia began to stroll amongst her guests.

Matilda was equally impressed by her daughter-in-law's musicianship, along with every man in the room, she decided looking around at their rapt expressions. Only Adam appeared immune to his wife's charms, and he was standing at the back of the room paying no attention to her at all. At this obvious snub to his wife, Matilda shifted uneasily in her chair. Did he not love Isabelle? And if he didn't, why had he married her? But the die was cast now, and at least there was no possibility of him running back to the Fairfax girl, thank heaven.

When Isabelle had run through her repertoire of songs, Judith went over and congratulated her on her French. 'You sing it beautifully.'

'My father was French,' Isabelle answered.

'Well that explains it. What part of France?'

Isabelle shrugged. 'I'm sure I have no idea. Paris perhaps, he never said.'

'You should get Adam to bring you over for a visit. It is a fine city, you would love it and there is so much culture. Unlike Leicester,' Judith added *sotto voce*. 'Perhaps next time Olivia comes we might arrange something.'

'Yes, I would enjoy that. You and Adam and Olivia were all good friends at one time, I believe?'

'We still are, I hope.'

Isabelle looked across at Adam and Olivia, who were standing talking together. 'Do you know, they could almost be brother and sister, don't you agree? It's strange, too, that they share the same name.'

'It isn't really. Many of the families around here are connected and Adam's mother was married to my father's uncle.'

Isabelle nodded her head. 'I see.'

Judith yawned. 'People are drifting off to bed. I think I'll do the same. The trip to Matlock Bath starts early.'

'I shall wait for Adam,' said Isabelle and wishing Judith good-night, she moved across to where her husband and Olivia had been joined by Sir Austin Beauchamp.

Four carriages set off the following morning into an accommodating day of fresh blue autumn skies. Narrow, high banked lanes drew the horses into deep tunnels of trees then back out again into bright sunshine, and at each village they were accompanied for several miles by packs of half-wild dogs. Gradually the terrain became steeper, the horses slower until finally they were out on open rolling moorland. Here, while the horses rested, everyone got out to stretch their legs and admire the scene stretched out before them; isolated farmhouses, small green fields stitched together by dry-stone walls, as well as the lime kilns and abandoned lead mines that had left their industrial mark on the landscape.

The horses rested, the party moved on, finally reaching Matlock Bath around midday. It was a picturesque town, set in a deep limestone gorge with the River Derwent cutting through it and since Olivia and Max were keen to show off its many attractions it was decided they should leave the carriages and walk.

Gazing upwards at houses built on the almost sheer cliff face Matilda wondered out loud how anyone would dare erect a home there.

'It's for the wonderful view,' Max explained. 'But see, what do you think of Sir Richard Arkwright's cotton mill, isn't it a fine building, Mr Bennett?'

'It certainly is,' agreed Harry.

'There's nothing to compare with it in Leicester, I'll be bound.'

'Indeed there isn't,' Harry had again to concede.

Retracing their steps, they tasted the health-giving water, threw some coins into the petrifying pool, after which Max led them to a hotel in the centre of the town where a magnificent luncheon of game pie, a whole salmon and cold roast beef plus some excellent wine, had been laid out for them.

It took a good hour to consume the food, a little longer to digest it and several of the party settled down for forty winks in comfortable chairs. Olivia, however, had other plans for her guests. 'Who would like to go for a walk and see if we can get up as far as the Heights of Abraham? There is a magnificent view from there, I believe.'

Matilda made a face. 'I think I'll leave

such activities to you energetic young things.'

Harry leaned back in his chair and lit a cigar. 'I second that.'

But Sir Austin, who had no wish to appear like an old fuddy-duddy to the younger element, patted his stomach. 'After that lavish repast, I feel a stroll would do me good.'

'Me, too,' said Isabelle, jumping to her feet.

In the end six of them went, including Adam and Judith. But the path seemed almost vertical, the ground stony, her shoes unsuitable and Isabelle's enthusiasm quickly waned. Soon she was lagging behind. Pausing, Isabelle called plaintively to her husband, 'Wait for me, Adam, please.' But he pretended not to hear and she watched with marble-cold eyes, as he forged on ahead with Judith. 'You'll regret this, *dearest,*' she promised through gritted teeth then, noticing Sir Austin struggling up the path behind her, she let out a squeal of pain, hobbled to a lump of rock, sank down on it and began to rub her ankle.

'What is the trouble, Mrs Bennett?' Sir Austin puffed to a stop beside Isabelle and his sad, liquid eyes gazed down at her in concern.

'I fear I have twisted my ankle, Sir Austin.'

'Oh, dear.' His brow furrowed and he looked about him ineffectually.

Bravely biting on her lip, Isabelle stood and tested her foot on the ground, gave a small gasp of pain and collapsed again on to the rock. 'I think I am going to need some assistance to get back to the hotel.'

'Yes, of course.' Austin Beauchamp cleared his throat nervously, moved forward and placed a tentative arm round Isabelle's waist, easing her to her feet as if she were spun sugar. As he did, Isabelle gave another small cry of pain and fell against his chest. Her head was just level with his heart and Austin smelt the warm, womanly scent of her with an acute sense of loss and longing. He knew he could have amused himself with lewd women like many of his kind did, but he wasn't a carnal man by nature. Truly loving another human being was about many things, not just sex. Although he doubted if he'd ever be that fortunate a second time, what he desired, with all his heart, was the union of body and mind he'd had with his late wife. Like nothing else, he wanted to hold a woman he loved in his arms again, to sleep with her and wake up to her smile each morning. Now here was this little creature, so delicate, so appealing, gazing up at him with a special look in her eyes. *Compose yourself, Beauchamp, for heaven's sake,* he berated himself. Remember, this is a young married woman and you are a gentleman of honour. With a roughness uncommon to him, Austin put Isabelle away from him then, taking her arm firmly, he helped her back to the hotel.

'I thought your ankle hurt?' Adam said to his wife the following day after luncheon.

'No, it's really much better now. See, it can take my weight with no trouble at all.' Isabelle stood up to prove her point.

'Well, go if you want to, Isabelle, but I can hardly imagine there's much to see. The mine is still in the process of being sunk and I never knew you were much interested in machinery.'

'I am interested in a great many things, Adam,' Isabelle answered tartly and glided to the mirror to tie the ribbons of her bonnet in a enormous bow under her chin. Picking up a small parasol, she enquired, 'Do I look all right?'

Adam appeared to think about this. 'I would have chosen something a bit darker to wear. A blue silk dress hardly seems the appropriate attire for trudging across muddy fields.'

Isabelle chose not to respond to this criticism. Anyway, she had no intention of going within a mile of a muddy field. Smiling at her husband she said instead,

'We won't be long, Sir Austin says he'll have us back here by five o'clock. What will you do, dear?'

'Have a game of billiards probably, since the weather doesn't look too good.'

Isabelle gave her husband a quick kiss. 'Do you love me, Adam?' she asked.

Adam picked up a book and rapidly turned the pages. 'Why, of course I do.'

Liar, Isabelle thought, and wondered whom he did love. Olivia perhaps? 'And I love you, too,' she answered equally untruthfully and winding her arms around his neck, she kissed him again. 'You could come, you know. Olivia's going,' she added, as an inducement.

But even the prospect of Olivia's company couldn't tempt Adam and on the trip to Chalcombe, Isabelle had to delete Olivia from her list of possible mistresses anyway, because it was obvious she only had eyes for Theo Bartlett. Could it be that Adam was staying behind to have a dalliance with Daisy, or perhaps Theo's sister, Dorothy? Not that either of them had much to attract a man; no beauty, no sparkling wit, no particular accomplishments. In fact, both of them, poor things, were lumpy and charmless. She on the other hand had been reared to charm and flatter men. And how these Englishmen fell for it, Isabelle thought, with a sly glance at Sir Austin, who was sitting opposite gazing at her with dog-like devotion.

'Here we are, Chalcombe,' said Sir Austin with obvious pride as they drove through the enormous wrought-iron gates, topped by the family crest figured in gold leaf. The lodge-keeper's wife rushed out to drop them a curtsy, then they continued through what seemed like endless woodland until finally they crossed a small bridge into parkland dotted with grazing deer. Her first glimpse of Chalcombe, with its mullion windows and crenellated roof, momentarily silenced Isabelle then, hiding her excitement as best she could, she turned to Sir Austin.

'You didn't tell me you lived in a castle.'

'It's not a castle, more a fortified house,' Austin explained. 'I'll show you round after we've been out to the mine.' Isabelle's objective in coming on this trip was to ascertain what sort of style Sir Austin lived in, not gaze at some wretched machinery and pretend interest. She was wondering if her ankle might come to her rescue when there was a rumble of thunder, a flash of lightning, then the sound of hailstones bouncing off the carriage roof. 'Well, that's put paid to the visit for today,' Sir Austin apologised.

'What a pity.' Isabelle looked genuinely crestfallen, but then she brightened. 'But there will be other times, I'm sure. That is, if Olivia invites me here again?' She smiled at her friend.

'Of course I will, dearest, I love having you. Come any time you like.'

'You are too kind, thank you.' Isabelle kissed Olivia with great affection. 'We've been acquainted for only a short while and yet I feel you've been my friend all my life.'

'What a lovely thing to say.'

The horses had drawn up now and, protected by umbrellas, they stepped down from the coach and hurried in through a massive studded door to an oak panelled hall.

'Are you impressed, Isabelle?' Olivia whispered as Isabelle gazed about her.

'Quite impressed,' admitted Isabelle, swinging round on her heels and trying to calculate what sort of income a man would need to maintain a establishment of this size. And while Sir Austin showed them the rest of the house and room after room of fine furniture, silver plate and paintings, Isabelle kept thinking to herself, *oh, to be mistress of all this.* And fast on this idea she made a pact with herself, one day that's exactly what she would be: Mistress of Chalcombe.

Chapter Six

Emily had been quite specific about where she would meet William Jackson: outside the shop; so when she came down the following morning and found him chatting to her mother, she felt a curl of irritation.

'The Reverend Jackson tells me you are going *together* to look for second-hand boots in the market,' said Rachel, putting far too much emphasis on the word, 'together' in her daughter's opinion.

'Yes, but I shouldn't imagine that will take long,' Emily answered shortly, cottoning on immediately to her mother's thought processes. It took a dyed-in-the-wool romantic to imagine that love could blossom over a pile of stinking leather, but time was slipping by, and here was a respectable young bachelor, her mother would be thinking, and she had a twenty-eight-year-old unmarried daughter. That she was still licking very open wounds seemed to have slipped her mother's mind. And couldn't she grasp, Emily wondered, that the possibility of her ever being interested in a man again was about as likely as snow in August.

'Well, you don't have to hurry back, we're not very busy.'

Emily's lips tightened with annoyance but she was determined to smother at birth the hopes printed so plainly on her mother's face. 'The boots are for Mary Todd, one of Reverend Jackson's parishioners. He just wants a bit of assistance with the size.'

But Rachel, who was an inveterate matchmaker, ignored her daughter's comments and smiled with a bright optimism at William, who'd already metamorphosed into a son-in-law.

The young curate, unaware of this silent tussle between mother and daughter, bid Rachel goodbye, adding that he hoped he'd have the pleasure of seeing her in church on Sunday. Assuring him that he would, Rachel saw them to the door.

Acutely conscious of her mother's hopes following them down the street, Emily kept as far apart from William as was possible without falling into the gutter.

'I gather you're not coming with me to give Mary her present, Miss Fairfax,' said William, closing the gap between them.

'No, sorry.'

'I must say I'm disappointed, she responded so well to you yesterday. I thought you might actually persuade her to come to Sunday School.'

'I doubt if I'd have that much influence.

Besides, I haven't the time. My father and I leave for Manchester in the morning, and there's still packing to be done.'

Manchester invoked so many painful memories, Emily had wondered for some time how she would feel about returning. For if she hadn't fallen sick, if irate parents hadn't caught up with them, if she and Adam had succeeded in reaching Gretna Green and marrying, how differently her life would have turned out. So many 'ifs'. Emily gave a small sigh. No doubt she'd be the mother of several children by now, totally immersed in domesticity and with scant interest in the Chartist movement or much else, certainly not the soul of one young street urchin.

'Sorry, what did you say?' asked Emily suddenly aware that the young curate was talking to her.

'I asked if you were visiting relatives in Manchester,' William repeated.

'No, I'm attending a Chartist meeting with my father.' It was daring of her to admit her radicalism, but Emily was keen to test William's reaction.

'Oh, I see.'

'Do you? Well you're the exception then. Most people don't. I'm always being told that politics are best left to men, although I fail to see why. In my opinion, women, as members of the human race, are entitled to the same rights as men.'

'I've read the People's Charter and as I recall, it demands the vote for every man over twenty-one, but it made no mention of women anywhere in its six points.'

Slightly stumped, Emily answered, 'You're quite right. Votes for women will come later, once we've achieved our objective, which is a democratically elected parliament. Actually, I'm addressing the meeting.'

'Is that wise, Miss Fairfax? These events often get out of hand and flare into violence. People have even been killed.'

'Yes, by the Militia and the police,' Emily replied somewhat tartly.

It was plain by the Christian concern on his face that the curate wasn't used to women with firmly held political views, and her remarks obviously unsettled him. He was a nice man, though; kind and trying to do his best for humanity, Emily decided, studying his profile and the pale, undistinguished Anglo-Saxon features. Although tall, he was quite slender and even with his religious beliefs to sustain him, the curate seemed ill-equipped to deal with the harsh rigours of Sanvey Gate and Emily wondered how long he would survive in Leicester. His main asset was his voice which was pleasant, well modulated and ideally suited to the pulpit. And no doubt of a Sunday it sent a shiver of delight down the spine of many a young woman in his congregation. But definitely not hers, never hers, Emily decided.

'A mob can be just as dangerous,' William pointed out, for his overly-fertile imagination now had Emily being pursued by villainous cut-throats. 'And as a woman you would be particularly vulnerable.'

'Well, no one's attacked me yet. Besides, my father would protect me.' They had now reached the marketplace and anxious to move the conversation away from her and back to their reason for being there, Emily lightly touched William's arm. 'Let's see if we can find that shoe stall, shall we?'

Although it wasn't market day, a few enterprising farmers' wives had brought in baskets of eggs and apples and set them down on the cobbles. At the edge of the marketplace several second-hand clothes stalls were being assiduously picked over for a bargain and the rank, cheesy smell of shoddy leather guided Emily and William to a stall piled high with every conceivable kind of footwear. Tiny babies' shoes, ballet slippers with trailing pink ribbon, spurred riding boots, shoes with the soles half off or a heel missing, and probably dead mens' shoes, too, thought Emily and wondered what stories lay behind each abandoned pair. Just visible above this mountain of leather was the stallholder. 'Is there anythin' perticuler you wa' lookin' for, Reverend?' he enquired.

'Yes, a pair of shoes or boots suitable for a young woman.'

'This young lady?'

Emily shuddered. 'Oh no, not me,' she answered then felt ashamed at her own snobbery.

'How big would you be wantin' them?'

Emily presented her foot for inspection. 'About this size. Or maybe a bit bigger,' she added, deciding that Mary probably still had some growing to do.

The man sorted around in the pile, pulled out shoes in various styles and state of decrepitude, and held them up in turn for inspection. But they were either too big, too small, too shabby or they didn't match. Finally, at the bottom of the heap, he found a rather pretty pair of brown button boots with small heels and a bow on the front, which Emily was certain any girl would be proud to wear.

Emily measured them against her own foot for size, imagining Mary's delight when they were handed to her. 'How much?' she asked.

'A shilling to you, lady.' Emily dithered. That was a great deal of money to spend on someone she hardly knew. 'They're proper leather and none of yer cheap cloth.' Anxious to assure them of the verity of this remark, the man spat on the boots then buffed them up on the sleeve of his jacket. 'Last you for years, these will. Tell you what, you can 'ave 'em for ninepence, and don't say I in't generous.'

'I wouldn't dream of you paying for them, Miss Fairfax. Mary is my responsibility,' insisted William, hunting around in his pocket for the money. While the stallholder wrapped the boots in a sheet of newspaper and handed the parcel to Emily, William found a sixpence and three pennies in his pocket. He was counting them into the man's hand when he was distracted by an almighty commotion behind them. 'Whatever ...?' He and Emily swung round simultaneously to find, close by, a peeler holding a screeching, spitting, writhing girl by the scruff of the neck.

'Lemmee go! Lemmee go! you old sod,' the girl hollered, flailing her legs and, catching the policeman a sharp one on the shins, she was rewarded with a sound box around the ear. 'Bastard!' The girl's shrieks and curses echoed round the square, flocks of pigeons rose in a flutter of panicking wings and passers-by paused to gape.

'Why, I do believe it's Mary!' William

exclaimed and strode over to the policeman. 'What's going on here, constable?' he enquired.

'I caught this ... this alley-cat red 'anded, stealin' an apple out of a basket.'

'May I suggest you put her down, before she chokes to death.'

Her small face red and furious, Mary glared at the bobby. 'You 'eard, let me go.'

The policeman dropped the girl as if she were dog mess. 'The way this thievin' wretch is goin', she'll have a rope round 'er neck soon enough, without me bothering. A right bad lot she is, like the rest of 'er tribe.'

'Nobody is beyond redemption, constable.'

The policeman's lips gave a cynical twitch. 'I know yer a man of the cloth, sir, but don't you believe it. I've met some real evil specimens in me time. Perhaps we should swap jobs for a while, then maybe me faith in human nature would be restored.'

William didn't reply to this suggestion, instead he looked down at Mary who, after adjusting her rags, had gone unnaturally quiet.

'Did you steal the apple, Mary?'

'No, Reverend. I swear on me mam's life.' Mary looked up at him with an unnaturally pious expression then made the sign of the cross over her left breast. 'Cross me heart and hope to die.'

'All right, there's no need to overdo it, Mary,' William retorted.

'If you don't believe me, take a look for yerself. Me pockets is empty.' To prove it, Mary turned them inside out.

'There you are, constable.' William smiled at the policeman. 'Miss Fairfax and I know this girl and can vouch for her character. She will also be attending our Sunday School, won't you, Mary?'

'Oh yes, next Sunday you'll see me there awright.'

'Well I won't take 'er in this time. But if I find you round 'ere again with yer thieving mitts, it'll be the jug for you, missie. A nice long stretch too, which you've 'ad coming to you for a while.'

The peeler wagged a final warning finger at the pint-sized miscreant then walked off, making his way to one of the stalls where he knew tea was being brewed up on a brazier. When there was sufficient distance between them, Mary put her thumb to her nose and wiggled her fingers derisively at his departing back.

'Stop that, Mary, at once!' Emily's tone was sharp, the rebuke meant and the girl was so astonished her hand fell to her side.

'Look, we've got something for you, like we promised.' Emily held out the parcel. Mary, who had no concept of charity, picked her nose and wondered what their game was. 'Go on, take it.' Emily pushed the package at the girl, who grabbed it and tore away the paper.

Mary stared at the boots. 'Are they really mine?' There was still a measure of doubt in her voice.

'They are indeed,' William smiled.

'Shall I try 'em on?'

'Of course.'

Mary pushed first one filthy foot, then the other into the boots, twisting and turning them this way and that and admiring them from every possible angle. Clearly pleased as punch she began mincing round the marketplace for the benefit of the populace. 'In't I the lady then?' Her grin displaying a row of discoloured teeth, she turned finally to face William, and Emily.

'You are indeed, and there's nothing to stop you coming to Sunday School now, is there?' the ever-hopeful William ventured.

'I'll come, never you fear, Reverend,' Mary assured him with a cheerful wave then, after making sure she was out of sight of her benefactors, she skipped off in the direction of the nearest pop shop. Pawnbrokers, with their trade sign of three golden balls hanging above the premises, could be found in virtually every street in Leicester and Mary reckoned the boots were worth at least a tanner. But as she trotted along, the gin the sixpence would buy suddenly didn't seem so important. Mary was unaccustomed to anything other than the most broken down footwear and more often than not she went barefoot, so her toes, living this unrestricted life, were naturally splayed. What surprised her most was that, in these boots, her feet didn't feel all squashed up. The soft leather wrapped itself round them and she noticed she was walking twice as tall, with her head thrown back, same as the rich lady they must have once belonged to.

Deciding she might as well hold on to the boots a bit longer, Mary managed quite a swagger as she sauntered down Sanvey Gate. But she could have been invisible for all the notice anyone took. Smart boots or not, to passers-by, she was just another scruffy urchin.

Passing the Anchor, Mary paused, tempted by the sounds of well-lubricated bonhomie coming from inside the tavern. It was almost her second home and Mary loved the familiar smells of sweat, shag tobacco, and spilt beer on sawdust, but best of all was the warm blanket of fug that enveloped her as soon as she walked through the door. A couple of tots of gin would go down a treat right now, she mused, and put a rosy glow on the world for an hour or so. But she hadn't a farthing to her name. She could try scrounging a drink, but her slate was full and she didn't want to wear out her welcome entirely.

Mary stared at her boots, regretting her earlier decision. What good were they to her, really? If she'd pledged 'em she could have put the money to far better use, and she was parched. She was about to go and look for a pawnshop when she noticed a chap coming towards her and she had a sudden brainwave. Here was a way of killing two birds with one stone. Keep her boots and wet her whistle. Arranging herself languidly against the wall, she ran her tongue round her lips, rested her hands on her narrow hips in a fair imitation of her mam, waited until the man drew level, then rolled her eyes provocatively. 'Fancy a quick one, deary?'

The man stood back a little, gave her a quick once over then laughed in her face. 'Have a heart. I'm not that desperate, me dook, I like a full-blooded woman, not some half-starved kid who could do with a good scrub in carbolic. Get some flesh on you, have a good wash then ask me again.' After flinging this final insult at her, the man walked on, chuckling to himself as if it were the greatest joke in the world.

Mary had learnt early on in life that tears were a waste of time, for all they ever earned you was a crack on the head. But try as she might, she couldn't prevent them now and tears of rejection slid down her cheeks. Bloody 'ell, she couldn't even make a success of pickin' up a chap. In fact, she was useless and it would be better if she wa' never born.

Choked-up with self-pity she wandered in a directionless manner towards the canal, sat herself down on the towpath and gazed morosely at the passing traffic. 'Cheer up, lass, it may never happen,' a bargeman called to her and Mary smiled wanly, remembered the stolen apple and perked up a bit. With the skill of a magician she produced the apple from the sleeve of her jacket and bit into it. Chewing it reflectively, Mary stared into the murky water, then at her boots and felt the first stirrings of ambition. *Who was to say she couldn't be a lady? Who was to say she couldn't learn to read and write and get out of this shit-hole?* There was a better life to be had, she knew that because one of her favourite pastimes was to take a stroll at dusk past the houses in Granby Street when the lamps had been lit but before the curtains were drawn. It was almost like they lived in another country, these families, because there was no scrapping or bawling drunkenly at each other. Instead, they sat round tables, eating, talking and laughing or just reading or playing cards.

Most of Mary's waking hours were spent in the grim struggle to avoid starvation by fair means or foul, so she'd never had time for deep contemplation. Now, however, she thought long and hard. If she did go to that there Sunday School the reverend went on about and got a bit of learnin', maybe she could give up the thievin' and get an honest job with a wage at the end of the week, enough to pay for a room well away from her mam.

Mary laughed at the very notion. *Daft cow, yer gettin' ideas way above yer head, so stop it,* she rebuked herself then thought, *But what was there to lose in trying, anyway?* Mary sat there for several more minutes seesawing between doubt and optimism and finally stood up. Come Sunday she would present herself at the church she decided. Then, having made this momentous decision, Mary headed back to Bees Court.

Home wasn't a refuge or place of comfort, merely somewhere to rest her head and often on summer nights, when the weather was warm she would sleep out in Abbey Meadows, then come dawn, strip off her clothes and swim naked in the Soar.

It was a bit late in the year for that now but the man's remarks about her needing a good scrub had hit home so, as she turned into Craven Street, Mary decided she would go down first thing and take a dip in the river. In the entry that led to Bees Court she paused, pulled off her boots and stuffed them up her skirt. Whatever happened her mam mustn't get her hands on them or it would be the last she saw of her lovely boots.

Sunlight avoided Bees Court, as if fearful of picking out its true squalor, but Mary could see her brother crouched in the yard, drawing in the dirt with his fingers. 'Hello, Joe,' she called, and splashed barefoot through the pools of stagnant water towards him. 'See what I've got for you.' Bending down she gave him the core of her apple.

He grinned, snatched it from her, stuffed it in his mouth, swallowed it almost whole, then made a few excited quacking sounds, his only means of communication. Mary knew he was showing his gratitude and she ruffled his hair affectionately. 'Poor little boogger, nobody gives a fig about you except me, do they? And not bein' able to talk must be like bein' in prison, with no chance of ever gettin' out.' But she always made sure she shared what she had with him, whether it was the crust of a pork pie or a tot of gin, although he got nothing from their mam except beatings.

Pulling him close, Mary said quietly, 'I'm gonna leave this 'ole one day, Joe, and when I do I'll take you with me, and I promise I'll take care of you for the rest of me life.'

The morning service was over and William Jackson was standing at the door of the church, smiling and mouthing the normal platitudes to the departing congregation, when he noticed Mary hanging about on the other side of the street. He waited until the church was empty and he'd shaken the last hand, then went over to her.

'Hello, Mary, this is a nice surprise.'

Mary twisted her foot in the dust in an embarrassed way. 'I've come to Sunday School. I want you to learn me to read and write,' she finally found the courage to say.

'I'd be delighted teach you. But could you come back at two o'clock this afternoon? That's when we have our Sunday School.'

'Probably.'

'Promise me you will come, Mary,' said William, looking her directly in the eye, for he was most anxious to add this straying lamb to his flock. Like many of the poor in Leicester she was crushed under the wheels of ignorance and had no concept of God. But then perhaps it *was* easier to believe in the Lord with a full belly. He had taken as his text for this morning's sermon, 'If we say that we have no sin, we deceive ourselves' and although he appeared initially to have the full attention of the congregation: honest hardworking men and women and the backbone of the town, William could tell a short way into the sermon that their minds were wandering elsewhere, possibly to the coming pleasures of roast beef and Yorkshire pudding.

If I could just convert one soul to God, thought William, his gaze settling on Mary, then my years of training won't have been wasted. After all, wasn't that why he had taken Holy Orders? It was pretty evident, though, that even with these advantages he handled the girl less successfully than Miss Fairfax. She was a little misguided in her politics, perhaps, but her compassion shone through and she was sympathetic and in tune with Mary's needs, and he wished she was here instead of Manchester. Handing the girl threepence, William said, 'Here, get yourself something to eat, Mary.'

'Ta.' Mary grabbed the money and sped off.

As an extra bribe, William called, 'After Sunday School there will be buns and lemonade. So make sure you're here.'

But with the coppers already burning a hole in her pocket, Mary closed her ears against his promises and made for the nearest tavern. It was bloody ridiculous thinking she could be somebody. This is where I belong she thought, gazing round her as she supped her gin. With the riff-raff of the town, its forney-squarers, chanters, thieves and vagabonds, it's all I deserve. And at least they're me own kind and I was a stupid cow thinkin' I could better meself anyway. Having come to this depressing conclusion, Mary poured the rest of the drink down her throat and ordered another one.

At closing time when the publican came to throw her out, along with the rest of the rag, bag and bobtail of the neighbourhood, Mary could hardly stand. And when he closed the door on her she collapsed onto the pavement, then rolled dead drunk into the gutter.

And while she lay there amongst her vomit, sometime during the darkest hour, a thief came stealthily, removed the boots from her feet and stole away unhindered into the night.

Chapter Seven

Emily's only other visit to Manchester had been with Adam by coach and that had taken sixteen hours. But in the space of nine years such rapid changes had taken place that she and her father were able to catch a train from Campbell Street and be in Manchester four hours later, even after changing trains at Rugby and Crewe and waiting for connections.

But these advances in machine and steam didn't mean passengers journeyed in more comfort and it required a certain hardiness of spirit to even contemplate travelling in the third-class open trucks. Fortunately, Jed had splashed out and bought second-class tickets, although Emily quickly realised that the extra money was no guarantee of a comfortable journey.

To the accompaniment of a great deal of grinding and hissing the engine pulled out of the station, gradually picking up speed then rattling along at such an alarming rate Emily began to fear that the train would fly off the rails. As if this wasn't enough to cope with, a fierce, bitter wind blew in through the unglazed windows, causing people to withdraw like tortoises into their heavy coats and blankets. The worst moments for Emily, though, were when they were sucked into the pitch-black tunnels. The noise resonated in her head and the acrid taste of smoke filled her mouth, and when the train did emerge into the light, she was treated to the unedifying spectacle of fellow passengers hawking and spitting onto the carriage floor.

By the time they left the train at Manchester, Emily knew she must look a fright. Her hair, clothes and skin were covered in a film of dirt and she tried in vain to blink away the grit in her eyes. Although she didn't say as much to her father, Emily decided that if this was progress, they could keep it. In her opinion, coaches were a far more civilised mode of travel. In fact, she couldn't really see trains taking on.

Fortunately, it was only a short walk to the Crown Inn where her father had arranged accommodation for the night, and as soon as they arrived Emily ordered hot water to be sent up to her room. The water the chambermaid brought was in a large jug and steaming hot. A fire had been lit in her room and stripping off, Emily soaped away the soot and grime and changed into a fresh dress. Glad to feel human again, she took out her speech and read it through to her reflection in the mirror, making what she felt were the appropriate gestures and pauses. But even after several rehearsals, she still felt unprepared and she went downstairs to meet her father, struggling to keep terror at bay.

'Posters and hand-bills advertising the meeting have already been distributed around outlying villages,' her father told her as she sat down to eat, 'and local Chartists will be waiting at mill gates to catch hands leaving work, so as long as the weather stays fine, we should get a sizeable crowd tonight.'

Emily had a sudden vivid picture of this crowd, their faces expectantly upturned, waiting to hear from her lips words that would change their miserable lives. Promises that Chartism would put food in their children's bellies and give them a living wage. Realising that in less than a couple of hours she would have to disappoint them, the roof of Emily's mouth went dry and she could hear strange erupting noises in her stomach. 'I'm sorry, I don't want anything to eat,' she said to the girl who came to take their order.

'You must have something,' her father insisted. It was natural she should be suffering from nerves, but having talked

Emily into addressing this meeting in the first place, Jed knew it was up to him to see she didn't lose her confidence. There were also signs that his ageing body wouldn't be up to the hurly-burly of political life much longer, and he wanted Emily to carry on the struggle to achieve the rights every free-born Englishman was entitled to. He was immensely proud of her, too, and he knew she had that fire, that gut belief required to succeed. Understandably, she wanted votes for women, and they'd discussed this more than once. But, as he pointed out, they had to get the six points of the Charter through Parliament first. Once they became the law of the land, then they could concentrate on universal suffrage and she'd understood this, bless her heart. Reaching out, Jed gave his daughter's hand a reassuring squeeze. 'I know how you feel, but you need a bit of food in your turn to keep you going for the evening.'

'I'll be sick if I eat one mouthful.'

But Jed was having none of it. 'Bring two plates of cold sirloin, with apple pie and cream to follow,' he said to the serving girl, who'd been waiting with barely contained impatience for their order.

She returned with the food and was placing it in front of Emily when a pronounced Irish accent hailed her father from the across the room. 'Why, hello there, Jed Fairfax.'

Emily looked up to see striding towards them with his right hand outstretched, a man of such commanding presence every diner paused in eating to watch him. Jed leapt to his feet, gripped the man's hand and slapped him on the shoulder with genuine delight. 'My God, it's good to see you, Rory, when did you get out?'

'About a month ago.'

'Sit down, Rory, sit down,' Jed ordered, called the girl over, ordered a pot of ale for him, then remembered Emily. 'Sorry, this is my daughter, Emily. Emily, this is Mr Rory Aherne, a brother in arms.'

As they shook hands across the table, Emily assessed Rory Aherne and he assessed her. What Emily saw was a man in his late thirties with a head of thick brown hair with a hint of copper in it, grey combative eyes and a full sensual mouth. In the assured way he held himself she also sensed a man of immense appetites. And she was spot on there. Rory Aherne *was* a man of immense appetites: for food, for life, for politics, but particularly for women, and what he saw opposite him was a handsome young woman he intended, by every means available to him, to lure eventually into his bed.

Having made this none-too-difficult decision, Rory promptly forgot about Emily and turned his attention to Jed. 'Where's Cooper? I thought he'd be with you.'

'No, the years in prison knocked the stuffing out of Thomas, poor man. When he was released he didn't return to Leicester and to tell the truth, the heart seems to have gone out of Chartism in the town. What we need is someone like you, Rory, to put vigour back into it.'

'I'd like to help, but I need to find work myself and London is the place for that.'

'Of course.' Jed turned to Emily and said with immense pride, 'Rory was jailed for a year for causing a disturbance of the peace at a Chartist meeting in Birmingham.'

'Was he now?' answered Emily, making it clear by her tone she wasn't impressed. She could definitely see him as a physical rather than a moral force Chartist, he had that look about him. A real stirrer and troublemaker.

'Put up job, of course.' Rory took a sup of his ale then banged the tankard down on the table. 'My residence in Her Majesty's prison was not exactly a pleasant experience, as you will remember yourself, Jed.'

'Indeed I do, although I consider it an honour to be thrown in jail for a political belief. All the best men are.'

Rory rested a brotherly arm on Jed's shoulder. 'So do I. Shall we drink to that, my friend?' He waved to the girl, ordered two more tankards of ale without having the manners to ask Emily if she wanted a drink.

Ignorant oaf, she thought, as she pushed the cold beef round her plate and pretended to eat. Neither did his conversation give her any cause to alter her opinion, for listening to him it quickly became apparent that his ideas on democracy didn't extend to women. Emily knew, too, that he'd take it for granted that it was her father who would be standing up on a wagon and facing the crowd later that evening. Well, his smug assumption that she was here in Manchester merely as his handmaiden would take a knock tonight, and the notion so pleased her that when the apple pie came she found that her appetite had returned and she tucked into it with great enjoyment.

Later, as her father helped her up onto the wagon, her makeshift platform, and introduced her to the crowd, Emily couldn't resist a quick glance in Rory's direction. The look flitting across his face was one of pure astonishment. Gratified to have dented his certainties, Emily's nervousness receded and she turned to face the crowd with her shoulders squared and chanting under her breath the last bit of advice her father had given her: *'No matter how terrified you are, don't let the crowd see it'.*

Before this moment she hadn't dared think about the size of her audience, but as she drew her notes from her bag, she surveyed the vast sea of faces, some mere blurs in the lamplight. Poles, topped with the red cap of liberty, bounced amongst the crowd and banners proclaiming, 'Reform and Universal Suffrage', fluttered in the night air. Emily also knew that as a woman, she had a certain novelty value and she could sense that the crowd was with her. In fact all, the signs were propitious.

Her father called up, 'You can do it, Emily, good luck,' and gave her the thumbs-up sign.

'Thanks, Papa.' Emily gave him a grateful smile, caught Rory Aherne's sardonic glance, flicked her notes with an irritated gesture and noticed, for the first time, policemen placed strategically around the edge of the crowd. Now why should they be here? she wondered. Were they expecting trouble?

Emily half expected to stumble over her opening sentence, but to her surprise she heard herself speaking in confident, articulate tones.

'The Barons got the Magna Carta, the

middle-classes the Reform Bill, but what has the working man had, I ask you?'

'Sweet bloody nothing,' a chorus of voices shouted back.

Emily smiled. 'You are right, gentlemen, instead they are ground down by unjust laws. What the People's Charter demands is a democratically elected Parliament ...'

Emily was going along nicely when a heckler shouted provocatively, 'Get back to the kitchen where you belong, lady. You she-Chartists are a disgrace to yer sex.'

Emily's neck reddened and her instinct was to retaliate, but her father had warned her about provocateurs, men planted by the government, so she ignored the insult and went on with her speech. 'Women, as much as men, are aroused to anger by the gross injustices inflicted on our class ...'

'Stay at home, then, stay at home ...' another man, this time in the front row, began to chant and this was taken up by several of his cronies, accompanied by a slow hand-clap.

Emily now did what she'd been warned by her father not to do, she lost her temper. 'Shut up!' she snapped, her foot shooting out at the same time to give one of her tormentors a sharp dig in the shoulder.

'Bugger you, woman!' the man exploded and made a grab at her ankle.

But in time, a sympathiser to the cause swung him round and with a warning, 'Don't you dare touch 'er,' punched him hard on the jaw. The man staggered back, recovered and then came for his assailant with both fists raised. Soon they were going at it hammer and tongs, bets were being placed on a likely winner, and as several more skirmishes broke out, the police moved in with staves and truncheons.

Emily stood her ground. Holding only the suggestion of a tremor, her voice rose above the hubbub, until to her horror, she saw that the police were cutting a swathe through the crowd and laying about them brutally and indiscriminately with their truncheons. There were screams of pain, shouts of terror but no one was safe, neither man, woman nor child. In less than five minutes a peaceful demonstration had turned into a battlefield and people staggered about half-conscious, with cracked skulls and blood-streaked faces.

As the police moved in behind her, Emily heard Rory shout, 'Run for it!'

But although by now her vocal cords had just about seized up in terror, Emily was determined to show the arrogant Irishman that, like her father, she was ready for martyrdom and so she pressed on. 'The agitation will continue until every man has obtained his long withheld rights and it is the duty ... Ouch!' Emily exclaimed, winded by the impact of an arm grabbing her roughly round the waist.

'Damn fool, let's get the hell out of here before you're torn to shreds,' a hated Irish voice snarled in her ear, then she was lifted bodily from the wagon.

Pinned to the vast plain of Rory's chest, Emily was conscious of his rapid heartbeats as he pushed his way through the crowd like some juggernaut. Initially she'd been too dumbfounded to protest, but then she remembered her father. 'Put me down, I've got to find Papa before he gets hurt,' she squeaked into his jacket.

'Your father has gone home,' Rory gasped, as they turned into a back street of factories and warehouses and finally found cover in a doorway. There was still a distant sound of mayhem and the occasional spark from hobnailed boots as a shadowy figure fled past but deciding they were relatively safe, Rory lowered Emily slowly to the ground, brown eyes gazing into grey.

Discomfited by this strange man, Emily straightened her jacket, pulled on her bonnet which had slipped onto her shoulders, then asked, 'Did I hear you say my father had gone back to the Crown?'

'You did,' answered Rory, still fighting to get his breath back.

'Excuse me for doubting your word, but I know Papa would never leave me to fend for myself in such a dangerous situation.'

'Which you started,' Rory accused. 'It really isn't a good idea for the speaker to assault a member of the audience, you know.'

'It was unintentional, the man's shoulder just happened to get in the way of my shoe,' Emily shot back.

Rory allowed himself the merest smile. 'Well, you're new to this game, but I suggest next time you act with more restraint. That is, if there is a next time, because in my opinion, politics is too rough a sport for a woman.'

Emily gave a derisive snort. 'Don't worry, I'd summed you up along with your opinions a couple of minutes after meeting you, Mr Aherne.'

'Did you now?' he mocked.

'In fact, men like you are no better than those Tory die-hards in Parliament. Your minds and opinions are set in aspic.'

'Thank you.' He gave a slight bow, but Emily could see that for the second time that evening she'd ruffled his complacency and this pleased her enormously. 'Anyway, since you had a spot of bother yourself and were put in jail for it, isn't it the pot calling the kettle black?'

'That was different,' Rory answered and strode off up the road.

'I hardly see why,' she said catching up with him.

'Because I happen to be a man.'

'And one of the lords of creation.'

'You could say that.'

Emily ground her teeth. 'You men are always so sure of yourselves, aren't you?'

Rory stopped suddenly. 'You seem to have some trouble dealing with men as a species, Miss Fairfax, now why is that, I wonder?'

Emily was almost, but not quite, speechless with anger. 'I refuse to respond to such cheap jibes. Good-night to you, Mr Aherne.' Overtaking him she hurried to put as much distance as possible between Rory Aherne and his opinions. But his comment had caught a raw nerve. Is that really how I sound, like some querulous spinster? she wondered. Was she allowing her bitterness at Adam's betrayal to seep into all relationships with men? It wasn't entirely due to her that the meeting had ended in mayhem, but she did have to accept some responsibility, although she would rather die than admit it to *that* man.

The evening had been a disaster, she felt emotionally drained and just a little weepy. But the enemy was just behind her, and he would delight in having his prejudices confirmed. *So, stiff upper lip,* Emily reprimanded herself.

However, it was with a sense of relief that, a short way ahead, she detected the glow of lights and heard the rumble of traffic. 'The main road, thank heaven,' she murmured and hurried towards it, making a bee-line for the cab-stand on the opposite side of the street. Calling to a cab driver, 'Take me to the Crown Inn, please,' she jumped in and was about to close the door when the handle was grabbed by Rory Aherne.

Emily gave him her best glacial stare. 'Haven't you got a home to go to?' she asked as he slid in beside her.

'Since you ask, my dear Miss Fairfax, no. So, if you've no objection, I might as well spend the night at the Crown Inn in the agreeable company of yourself and your father.'

Emily remained coldly aloof. 'You might have my father's company, but I shouldn't count on mine,' she replied, then hoping her snub had humbled him, she turned and stared out of the window for the rest of the journey. Hardly giving the cab time to draw up outside the Crown, she opened the door and jumped down. Determined at any cost not to accept Rory Aherne's charity, she smiled up at the driver. 'How much is that, please?'

'A shilling to you, miss,' the man replied as if this were some great bargain. Emily was taken aback at the price, considering a shilling to be daylight robbery. But she couldn't bring herself to haggle in front of Rory Aherne, and she was fumbling in her purse for the fare when he tossed the man a coin.

'Now, why did you do that?' Emily asked in a peeved voice as the cab moved off.

'Generosity of spirit, shall we say.'

'I'm sorry but I don't accept charity.' Pressing sixpence into Rory's hand, Emily strode off into the inn, making her way immediately to the coffee-room where she expected to find her father enjoying a bite of supper. But he wasn't there, neither was he in the jug-room. Puzzled, she turned to Rory, who was still shadowing her. 'That's funny, there's no sign of Papa. Do you think he met up with a friend and went on somewhere else?'

'I very much doubt it. He left the meeting because he was feeling unwell.'

Emily's heart missed a beat. 'And you didn't even bother to tell me?'

'That was your father's idea, not mine.

With your speech coming up, he wanted to spare you any extra worry.'

'Well, I'm certainly worried now,' Emily retorted and, pushing past him, she raced upstairs to her father's room.

'Papa,' she called in an anxious voice through the door, 'Are you all right?'

'I'm fine, dear, come in.'

Her father was sitting up in bed reading pamphlets. There was an oil lamp on a small table by the bed and Emily moved swiftly to his side. Studying Jed's face intently by its light, she decided he looked pale and tired. 'It's unheard-of for you to leave a political meeting, so you can't be all right.'

'It was the noise and crowds, it brought on a dizzy turn, that was all. I thought it best to come back here.'

'I'm fetching a doctor.' Emily turned to go but Jed reached out and grabbed her hand.

'You'll do nothing of the sort. Neither will you mention this episode to your mother. Is that clearly understood?'

Emily sighed. 'Yes, Papa.'

'Anyway, enough of me. How did the meeting and your speech go?'

'Very well,' Emily lied, wondering if Rory could be relied upon to keep his mouth shut and spare her father the true facts.

'Good girl, I knew you could do it. And did Rory look after you properly, like I asked him to?'

'He did.'

'Quite a character, isn't he?'

'Well he's certainly got a big opinion of himself.'

'With good cause. A great orator is Rory. He can hold the rowdiest mob spellbound.'

'What does he do for a living?'

'He earns money by his pen and has a good knowledge of the law, which he studied in Dublin, I believe. But he's committed to politics.'

'Has he no family, then? No wife, no children?'

'Not that he's ever talked about. But then Rory's something of a loner. In fact you never know where he'll turn up.'

'Like a bad penny, eh?'

'Not exactly. He does have this ability to rub people up the wrong way, I grant you, but along with his faults Rory has many virtues, one being his concern for justice. It's a cause he would die for.' Jed yawned and laid his pamphlets aside.

'You're tired, I'll leave you now.' Emily leaned over and kissed her father. 'Sweet dreams, Papa.'

At breakfast the following morning it was apparent by the way her father glanced up every time someone entered the dining room that he was keeping a look out for Rory. But no ebullient Irish voice hailed them from across the room and at last, with a note of disappointment in his voice he said, 'Rory must have left already.'

And you don't know what a relief that is, thought Emily, as she buttered a piece of toast.

'A pity. You were too modest to say much, but I wanted Rory to tell me how you got on last night.'

Emily bit into her toast. Yes, he'd tell you all right, how I was a miserable failure who caused a riot. *My, how he would enjoy that.*

'Never mind, he's coming to Leicester in October.'

Emily gave her father a sharp look. 'Coming to Leicester? What for?'

'I've asked him to give a talk at All Saints' Open. He'll get the people back.'

'Well, I hope he's not expecting to stay with us, we've no room.'

'But we will make him welcome, won't we, Emily?'

'Of course, Papa. Very welcome indeed,' Emily answered through tight, disapproving lips.

Chapter Eight

Adam understood very well the feeling that gnawed away at him: it was guilt. He could have made it easier for himself by blaming Isabelle for the whole sorry mess, but he was honest enough with himself to know that his betrayal of Emily had begun long before he met his wife. It had started with the first kiss he'd given another girl under a magnolia tree, and from there it slid inexorably towards all those unanswered letters and debauched nights in New Orleans whorehouses.

Adam knew, too, that he had relinquished the right to go within touching distance of Emily. However, there was nothing to prevent him dreaming about her, which he found himself doing more and more frequently. On one particular night she appeared smiling and beckoning to him, and the dream was so vivid, the message was so clear, he no longer felt the need to wrestle with his conscience. So, without even bothering about breakfast, the following morning Adam galloped at a reckless speed to Leicester, spurred on by the dream and its promises.

Adam was acting purely on impulse, and when he and his weary horse arrived in town, he didn't even know what he would say to Emily. But he was certain about one thing, if they did meet, excuses and apologies would be a waste of time.

In the event he spent two purposeless hours striding up and down High Cross Street and returned home deeply dejected. Within a day, though, Adam was back pounding the Leicester streets and hurrying after every dark-haired girl who bore the slightest resemblance to Emily. This went on for over two weeks and Adam had just about given up hope when one afternoon in Cank Street he saw her approaching. She was in the company of a young man and although he'd imagined the occasion often enough, it was such an emotionally charged moment, he stopped dead in his tracks.

It was his first glimpse of her after nine years, but even so Adam wondered how he could have possibly mistaken any other young woman for Emily, because there was no girl in Leicester who could match her luminous, dark-haired beauty. Her companion's garb told Adam that he was a clergyman, and although he didn't dare speculate on their relationship, when she laughed out loud at some remark he made, Adam's heart was pierced with jealousy and regret.

'Oh, Emily, my love, what an idiot I've been,' he murmured and the urge to call out to her almost overpowered his common sense. But to approach her was to risk seeing her dark eyes flicker over him with contempt, and that he couldn't have borne. Darting into a shop doorway, Adam pulled the brim of his hat over his eyes then turned up the collar of his coat. Confident in his disguise, he was about to walk on when, to his consternation, they paused to look in the shop window. He heard Emily say, 'They should have the music we want here.' Then, with barely a glance at Adam, she brushed past with a polite, 'Excuse me.'

The fluid grace of her body, the faint scent of eau-de-cologne he remembered so well, made him dizzy with longing. Instead of doing the sensible thing and moving away, Adam stood staring at Emily through the window, watching every movement, every gesture as she flicked through the sheets of music. After a lengthy discussion between her, the shop assistant and the clergyman, Emily finally handed over some money. The transaction concluded, the assistant rushed to see them off the premises, and Adam slid quietly away.

So what was the relationship between

Emily and the clergyman? Adam brooded. A good friend? Perhaps more? And why not? He had everything to offer her: security, respectability, loyalty, children; perhaps, even some happiness. Certainly not the pain he'd made her suffer. Unable to think of anything but his own wrecked life, Adam turned into the first tavern he came to and spent the rest of the day trying to drink himself insensible.

That evening after dinner Adam sat slumped in his chair, morose, uncommunicative and with a very sore head. When Isabelle left the room briefly, Matilda, who'd been watching him with concern, rose from her chair and went over to him.

'What's wrong, darling?' she asked, stroking her son's hair back from his forehead. 'You look very rather down in the dumps.'

Adam lifted his head and stared straight at his mother. 'I saw Emily in town.'

Matilda squeezed her fingers nervously together and walked to the window. 'Oh. And how was she?'

'She looked remarkably well. Even happy.'

Matilda swung round. 'Did you speak to her?'

'No, she was with someone. A clergyman. But what do you say anyway to someone you've betrayed.'

'Listen to me, Adam, you didn't betray her, you just grew apart. You were both so young when that other incident ...'

'What incident is this, dearest?' Isabelle stood in the doorway stroking the small dog she'd recently acquired and covertly studied mother and son. There are secrets here, she decided, the atmosphere reeks of them.

'Nothing, Isabelle.' Matilda smiled at her daughter-in-law then sat down and took up her embroidery.

Liar, thought Isabelle and almost laughed. But although she'd only caught the tail-end of their conversation, she found it paid to move around with stealth, occasionally pressing an ear to a door. It was surprising what snippets of gossip and snatches of intimate conversation you could pick up, and these were always useful weapons to have.

So, don't think you can hide your family skeletons from *me,* mother-in-law. Give me time and I'll winkle them out. Hiding her various plots and schemes behind a serene smile, Isabelle sat down and while she fed Mimi small pieces of cake, said, 'By the way, I've had some very pleasant news today. Olivia has written to say she's coming to stay at Fern Hill for two weeks. Judith has apparently had enough of England and wants to return to Paris. Her father will accompany her as far as London, where she's meeting a friend, and Olivia has decided to go too, to see her off.'

'That will be nice for you, dear, I know you how much you and Olivia enjoy each other's company.'

'Yes, but even better, she's suggested we go down to London with them. May we go, Adam? I've never been and I would so love to see it.'

Matilda looked across at her unhappy son. 'Yes, why don't you take Isabelle? Go to the theatre, enjoy yourself for a few days.' Anything to get you away from the malign influence of that Fairfax girl, Matilda thought.

Suddenly Adam roused himself out of his torpor. 'You know I can't, Mother, not with all this sheep stealing going on in the County at the moment, it wouldn't be fair to other farmers. We're determined to catch the blighters so we've set up a night watch, and I'll have to do my share along with everyone else. But why don't you go, Isabelle? I'm sure Olivia's father will be quite happy to chaperon you both and he knows London a great deal better than I do.'

Isabelle leapt to her feet and ran to embrace her husband. 'Are you sure?'

'Absolutely. You must write to Olivia, of course, and find out if it's in order for you to go without me.'

'Oh, Adam, you really are the dearest, sweetest man and I know Olivia would be quite happy for me to go alone, for we do get on so well. In fact, I often feel she's more of a sister than a friend.'

Several days later, with letters exchanged and the date of departure fixed, Olivia and Harry drove over to Trent Hall. After a great deal of discussion about the length of their stay in London and the number of gowns they would require for all the social events Harry had lined up for them, Olivia drew Isabelle aside. 'Let's go outside,' she whispered, 'there's something I need to ask you.'

Isabelle's eyes brightened for she adored confidences. 'We'll walk down to the village,' she said. Then, after glancing round the room, she linked arms with Olivia and drew her out of the house and down the drive.

It was early November, a bright cold day with the occasional late leaf spiralling down to join the golden carpet that crunched under the girls' feet. Olivia said nothing until they turned into Blackthorn Lane then, after a final glance over her shoulder, she gripped Isabelle's hand as if for reassurance. 'I find myself in a bit of a fix, and you're the only one I feel I can talk to, dear, for Judith would never understand my predicament.'

'Is it money? Have you been gambling?' Isabelle asked although, having a keen awareness of Max's wealth, she couldn't see this as a problem. She knew that some husbands could suddenly become quite mean however, when it came to their wives' debts.

'Nothing as simple. I'm with child.'

'Congratulations,' Isabelle replied automatically although she knew from previous conversations with Olivia, that her friend found no great joy in motherhood and in producing two sons, she considered she'd fulfilled her purpose as far as the continuance of family line was concerned.

'Don't congratulate me. I don't want the child. Besides,' she added nervously, 'I know for certain it's not Max's. He hasn't been near my room in months, and even he can count.'

As these indiscretions tripped off Olivia's tongue, Isabelle was all ears. 'Whose is it, then?'

An edgy smile touched Olivia's lips. 'Why, Theo's of course. Look, I need your help. You said not long ago that there were ways of dealing with unwelcome pregnancies. Herbs and potions you can take.'

'Well ... yes.'

'Can you get hold of some of this stuff for me?'

'Perhaps.'

'Where?'

'In Leicester.' Isabelle, in fact, had some very effective concoctions secreted away, for she disliked children intensely and had no intention of ever having one. But although she'd treated herself, she'd never done it for anyone else and the idea made her nervous. 'It could be dangerous,' she warned. 'You would bleed afterwards and you might have to spend several days in bed. How could you hide that from Max or the servants?'

'That's why it's got to be done while I'm at Fern Hill. Papa is a man of the world and very understanding about such matters, so he wouldn't ask any questions. Please, please help me, Isabelle, I would be eternally in your debt.'

Isabelle, who wasn't inclined to put herself out for anyone unless it benefitted her in some way, thought of Sir Austin and began to weaken. To have any chance of fulfilling her plans there, she would need plenty of invitations to Lindfield Hall. 'All right, but we'd need to go into Leicester.'

Olivia squeezed Isabelle's hand with gratitude. 'You *are* a good friend. We'll go tomorrow in my carriage, say we're going to order new dresses for London. You can slip out while I'm being measured for my dress and as a present I'll let you into a big secret.'

'Oh, what's that?'

'Before I tell you, you must fulfil your side of the bargain,' answered Olivia, who wasn't without guile herself, then leaning over, she kissed Isabelle with a display of great affection.

Although Isabelle had more than enough of her various remedies at home to deal with Olivia's particular problem, she chose not to tell her. Instead, while her friend was having a fitting at Dumbelow's, she trotted off to a chemist's. When Isabelle returned to the shop, she was shown to a seat by an assistant who brought samples of materials and pattern books in the hope of making a further sale. 'These are our latest patterns, Madam, they arrived from Paris only last week,' said the fawning girl.

Isabelle flicked over the pages of the pattern book and fingered the material with an increasingly dissatisfied expression. 'These styles are too dull for words,' she complained. She almost added that they might be all right for the matrons of Leicester, but thought better of it. After all, Olivia was one of their most valued customers and hardly dowdy. But in Isabelle's opinion she was too fond of frills and bows, and she considered her own dress sense far superior to her friend's.

'I'll leave it, thank you,' Isabelle said and to the young assistant's consternation, pushed the pattern book aside. She would wait until she reached London, she decided, then order a dozen gowns in the most expensive silks and up-to-date fashions, which couldn't fail to dazzle Sir Austin when next she was invited to Lindfield Hall. And considering the enormous favour she was doing her friend, it had better be pretty soon.

Having failed to tempt her into ordering a dress, the assistant now brought a tray of gloves in fine kid and pressed her customer to try them on. But Isabelle tossed them around with an indifferent expression and, realising she was going to have no luck here either, the girl, desperate to make a sale, drew out a box of white silk stockings. Finally, Isabelle snapped, 'I've told you, I do not require anything, now will you leave me alone.'

'Sorry, Madam.' The girl bit her trembling lip and retreated from Isabelle's presence with a sense of impending doom.

126

She'd really tried, but all her employer would be interested in was why she hadn't sold a single item to the wife of one of the most prosperous landowners in the County. Not that the snotty nosed madam, with her peculiar way of talking, would care, but she could be slung out of this job without even a testimonial, and what would become of her then?

The assistant's assessment of Isabelle's character was pretty accurate. Although she'd spent much of her life living on her wits, she was completely indifferent to the girl's distress. She'd clawed her way out of poverty, worked in places the assistant probably didn't even know existed, all to keep body and soul together, so she never wasted her time on such emotions as pity.

Isabelle gazed around her imperiously. And now she had all this, toadying assistants, a fine house. But she wasn't finished. There was still a way to go before she reached the pinnacle of her ambitions. Of course, circumstances had dictated she leave Louisiana but she couldn't have guessed what a dreary town Leicester was. Engulfed by a great wave of homesickness, Isabelle leaned back in her chair, closed her eyes and smelt the scented air, felt the languid heat of summer afternoons, heard through the shuttered windows the sound of slaves singing in the cotton fields. In comparison, the dripping autumnal mists of England left her feeling so low spirited she often wanted to stay in bed all day. But what irritated her above all were the inhabitants of the County, with their bland assumption that they were quite something, when in reality they were nothing but dreary provincials, and that included her mother-in-law. Not that Isabelle would ever make the mistake of openly showing her contempt. Matilda looked on her favourably and she didn't discount the importance of an ally.

After an age, Olivia finally emerged from the fitting room throwing apologies in Isabelle's direction. 'Sorry, dearest, but the waistline wasn't right.'

Isabelle adjusted her expression and smiled sunnily. 'Oh, I've been quite happy sitting here,' she lied and stood up, for the proprietress was holding the door open for them.

As they stepped out on to the street, the woman gave a deferential bob. 'Good-day to you, Lady Collins, Mrs Bennett,' she simpered.

'Adieu,' Isabelle nodded but Olivia, who had far more urgent matters on her mind, didn't bother to reply. In fact the door had hardly closed behind them before she turned to Isabelle with an anxious expression.

'Did you get the stuff?'

Isabelle nodded and patted the purse hanging from her wrist. 'It's in here.'

'Will it work?'

'I hope so. But there's never any guarantee with these things.'

'It must work or I'm done for.'

'How far gone are you?'

'I'm not sure, but not long.'

'Can't you get Max to make love to you? Babies often arrive early.'

'It required a great deal of effort for Max to sire three children. He has some trouble, you know ...' Olivia hesitated, '... down there.' Pointing to a fishmonger's slab, they were passing, she went on, 'In fact, it's got about as much life in it as that piece of wet cod.' Not sure of Isabelle's reaction, Olivia gave a slightly self-conscious smirk.

But this rather cruel disclosure of the inadequacy of Max's private parts was too much for Isabelle, and she started to giggle and soon the girls were clinging to each other in helpless mirth, while heads turned to gaze at them reprovingly.

'Hush.' Noticing the strange looks, Olivia managed to compose herself and clear her throat.

'Is that ... the secret you promised ... to tell me?' asked Isabelle, her voice still trembling with laughter.

Olivia's eyes gleamed. 'Oh, *no*. That's something even more interesting. Come with me, you are going to purchase a book.'

'What sort of book?'

'A novel,' replied Olivia. Pausing outside Jed's shop she turned and said in a low voice, 'Now I want you to take a good look at the young woman behind the counter. Her name is Miss Emily Fairfax, and she's the owner's daughter. I'll fill you in on the details afterwards.'

'Good-afternoon. Can I help you?' The young woman rather startled them by coming to the door and holding it open, leaving them no choice but to step inside.

'Is it all right if we just browse for the moment?' asked Olivia, and without waiting for a reply she moved over to study the shelves of books.

As she'd been instructed to, Isabelle studied the girl closely, half expecting her to be deformed in some way. However, she looked perfectly normal. Mystified, she followed Olivia to the far end of the shop.

'Have you any particular book in mind, Madam?' asked the young woman, who had come up behind Isabelle.

'Well, no we haven't, actually,' answered Olivia, smiling sweetly at Emily. 'You see,

130

my friend, Mrs Bennett, hasn't been long in this country and she's unfamiliar with English novelists, so I'm sure she would be glad of some advice.'

At this seemingly innocuous request, the blood rushed up from the girl's neck and turned her face scarlet. Almost immediately it drained away leaving her skin ashen. Then, with her hand clutching her throat, she turned and rushed from the shop, pausing to call over her shoulder in a choked voice, 'I'll ... I'll get my mother to come and serve you.'

'Come on, let's go!' Olivia hissed, and having stirred up a hornets' nest, she pushed a startled Isabelle out of the door. 'Now *run*,' she ordered.

But Isabelle refused to do anything so undignified. She was still obliged to move at a fair pace, though, and with her dress bunched in front of her to prevent herself tripping over, she pattered after Olivia. But she hadn't gone far before she'd had enough. Her mouth pinched into lines of irritation, Isabelle paused. 'Will you please wait? I'm out of breath,' she called to her friend. Checking first that they were a safe distance from the shop, Olivia slowed down. 'Now, please explain to me what all that business was about, back there?' Isabelle asked, when she caught up with her.

Olivia gave Isabelle a knowing smile. 'Did you notice how distraught Miss Emily Fairfax became when I said you were Adam's wife?'

'I could hardly fail to. But why?'

'I am now going to let you into the most enormous secret. It was because she had every expectation of being Mrs Bennett herself one day.'

Olivia watched Isabelle with interest, as various expressions flitted across her face, but the most gratifying was her look of utter surprise. It even, briefly, deprived her of speech. However, she quickly collected herself again. 'My Lord!' she exclaimed, 'Are you telling me she and Adam were betrothed?'

'No, there was a great deal of bad feeling between the families and both sides were opposed to them marrying, so Adam and Emily took matters into their own hands and eloped to Gretna Green. But her father and my Papa went after them and were able to put a stop to it. They were both very young, hot-headed and in love. I suppose it was a foolish thing to do, but I envy them in a way, experiencing that intense kind of love, and being prepared to take those sorts of risks.'

So, thought Isabelle, this was who her husband loved, no fine lady but a mere shop girl. Well, she would never have him.

'Of course, it could have caused the most terrific scandal,' Olivia went on, 'so it was hushed up, which means you must promise me that you will never repeat what I've told you to a living soul.'

'Of course I won't, my dear,' Isabelle assured her, but her smile hid her true thoughts. That girl probably thinks she's suffering right now, but by the time I'm finished she'll know what real pain is.

'That's why Adam went to America,' Olivia continued. 'It was agreed that if he still wanted to marry Emily after two years away, neither family would stand in their way.'

'Well, he obviously didn't love her that much, did he?' Isabelle snapped, 'Otherwise, he wouldn't have married me.'

Olivia squeezed her hand. 'And we are all very thankful he did, me in particular, because you are a true friend. But enough of them.' Olivia lowered her voice. 'When shall I take this potion?'

'I'll ride over tomorrow. You must drink it, then have a very hot bath. You'll feel ill afterwards, and bleed.'

'I'll say it's my monthly problem and stay in bed.'

'You've made me take a vow of secrecy,

Olivia, and now so must you. No matter what happens, you must never tell anyone, for if it was discovered I'd given you something to bring about a miscarriage, I could be in very deep trouble.'

Chapter Nine

The false smile, that slight baring of the teeth should have warned Emily it wasn't chance that had brought Olivia into the shop, but a twisted desire to make mischief. And she, of course, had played right into their hands and exposed her pain to their ridicule. Deciding that Adam must have changed from the person she knew if he could love such a woman, Emily fled.

Rachel, who was standing over the fire stirring something in a pot, thought at first that her daughter was ill when she staggered into the room pale and large-eyed. But a heartbroken sob followed by a wail of, 'Oh, Mama,' quickly caused Rachel to change her mind. Opening her arms, her daughter fell into them and abandoned herself to tears.

'Whatever is wrong, dear?' asked Rachel, alarmed at the strength of her daughter's grief, although a sixth sense told her that Adam was most likely somewhere at the bottom of it. As she considered the possibility, Rachel's lips tightened in anger over her daughter's head. Any happiness Emily had had with him was far outweighed by the pain he'd since caused and as if that wasn't enough now, with impeccable timing, he had to come along and upset the apple-cart again. And just when things were going along so nicely with the young curate.

'I've ... I've ... just seen Adam's wife,' Emily sobbed, confirming Rachel's suspicions.

'His wife? Where?'

'In the shop. She came in with that Lady Collins.' *Ah, Harry's daughter,* thought Rachel. *Now, what's that young madam been up to?* 'She brought her in to make mischief and humiliate me.'

Rachel felt a rush of protective love for her eldest child and conversely, a curdling hatred for Harry's daughter. 'Unfortunately, having the title "lady", doesn't automatically make you one,' she said acidly.

Emily lifted her head. 'You're right, she's just a spiteful bitch.'

'Emily!' Although Rachel felt bound to remonstrate with her daughter at her coarse language, secretly she was inclined to agree with her.

'Well, it's the truth!'

'Actually, she sounds like the sort of woman who gives bitches a bad name. As you know, dear, I don't always agree with your father, but he's absolutely right about one thing. That whole bunch, the Pedleys and the Bennetts are nothing but a curse on this family. I just wish they'd vanish from our lives. From the face of the earth, in fact.' Then, rather shamefully succumbing to curiosity, Rachel asked, 'But what does she look like? This wife of Adam's.'

Emily drew away from her mother, tucked a strand of hair behind her ear, blew her nose and considered the question. 'She's not very pretty.'

'Not pretty?' This surprised Rachel. Knowing men and their weaknesses, she rather imagined the American girl to be a striking beauty. For why else would Adam have cast her lovely daughter aside?

'Sly-looking, too,' Emily went on, 'and I've never seen eyes the colour of hers before. They were really strange. Sort of transparent, like a ghost's. Without her fine clothes you wouldn't give her a second glance. But go and take a look for yourself, she's down in the shop, waiting to be served.'

'Shall I?' Feeling rather daring, Rachel

took a couple of steps towards the door then stopped.

'Go on,' Emily urged.

'You don't mind?' Rachel was now grasping the door handle.

'Why should I? There's no turning the clock back. Adam is married and that's that.'

'Yes, and remember, he isn't the only man in the world. There are other, equally acceptable ones around,' Rachel pointed out, then went before her daughter could make some acid retort. But she quickly returned. 'Those young madams have buzzed off.'

'I'm not surprised. They didn't come here to buy a book, only to stir up trouble.'

'Just let either of them set foot in this shop again ...'

What her mother intended to do, Emily never discovered because the bell over the shop door tinkled. Mother and daughter looked at each other. 'Do you think it's them back?' asked Emily.

'It would be nice to think so because I've an awful lot to get off my chest. But I doubt it. Mischief-makers don't hang around. They cause havoc then disappear. But I'll go and find out.'

Rachel descended the stairs again, and Emily tiptoed to the door and listened.

There were no raised voices from below and remembering she was supposed to be keeping an eye on the stew, she went over and gave it a stir. While she tasted it, added a pinch of salt then a shake of pepper, Emily wondered how much Adam loved this new wife. Deeply, passionately, like he had claimed to love her? She supposed so, or he wouldn't have brought her all the way from America. Emily gave a small sigh. For weeks she had struggled to come to terms with the sad truth that although they'd been through so much together, Adam's love had been at best, transitory. Acknowledging this brutal fact had been like lancing an abscess, painful but cleansing. Slowly, acceptance had come, her damaged self-esteem repaired itself and she no longer greeted each day with dread. And now this.

Deciding it would give her the greatest pleasure to stick pins in the most sensitive parts of Adam's wife's body, Emily began setting the table. She heard Natalie greeting her mother, a thump, thump on the stairs then her sister burst into the room, young and exuberant and as yet unaware of life's disappointments and tragedies.

'Mmm, that smells good.' Natalie sniffed appreciatively, and let her school books drop on the floor. 'I'm famished, when can we eat, Em?'

'Well, certainly not until you've picked your books up and washed the ink off those hands,' Emily answered sternly. 'As for Mama and me, we'll sit down as soon she gets rid of her customer.'

'It's not a customer, it's a man come to see Papa.'

Emily went to the cupboard for three dinner plates. 'Well, he'll be unlucky, I'm afraid. Papa is out.' She was about to set the plates down to warm by the fire when her mother entered the room followed by a man whose size filled the doorway.

Emily nearly dropped the plates in astonishment. 'Mr Aherne!' she exclaimed, 'What are you doing here?'

'Good-day to you, Miss Fairfax.' Rory Aherne gave a slight bow. 'I happened to be passing through Leicester so I thought I'd drop in to see how your father was keeping.'

'Yes, and Mr Aherne has just told me about your father being taken ill in Manchester. Why was I never told about this, Emily?' There was a definite reprimand in Rachel's voice.

Emily threw a hostile glance in Rory's direction. Trust him to open his big Irish mouth, she thought. 'Papa forbade it. He said you would worry unnecessarily.'

'Or I'd stop him going on his precious political rallies, more like it. I shan't say any more at present, but it was irresponsible of you in the extreme not to tell me.'

Mortified at being rebuked by her mother in Rory Aherne's presence, Emily's dislike for him ballooned. However, he was quick to jump to her defence. 'It was Jed, he forbade her to say anything to you, Mrs Fairfax. Your daughter was deeply concerned about her father.'

'Well, I suppose Jed is hard to oppose,' Rachel answered, slightly mollified. 'But now that you are here, Mr Aherne, will you stop and have a bite to eat with us?'

'If it wouldn't be imposing, I would be delighted, Mrs Fairfax,' Rory answered, already removing his coat.

'There's hardly enough for the three of us, Mother,' Emily said pointedly.

'Rubbish,' Rachel replied. 'Now, come and sit down, Mr Aherne, while I go and close the shop.'

Emily and Natalie stood watching in silence as Rory made himself comfortable by the fire, feet on the fender, large hands spread towards the flames. Too thick-skinned even to know when he's not welcome, Emily decided, but Natalie was obviously intrigued by the stranger. 'Where are you from, Mr Aherne?'

Rory turned at Natalie's question and smiled at her. 'Why from the Emerald Isle.

Dublin, to be exact.'

'I'm Irish, too.'

Rory looked from Emily to her younger sister, obviously wondering how this could be. 'Natalie was an orphan, my parents adopted her. We think her mother might have been Irish,' Emily explained.

'Well, with that lovely red hair, I would say she was a real colleen and she should hold her head up high and be proud of the fact.'

Talk about the blarney, Emily thought disdainfully, but she noticed how Natalie's young face glowed with pride at the compliment, how she touched her flame-coloured hair with a sudden self-awareness. 'I'd like to visit Ireland one day,' said Natalie.

'One day, but not now. Things are pretty dire there at the moment. The failure of the potato crop is causing terrible distress. That's where I'm headed, to see if there's anything I can do to help. I'm catching a boat from Liverpool tomorrow morning.'

'A lot of Irish come to Leicester for the harvest and they often sleep fifteen to a room. There's a deal of fighting and drinking between them, as well.'

'You disapprove of the Irish by the sound of it, Miss Fairfax. But perhaps if you saw the sheer misery and squalor of their lives back home, thrown off their

141

lands by ruthless English landlords, you might feel slightly more compassionate.'

That combative look Emily recognised was there in Rory's eyes, but she answered robustly enough, 'I don't disapprove of them, Mr Aherne, but the area where they lodge around Wharf Street is crowded and unhealthy as it is. More people make a bad situation worse.'

'Well, Ireland should be ruled from Dublin, not Westminster.'

'Are you for Home Rule then, Mr Aherne?'

'What a strange question, Miss Fairfax. Of course I am.'

Emily, who was deliberately goading Rory Aherne, and enjoying it, watched him closely, He was obviously a man of extremes, easily driven to anger, and losing his temper with her would put him at a great disadvantage. However, he remained calm in the face of her provocation and the amused tilt of his lips told her it was beyond him to take the comments of a young woman seriously.

Deeply affronted, Emily headed off her own anger by pushing in front of him to check the potatoes were cooked and to give the stew a final stir. 'Mmm, I'm really looking forward to that,' said Rory. By way of reply, Emily slammed the lid back on the pot and went to lay an extra place. She was slicing bread when her mother returned.

'Would you believe it, we have another visitor.' Rachel was using the bright, optimistic tone she always adopted when William Jackson was around, and over her mother's shoulder Emily saw the curate's slightly anxious face.

'I'm sorry to interrupt you when you're about to have your dinner, Miss Fairfax, but it is urgent. I've got Mary down at the church, she's been involved in a fight. Somebody stabbed her with a knife.'

'Good Lord, is she badly hurt?'

'Fortunately not, but she does have a nasty gash on her arm which I think needs attention at the Infirmary. She won't listen to me, but she trusts you so I was wondering if you could come and have a word with her?'

'I really shouldn't have dragged you out in the middle of your dinner hour,' William Jackson kept apologising as he and Emily hurried towards All Saints', 'but you were the only person I could turn to.'

Although she could hardly say so, Emily blessed William for his timely intervention. It had spared her sitting through a meal being condescended to by Rory Aherne. 'Don't worry about it, Reverend Jackson, I quite understand. Mary is hardly an easy

143

girl to handle. Tell me what happened. How did she get into this fight?'

'She's gone dumb on me, won't say a word. I thought you might have more luck. I think she likes you.'

'Cynical of me to say so, I suppose, but the boots probably helped.'

'Except that she doesn't appear to have them any longer. They've probably been pawned.'

'Oh, no!'

'Well, we tried. We can't do more. And Mary is so brutalised by her circumstances, she's probably already had most of the finer human emotions knocked out of her.'

'Some people don't stand a chance, do they, Reverend? Not from the moment they are born,' Emily challenged and waited for his answer.

Since William's job was to minister, he wanted to disagree, to say that if only these people could find it in themselves to take God into their hearts, He would give them succour. But, anticipating Emily's snort of derision, he refrained and instead of entering into a robust defence of his faith, feeling a real Judas, rather weakly replied, 'No, I don't suppose they do.'

William's faith was total, unquestioning and he saw Leicester as merely a stopping-off point on his way to where he knew his true vocation lay: India, and the conversion of Hindu and Moslem to the True Faith. But the church didn't like its priests in foreign countries without a wife, fearing they would fall prey to all sorts of temptations, such as going native or falling in love with one of the local women. William glanced at Emily, intelligent, compassionate, young, strong, and thought: a little too radical perhaps for some, but otherwise she would make an ideal vicar's wife. She'd be a helpmeet and companion in the life he had mapped out for himself. Unfortunately, he had so little experience of young women, he hadn't the vaguest notion of how he should set about wooing her.

Blissfully ignorant of the drift of William's thoughts, Emily waited for him to pull open the church door for her. A few pale beams of sunlight had managed to pierce the sooty windows and in that dimness peculiar to churches, she saw Mary. The girl was sitting in a pew halfway down the aisle nursing her arm, and although she must have heard the door opening and their footsteps she didn't turn round.

Emily slid into the pew beside her. 'Hello, Mary, you seem to have been in the wars. Can I have a look?' Without waiting for the girl's consent, she took

145

her arm. Blood was seeping through a piece of rag, obviously William's somewhat awkward attempt to staunch the flow. Emily unwound the bandage and saw that the knife had scored the soft inside of her forearm just missing her wrist and, although not deep, the wound was long and jagged. 'This is nasty,' Emily exclaimed. It was apparent, too, that if it wasn't to become infected, the wound would need cleaning and a salve applied.

'T'int noothin'.' Mary was dismissive. 'I've had far worse.'

'How did it happen?'

'Me mam tried to steal some money off me.'

'Your mam? Surely not.' The thin, old-young face stared back at her with a ruminative expression and Emily thought, this girl's already crammed more experiences into her short life than I even know about.

'You don't know 'er.'

'But why?'

'She needed it for booze. She gets in a terrible state if she can't get hold of none. Shakes and sweats, she does. I caught 'er in the nick of time, but she went for me wi' a knife. She'd kill for gin, the old cow.'

'Good Lord!' William exclaimed as he listened to this tale of robbery with violence then felt obliged to add, 'But

146

you shouldn't call your mother names, Mary, it isn't nice.'

Mary scowled at him. 'Why shouldn't I? It 'appens to be true, 'cept that cows is nicer.'

'Honour thy father and thy mother, the Good Book says.'

'Sod the Good Book.'

'Yes ... well,' Emily interrupted. 'Mary, we'd better get you to the Infirmary and have that wound looked at.'

'I in't going to no Infirmary.' She did a furtive shuffle along the pew, and Emily knew she was going to make a bolt for it.

'All right,' she compromised, 'we won't bother with the Infirmary, but that cut is nasty. So would you come home with me, Mary, and let my mother clean and dress it?'

''Ome, wi' you?' Emily nodded. 'Oh, I'll do that awright.' Mary leapt to her feet, adjusted her rags and pulled her fingers through her matted locks with all the care of a lady preparing for a ball. The improvement was indiscernible and Emily just hoped the midday meal would be over because the girl's unwashed odour would dull anyone's appetite.

Her father had returned by the time they arrived back and he and Rory were sitting opposite each other, firing their opinions back and forth across the hearth like bullets, obviously relishing the verbal tussle. But when the three of them crowded into the small room and Emily pushed Mary forward, an unaccustomed silence fell. 'Mama, this is Mary and she has a nasty gash on her arm which I thought you'd take a look at.'

Rachel recovered from the shock of the verminous waif, remembered her own miserable beginnings and gave the girl, who was staring about her with the look of a cornered animal, a welcoming smile. 'Hello, Mary. Can I have a look at your arm?'

Mary, who looked ready to make a run for it, turned and buried her head in Emily's chest. 'No.'

'Perhaps you'd like something to eat first?' At the mention of food, Mary drew away from Emily, and managed a nod. Transferring her attention to Rachel, she watched with a ravenous expression as Rachel tipped the remains of the stew—*my dinner*, thought Emily—onto a plate. 'Here you are, dear.'

Mary approached the table warily, snatched up the plate and to everyone's astonishment, lowered her head and gobbled the food down like a dog. When she'd finished, she wiped her mouth with the hem of her skirt, belched then declared,

148

'I in't never tasted anythin' so nice as that in all me life afore.'

Guessing it would be a waste of time, Rachel curbed an instinct to rebuke the girl for her lack of manners. Mary had probably never used a plate in her life, let alone held a knife and fork, so a reprimand would be pointless. 'Well, I'm glad you liked it, Mary. May I look at that cut, now?'

'Yeah, awright,' Mary answered, prepared to humour these strangers now that she had a full stomach. The bustle her assent produced astonished Mary. Hot water was poured into a bowl, sheeting was ripped in two, and in no time the wound was washed and dressed. It was quite a novelty, being the centre of attention, and the bandaged arm lent her a certain importance. Wait till they see this back 'ome, Mary thought and her sharp eyes did a quick inventory of the room, searching for a knick-knack small enough to hide in the folds of her dress. But then, for perhaps the first time in her life, Mary had a glimmering of conscience. No, she decided, it wouldn't be right, not after these folks 'ave helped me. Her fingers itched though and the temptation was strong, but the eruption of virtue she felt was almost compensation enough. 'I'm off then,' she announced.

'I'd better go, too,' said William.

'I'll see you out,' said Emily.

'Ta-ra.' Mary waved her bandaged arm.

'Now, see you look after that cut,' Rachel called to her.

'Ooh, I will,' the girl promised.

Emily went down to see William and Mary off, but it wasn't until she had said goodbye to them both that it occurred to her that although Rory Aherne had been interested in everything that was going on around him, while Mary was there, he hadn't once opened his mouth to offer an opinion. And that, Emily decided, had to be some sort of record.

Chapter Ten

Isabelle put her plans into action with extreme care. First, she made sure Adam and his mother were out, then she went down to the stables and ordered a trap to be made ready. Finally, back in her bedroom again, she unlocked a drawer in her escritoire, removed several small bottles and slipped them into her purse. Intrigue was one of the great pleasures of Isabelle's life and her eyes glinted back at her with pleasure as she stood in front of the cheval glass and finished getting ready.

Isabelle had hoped to make a discreet departure so her brow creased with irritation when there was a tap on the door and her maid entered.

'Going out, Madam?' Hattie enquired as she began picking up various discarded garments lying about the room.

'Yes, Hattie, for a short drive. I have one of my headaches and need some fresh air.'

'On yer own, Madam?'

Isabelle swung round to face her maid. 'Yes, on my own.'

'Ooh, is it safe, Madam?'

Isabelle enjoyed tantalising Hattie and she advanced on her making clawing movements with her fingers. 'Why? Are there wolves and bears out there in the woods that might eat me up, or goblins, who might spirit me away?'

But Hattie, who knew she was being mocked, refused to back away. She was quite aware that her mistress considered her a dull, foolish country bumpkin but although she hid it under a fawning exterior, she hadn't much of an opinion of her either, and she certainly didn't deserve Mr Adam. 'No, Madam?' she retorted, 'but there's some strange folk around and t'int always safe for a young lady on her own.'

'Fiddlesticks.'

'Well, it might rain,' Hattie finished lamely, terrified that if any mishap should befall her mistress, she'd be blamed and sent back to work as a humble skivvy in the kitchen again. Being a ladies' maid was much more to her taste and it gave her a status in the household which she was determined to cling on to.

'Then I shall get wet, but I don't expect I'll melt. Now, fetch my cloak and help me on with it, please. And there's no need for anyone to know I'm out.'

'Supposin' they ask for you?'

'Tell them I'm walking in the grounds. Is that clear, Hattie?'

'Yes, Madam,' Hattie answered, with a quick bob, waited until the door had closed, then went and watched from the window as her mistress was helped in to the trap. She heard Isabelle order the horse to 'walk on', bade her time, but once she was certain she was out of sight, Hattie locked the door then danced over to the large cupboard which ran the length of the wall. 'Come on my beauties,' she said and, pulling open the door, Hattie sorted through her mistress's newest and prettiest gowns, dragging out those which most took her fancy. Quickly divesting herself of her maids' uniform, she began trying them on in quick succession, tossing them aside carelessly like her mistress did, when they didn't fit. The last dress she tried on, however, fitted her to perfection. It was a beautiful dark blue silk and cut low enough to do justice to her plump breasts. Pushing them up so that they spilled out over the tight bodice, she pinched her cheeks and wetted her lips.

'You are a fine young lady, and no mistake,' Hattie informed her reflection and swished the wide skirt back and forth in front of the cheval glass. If only Mr Adam could see her now, he wouldn't be able to resist falling passionately in love. 'A kiss, Hattie.' Playing the part, she lowered her voice to a masculine level.

Hattie cast her eyes modestly downwards. 'Oh, Mr Adam, it would be so wrong.'

'Never.' Moving close to the mirror, Hattie pursed her lips against the cold glass, closed her eyes and with a small swooning sound, collapsed to the ground. 'I'm your slave. Take me, Adam, now, please,' she moaned, yanked up the skirt of the dress and began writhing shamelessly around on the floor.

As she approached the house, Isabelle could see Olivia pacing up and down, sensed her agitation, recognised that her friend's need for her at this moment was total and felt a tremendous surge of power. And as soon as Olivia heard the wheels of the trap on the gravel her head jerked up, the tense expression on her face relaxed into a smile and she ran down the steps to greet Isabelle. Assisting her from the trap, Olivia asked in an anxious tone, 'Have you brought the stuff?'

'Yes, it's in here.' Isabelle tapped her purse and looked quickly about her. 'But where are your father and Judith?'

'Gone to Leicester. They'll be away all day.' Slipping her arm through Isabelle's, Olivia drew her towards the house.

But Isabelle held back. 'You know I want to help you Olivia, but you must promise me that whatever happens, you'll never tell a soul I've been here today.'

'Not a mention of it will ever pass my lips, I swear it.'

'I won't be able to stay with you, either. I have to be back at Trent Hall before luncheon.'

'I understand perfectly and I'm just grateful for what you are doing. But come, let's go up to my bedroom. I'm nervous but I want to get the business over and done with.'

'It might take a while to have any effect, so don't move far from the house,' Isabelle warned and drew out various bottles from her purse. With her back to

Olivia she measured the substances into a glass, mixed them thoroughly then handed the glass to Olivia. 'Now, drink it,' she ordered.

Olivia had gone very pale and her fingers trembled as she took the glass. 'It won't kill me, will it?'

'Of course not. If it did, I'd be dead now. But you will feel ill and bleed heavily, if it works.'

'Oh, God, please make it work,' Olivia implored then throwing back her head, she swallowed the concoction in one go. Olivia shuddered in disgust. 'It's absolutely revolting!'

'It has to be revolting to do you any good, that's the price we women pay.'

'What's in it?'

'That is a trade secret. But it's powerful stuff. Even so some babies won't budge. If it doesn't work you'll have to find some way of exciting your husband.'

'How?' Olivia was now lying stretched out on the bed with her hands on her stomach and Isabelle lay down beside her. 'There are all sorts of female tricks that can turn a man into your slave.'

'Such as.'

Isabelle smiled mysteriously, moved closer and, cupping her hand against Olivia's ear, whispered her secrets of the boudoir in her ear. As she did, her friend started back and

155

her eyes widened in astonishment. 'You do that? To men?'

'Yes. But not just me. Other women do it, too.'

But Olivia looked doubtful. 'Oh, I don't know if I could. I'd feel so ridiculous, I'm sure I would have a fit of the giggles.'

'You might not have any choice,' answered Isabelle practically.

'Anyway, where did you learn all these so-called tricks?' asked Olivia curiously.

Isabelle shrugged. 'They are what any woman of the world would know about, my dear.'

'Yes, I suppose they are,' answered Olivia, thinking at the same time that Isabelle was just about the most exciting and interesting friend she had ever had.

Doubled up with cramps and smothering her groans into her pillow, the unwanted lump flushed out of Olivia into the towel clamped between her legs sometime during the night. Sweating and shivering, she struggled to the edge of the bed, lit a candle, pulled a pillowcase from its bolster and stuffed the towel and the embryonic mass well down inside it. A hammer banged away incessantly in her head and her body felt as if it had been turned inside out. But never mind her pain, Olivia knew she had to keep her

156

mind concentrated, and the evidence of her crime got rid of before her maid came in to wake her. She was a girl who knew how many beans made five and it wouldn't take her more than a second to work out was wrong with her mistress. And these suspicions would be carried back to the servants quarters and in no time the whispers and gossip would reach Max's ears and what would happen to her then?

Her husband was willing to turn a blind eye to most things, but if his wife caused a scandal in the County, if the family name was besmirched, he might cast her off without a penny and even forbid the children to see her. With this image of herself, abandoned and alone in an attic, forced to take in sewing, Olivia inched herself slowly upright. As she did the room tipped, the candle flame became a mere pinprick and she felt the blood gush from her like a fountain.

In a blind panic that certain death was tapping on her shoulder, Olivia dragged the sheets from the bed and began tearing them in strips and stuffing them up her nightgown. But just as quickly the linen became saturated. Giving up, Olivia sank to the floor and wept. Her room looked as if it had witnessed a particularly bloody murder, and with an honesty not natural

to her, Olivia saw that it had in a way:
for tonight a child had been sacrificed.
Her child. She'd deliberately killed her
baby, deprived it of the right to life,
to happiness. Olivia pressed her hands
against her mouth to stifle the guilty
sobs that racked her. No, no she mustn't
think such thoughts or she would go
truly mad. Forcing her mind back to
happier times, Olivia remembered when
her other babies had been born and grew
calmer. Then there had been a nurse and
doctor in continuous attendance, servants
running around with hot water, her every
whim catered for. Now it was quite likely
she was going to bleed to death alone
in the dark, like an abandoned servant
girl.

With a fervour born of fear rather than
piety, Olivia's lips began to move in prayer.
'Please, dear God, don't let me die and
I promise that from now on I shall be
a good, faithful wife,' she bargained and
gradually, as if in answer to her petition,
the bleeding began to ease.

Briefly bowing her head, Olivia thanked
Him for his intervention, then got on with
the essential task of clearing up. Disposing
of the bolster case was her biggest problem.
She thought about hiding it under the
bed but eventually stuffed it away in
the bottom of one of her drawers and

covered it with clothes. But Olivia knew she couldn't leave it there because the contents would quickly putrify and the smell invade the room like a butcher's shop. Tonight, though, her brain was past making any more decisions. Tomorrow she would work out what to do, maybe take it out in the woods and bury it.

With every movement dissipating her small reserves of strength, Olivia crept along the corridor, found fresh bed linen, washed and put on a clean nightgown. Finally, completely exhausted, she fell into bed and slept. But the ordeal invaded her dreams and once or twice in the night Olivia called out, and it was the cry of a soul in deep torment.

The following morning when her maid came to draw back the curtains and wake her with tea and bread a butter, Olivia shouted bad temperedly, 'Go away,' and covered her head with a blanket. Later, though, when the timid maid dared to stick her head round the door and announce that Mrs Bennett was downstairs, to the girl's surprise, Olivia instructed that her friend be sent up immediately.

Being an expert on such matters, Isabelle knew from Olivia's wan features and the black circles under her eyes, that the potion had done the trick. Expecting grateful thanks she hurried to her friend's bedside, and bent down and kissed her. 'How are you, dear?' she asked solicitously.

But no thanks were forthcoming, just complaints. 'I'm ill.' Olivia pushed the pillows behind her back and eased herself up gingerly. 'I feel as if I've spent the night on a battlefield. In fact I thought I was going to die. It's far worse than having a baby.' As she started to relive the long terrifying night she'd just endured Olivia began to cry.

Isabelle sat down on the bed and put her arms round Olivia. 'But it's all over now, you are no longer with child, remember that and be grateful.'

But although her relief was intense, in a way Olivia recoiled from what she'd done and the guilt still clung to her. 'Well, it won't ever happen again. The next time I see Theo I shall tell him that our liaison is over. No man is worth what I've been through. If necessary I shall live the life of a nun.' Olivia pressed the palms of her hands together piously as if to make her point.

'But we are going to London shortly,' Isabelle expostulated. 'Do you intend to live the life of a nun down there?'

Olivia thought about it. 'Well, perhaps not,' she answered, and for the first time that morning, laughed.

Chapter Eleven

Emily knew that in a small town like Leicester she was bound to bump into Adam one day. The only question was when. So she'd spent many evenings in her room rehearsing various greetings and finally settled on a cool, slightly surprised, 'Oh, hello.'

However her plans were laid to waste when she saw him walking towards her one grey, snowy afternoon in February. Emily stopped, her good intentions collapsing in panic then, gazing about her with the frantic eyes of a deer cornered by a huntsman, she dashed across Hotel Street and up Friar Lane. But her way was blocked by a hackney carriage. In her haste, she darted round behind it, slipped on the hard-packed snow and fell face forward into the path of a carriage coming from the opposite direction.

Emily tried to wriggle out of the way but she was hampered by her heavy winter clothes and fear, which had sapped the strength from her legs. The wheels were almost upon her, the crushing horse's hooves no more than an inch from her head when she felt herself being yanked up by her collar and dragged unceremoniously to the other side of the road. Then a voice she hadn't heard for nine years asked solicitously, 'Are you all right, Emily?'

Emily leaned weakly against Adam and closed her eyes. 'I will be in a moment,' she answered, as his arms closed round her and she felt their healing spirit.

'Oh, Emily, my love,' Adam murmured into her hair and the words and the tone were a balm to her wounded spirit. *He still loves me,* Emily thought incredulously, and all the grief and bitterness of the last months faded from her mind, and he was forgiven.

'Look, can we go somewhere, Emily? I must talk to you, explain.'

She stared up at him. 'But where?' Although they were standing in a shop doorway, Emily began to feel exposed and conspicuous. 'Oh, Lord, there's one of our neighbours across the street, and she's a right busybody. If she sees me here with you it will go straight back to my parents.' Emily tried to melt into the shadows. 'Is she looking this way?' she asked, growing quite agitated.

Adam shook his head. 'No, she's gone.'

Knowing if she had a shred of common sense, she would follow suit, Emily backed away from Adam. 'I'm sorry, I'll have to go, too. You're a married man and we daren't risk being seen together. Tongues would start wagging and my reputation would soon be in shreds.'

But before she could make a run for it, Adam reached out, grasped her gloved hand firmly and pulled her close, so that their breath mingled in the cold air. 'Don't go yet, please,' he begged. 'Let's work something out. What about Lily? Wouldn't she help us? She was always so understanding in the past.'

'Life has changed for Lily, like it has for us all. She's not free to do as she pleases these days. The children take up most of her time.'

'Ask her, please, Emily,' Adam pleaded. 'She can only say no.' He put his finger to his mouth, kissed it, then pressed it against Emily's lips, holding it there until her blood quickened and her pulses raced. The naked need for her in his eyes weakened her resolve, even though a small cool part of her knew she was being manipulated. Although she was by nature cautious, when Adam pulled the strings, she danced. And that was how it had always been, she thought, remembering their disastrous elopement.

'I can't.'

But Adam detected a lack of conviction in her voice, so he pressed on. 'Yes, you can.' His tone was low, persuasive. 'And I do love you, Emily. Most desperately.'

Emily wavered. She knew she shouldn't allow herself to be seduced by honeyed words, and already she could imagine the end of their affair, saw herself clearly, an abandoned weeping figure. And yet she was hungry for the taste of his lips on hers and she'd been denied love for too long. What was wrong with trying to snatch a little happiness? Emily asked herself, seesawing between euphoria and doubt. I wouldn't be stealing him from that woman, either. Adam might not belong to me in the eyes of the church, but in every other sense he does.

Pushing aside any last lingering doubts, Emily pressed her face against Adam's heart and, heard its steady beat. 'I'll go and see Lily now. Follow me and wait at the end of the street.'

If Emily's request surprised Lily, she didn't show it. 'It will be just for a hour or two so that Adam and I can talk,' she explained.

'Don't you worry, I'll take the children round to Septimus's mother and give Bertha the afternoon off,' said the ever-accommodating Lily, who'd never lost her taste for a bit of intrigue in the cause of true love. 'Use any room you like,' she said with such a knowing wink, Emily blushed.

'I'll be gone by two and back at four, and the key to the front door will be under the flowerpot. Good luck.'

And as easily as that, the assignation was arranged.

Emily hugged her friend. 'Lily, you are an angel.' Then, because it had all been contrived so painlessly, she felt obliged to express some doubts. 'You don't think I'm a hussy, do you? After all, Adam is married.'

'I've got quite a lot of time for hussies myself, they enjoy life so much more. Besides, there's such precious little romance in this life, I came to the conclusion a long time ago that it's wise to take it where you can get it,' Lily retorted, making obvious reference to her own rather unconventional affairs of the heart. 'But do be careful. You are a single girl, all men are selfish by nature and Adam hasn't done a lot for your reputation so far. Don't let him ruin it completely.'

'I'll be sensible, don't you worry, we just want a chance to talk in private.'

Lily's lips gave a cynical twitch. 'Oh, yes?'

It was snowing heavily and the cold bit Emily's nose, toes and fingers as she walked up to Lily's front door, retrieved the key from under the flowerpot and

165

unlocked the door. Leaving it ajar, she removed her coat and bonnet, hung them on the stand then stood in the hall and waited, her mind raging with conflicting emotions. The snow muffled sound and she didn't hear Adam's footsteps until he slid in through the door. He leaned against it and Emily heard it snap shut. In the muted light, she noticed snowflakes melting on Adam's dark hair. They stood, regarding each other and in her heightened state of emotion the silence seemed to stretch like elastic between them.

'Come here,' Adam ordered at last and held out his arms.

Wishing her heart would quieten down, Emily moved towards Adam, and he enveloped her with his passion, kissing her with a man's kisses that were demanding and hungry. Swooning with love, she clung to him and he half dragged, half carried her to the parlour, where he lay her down on the sofa. Unbuttoning her dress, he pulled down her stays and took her nipples in his mouth. Emily arched her back in ecstasy and misreading her, Adam grew hasty, pushed up her dress and, his eyes drawn to the gap in her drawers and what he so desired there, he tried to force her legs apart.

Immediately, Emily remembered Lily's warning and her ardour drained away 'No,' she protested and sat up.

'But I'll go mad if you don't let me,' Adam wailed and pressed his face against her neck.

She pushed him away. 'I'm sorry, I know I'm as much to blame, but we shouldn't have come here, it was a dreadful mistake.' Emily's voice was unsteady as she attempted tuck in stray locks of hair and adjust her clothes. When she felt decent again, she went to stand up, but Adam pressed her back on to the sofa.

'Don't go, please.'

'Adam, what future is there in this for either of us when you are married?'

'It's a mockery of a marriage.'

'Oh, yes. How many women have heard those words before?'

'Don't be cynical, please. I'm not trying to win your sympathy, Emily. I dislike my wife intensely.'

'Why ever did you marry her, then?' *Particularly when we had an understanding,* Emily was tempted to add.

'I'm not trying to excuse myself and I know I've treated you abominably, but I swear that I never loved Isabelle. I met her quite by chance a few weeks before I returned to England. She told me some fanciful tale which I foolishly believed, then she hoodwinked me into marriage with further lies.'

'You make yourself sound rather gullible.'

'I was. I was stupid to be taken in by her, but I tend to assume people are telling me the truth. And Isabelle's a darn good actress. She doesn't know it, and you must promise never to repeat this to a living soul, not even Lily, but I'm having enquiries made about her in America. I intend to uncover the true story of my dear wife and her past.' Adam lifted Emily's hand to his mouth and kissed the palm gently. 'I do love you so much, Emily and the biggest regret of my life is that I stayed in America for so long, when I should have come home and married you.'

'Yes, it might have spared us both a great deal of unhappiness. Still, your mother got what she wanted. She at least, must be happy with the situation.' Emily, stood up. 'I'll go and make some tea. No, you stay here,' she added when Adam went to follow her. 'I need to think.'

The kettle was singing on the hob, and as she warmed the pot Emily mulled over in her mind what Adam had just told her. It seemed a bit far-fetched that any man should hate his wife after only a few months of marriage. She'd heard of marriages going sour, but not that quickly. Obviously it suited Adam's purpose to say he loved her, but it hadn't stopped him neglecting her while he was in America. Emily spooned tea leaves into the pot, poured on the boiling water and stirred thoughtfully. So who was the real liar here, Adam or his wife? And even if she was prepared to believe him, nothing changed the fact that he was still shackled to Isabelle, which meant for her a few snatched clandestine meetings. Exciting for a while but likely to soon pall. As always, it would be her who made all the sacrifices, risked her good name again. It wouldn't be long, though, before she started becoming viewed in people's eyes as a spinster, not a role she relished. She'd never known a man in the biblical sense of the word either, but above all, what she wanted was a fulfilling, loving marriage like her parents had. Not a hole-in-the-corner affair with the constant fear of an unwanted child hanging over her.

Of course, there was William Jackson, a highly respected member of the community. Emily briefly imagined herself as a vicar's wife. No, it was out of the question. She respected William and his good Christian soul, but that was no foundation for marriage. I will wait, Emily decided, and if the right man doesn't come along, then I shall devote my life to politics.

Emily looked at the kitchen clock and saw that it was three-fifteen. They would have to be out of the house in half an hour. Hurriedly, she shoved teapot, cups, milk and sugar onto the tray then, her spine stiff with resolve, she made her way back to the small parlour.

But her sense of purpose almost crumpled when she saw Adam sitting with his head in his hands in an attitude of despair. *Don't weaken now,* a voice warned her. Emily banged the tray down on the table, the cups rattling. Adam looked up, but she set her heart against the bleakness in his eyes. *You've made your bed, Adam ...* she recited to herself. Then brightly, with teapot poised, she enquired, 'Tea?'

'Please.'

Adam took the cup and as he stirred, Emily said, with barely a quaver, 'You must drink that and go. You see ...' and here she did falter. 'I ... I've come to a decision Adam, I'm afraid we won't be able to ... to ever meet again.'

Adam grabbed her hand and pulled it insistently. 'Please, Emily, don't be so cruel. Not when we have just found each other again.'

'I have to be cruel to save myself from further heartbreak. Please go now.' She shook his hand off and turned away.

'It needn't be heartbreak, it could be

happiness, but if that is what you want, Emily ...' Adam's voice broke and, unable to finish, he hurried from the room.

Emily heard him pause in the hall for his coat and she had to grip the table to stop herself running after him. The front door opened and there was a gush of freezing air before it closed again with an awful finality. Tears streaming down her face, Emily ran to the window and banged on the pane. 'Adam,' she sobbed, 'come back, I beg you.' But it was too late, he had already gone, swallowed up by the blizzard raging outside.

In the days that followed, Emily thought she'd be grateful for any diversion that would take her mind off Adam, until her father looked up from a letter he was reading. 'Oh, splendid, Rory's accepted my offer and he's coming to give a lecture at All Saints' Open on Sunday evening.'

'I thought he was in Ireland,' said Emily, somewhat put out.

'No, he's been back some time.'

'Where will he stay?' asked Rachel.

'He plans to take lodgings in Churchgate for a few days. Shall we invite him for Sunday dinner?'

'Of course,' answered Rachel, who was concentrating hard on picking up a stitch she'd dropped on the muffler she was knitting for her youngest son, Ben, who now worked in London.

'Oh, Mama must we have him here? I do so dislike the man,' Emily wailed.

Natalie, who was trying to work out the mysteries of fractions, stared at her sister in disbelief. 'How can you dislike a fine man like Mr Aherne?'

'I find it extremely easy.'

Jed turned to his daughter with a frown. 'Well, I find your dislike of Rory rather harder to understand, Emily. What is it exactly that you have against him?'

'Would you like a list? I promise you it will be quite long.'

'No, one good reason will be sufficient.'

'Well if you want to know, it's his arrogance. He's insufferable.'

'Perhaps Rory has something to be arrogant about, he is an extremely gifted man. As you'll discover on Sunday when you hear him talk.'

'I shan't be coming, Papa, sorry.'

'It will look extremely discourteous.'

'Not if I have another engagement. I will be spending Sunday evening at Lily's. She's invited me there for a game of whist,' Emily lied.

It was rather ill-timed of Septimus then, to come into the shop and while buying a book, happen to mention to Jed that he was off to London the next day on business, taking Lily and the children with him.

'So, it doesn't look as if you'll be going round there for whist on Sunday, after all,' Jed remarked, when Septimus had gone.

Emily reddened. She'd fibbed and been caught out. 'It seems not,' she answered, picked up some library books that had been returned and busied herself putting them back on the shelves.

'Good, that means you'll be able to come to hear Rory after all,' said Jed in a tone that brooked no further argument.

They walked in pairs: Jed and Rachel, Natalie and Rory, while Emily dragged along reluctantly behind. Natalie now identified strongly with Ireland and its people, and Emily could hear her questioning Rory about his recent trip there. She could understand Natalie's interest; being an orphan was bound to make you curious about your roots.

As if not trusting her, her father was waiting for her at the entrance of All Saints' Open. 'Come along, Emily,' he said and led her into the small room that had been booked for the evening.

'Looks as if Rory is going to have a good audience,' said Jed, gazing around him with satisfaction as the rows of seats filled up with men and women.

From their exhausted features and ragged clothes, Emily guessed that most of them were framework knitters, some of the most exploited workers in Leicestershire.

'I'll stand here at the back, Papa,' said Emily who wanted it to be known that she was there under sufferance.

'No, you won't, your mother has saved a seat for us,' answered Jed and strode down to the front row.

Emily clenched her teeth and followed. But at least she had free will in her head, she told herself, and no one could force her to listen to Rory's speech.

Her father introduced Rory and when he stood up the audience clapped enthusiastically. Emily knew her behaviour was slightly childish, but she didn't want to grow to like Rory Aherne, so she felt it was important for her to resist those persuasive Irish tones. But the voice was coated in honey and the words reached out seductively. Feeling like a sailor tempted by the sirens' call, she hunched her shoulders and pulled up her coat collar to stop her ears against his charm.

However, looking along the row it was hard not to notice the intent expressions of the audience. Rory had captivated them completely and they either nodded in agreement or smiled at almost every point he made. Gradually, Emily found her resistance crumbling, her shoulders relaxed, she smoothed down her coat collar and began to listen. She'd expected him to be a rabble-rouser but Rory was, in fact, fairly temperate in his use of language. Nevertheless, he wasn't above reminding the audience of some of the harsh measures used by the authorities to try and curb democracy. Counting the Government's crimes off on his fingers, he asked, 'Do you remember Newport?'

'We certainly do,' they answered back.

'Twenty left dead that day. And the workhouse riots here in the marketplace. A troop of horse sent from Loughborough and the poor starving blighters sent to jail, just because they objected to bad bread.'

'Don't forget the Battle of Mowmaker Hill,' a member of the audience reminded him, his pale face suddenly animated as he remembered the day.

'You are right, sir, we must forget none of the crimes committed against us. But we are little more than slaves without a vote.'

'That's right,' they shouted back.

'However, we must be prepared to continue to fight, and suffer martyrdom for the cause. I promise you that before the end of the decade our demands will have been answered by Government and we'll have annual parliaments, the ballot, and a vote for every man over twenty-one. And when we're in control of our own destiny you'll find no more beggars on the streets, for there'll be work and decent wages for everyone.'

On this optimistic note Rory ended to cheers and prolonged feet-stamping. People jumped up on the stage and crowded round him, wanting to shake hands or ask a question and no matter how trivial it was, Rory considered the point, and answered as honestly as he could.

When Rory had shaken the last hand and they'd finally managed to make their way out of the hall and into the street, Jed checked his watch. 'It's gone ten-thirty, Rory, so I reckon you can count it a successful evening. Congratulations.'

'Thank you, Jed. It did seem to go quite well. Now, what is your opinion of my speech, Miss Fairfax? Was it to your liking?' asked Rory, falling into step beside Emily.

'You pleased your audience, which is always a good thing,' Emily answered, noncommittally. 'But I think you're being optimistic about us getting the vote by the end of the decade.'

'You have to give these people hope, they have so little else in their lives.' Suddenly Rory paused, stared up at a long, dimly-lit upper window and shook his head. 'Now, will you listen to that.'

The creak of the stocking frame was such a familiar part of her life, Emily wondered why Rory had drawn her attention to it. 'It's some poor stockinger working late,' she commented.

'Yes, but ask yourself, should he still be slaving away at this time of the night?'

'Work is scarce, so when there is any they are glad to work any hour,' Emily explained.

'When people talk about being as poor as a stockinger they mean it,' said Jed, overhearing their conversation. 'Of all the exploited workers I think the stockinger is the worst. Most of them exist at starvation level.'

'What sort of wage do they earn?'

'If they are lucky, four and six.'

'Why that's twenty-seven shillings a week. Not bad, I would have said.'

'You've got me wrong, Rory, it's four and six a week.'

'But no man can bring up a family on that!'

'You're quite right. That's why they are often forced on the streets to beg.'

'But this is dreadful.' Deeply affected, Rory marched on, hands deep in his pockets, past the bookshop, on towards the end of the street.

'Are you not coming in for a pot of ale before you turn in?' Jed called after him.

Rory paused briefly, his mind obviously elsewhere. 'I've taken enough of your hospitality for one day, and thank you, Mrs Fairfax, for that splendid dinner.' He patted his stomach.

'Oh, don't go, Mr Aherne,' Natalie wailed, running up to him and tugging his arm.

'I must, young lady. I have important business to attend to in the town tomorrow. If it is successfully concluded within the next few days then I will come and tell you about it. Otherwise, I shall return to London.' Rory lifted his hat. 'In the meantime, I wish you all good-night.'

Chapter Twelve

Isabelle adored London, the shops, theatres and parties, but most of all the people; shallow perhaps, but smart and with a biting wit. Everywhere old buildings were being knocked down and replaced by new ones, and after seeing Judith off on her coach to Dover with tears and promises to visit, Olivia's father took them on a guided tour of the town. And he knew London well, was knowledgeable about its history and keen to show it off to Isabelle. So they visited St Paul's and the Monument, then made their way up Fleet Street and along the Strand, finally stopping to view the recently erected Nelson's Column. With barely a pause, it was on down Whitehall to the new Houses of Parliament an elaborate Gothic building, still in the process of being built.

'I was here the night the original building burnt down. That was a dreadful experience, in more ways than one,' said Harry, remembering Clare's ordeal and the terrible manner of her father's death. Of course, she was happy with Christopher but he imagined that that night must sometimes come back to haunt her. But what was he being morbid about? It was the past, gone and finished with and life had to go on. Taking each girl by the arm, Harry went on, 'But some good came out of it, for when it's finished our Parliament will make us the envy of Europe. Now, let's take a stroll down Birdcage Walk. If we're lucky we might catch a glimpse of Queen Victoria and her Albert.'

It wasn't warm enough to linger outside the Palace so with no sign of the royal couple, after a few minutes Harry suggested they stroll on down the Mall. But Olivia, who had still not completely recovered

179

from her recent considerable loss of blood, was beginning to wilt at the relentless sightseeing. 'Can we take a cab, please, Papa?'

'Of course, my dear.' Harry studied his daughter closely. 'You do look pale, are you all right?'

Olivia brushed aside his concern. 'I'm fine, Papa, truly, but we have done a lot of walking and I'm a little tired.'

'You're right, we have. We'll go home now.' Harry went to the edge of the pavement and was about to hail a hansom when a carriage drew up beside them and a head emerged from the window. 'Good afternoon. Can I offer you a lift anywhere?' Sir Austin Beauchamp called to them, and Olivia was quick to see how he looked straight at Isabelle, who lowered her eyes modestly.

'We'd be most grateful to you, old chap.' Harry replied. 'I think I've exhausted these young ladies with too much sightseeing.'

And so Sir Austin's carriage took them back to the Collins' London home and naturally enough, Olivia invited him in. Sir Austin's own residence was only a few streets away and over tea he told them he expected to be in town for at least two weeks.

Sir Austin being in London struck Isabelle as the most amazing piece of good luck and as she silently digested it, she began to wonder if he'd got to hear of their visit to London, maybe through Max, and had arranged to be here at the same time. If so, it would mean he was definitely interested and she could afford to hold off a little.

Even so, Isabelle was on tenterhooks waiting for him to make some move. It came the following morning, by way of an invitation to a small soireé. This was swiftly followed by a dinner invitation and from there it seemed only natural that the four of them should visit the theatre together.

Isabelle knew enough about men to be sparing in her favours, but she soon had Sir Austin spinning like a top. It didn't take much, a few meaningful glances, a hand brushed accidentally against his. Then she would watch him, confident that she had lost none of her skills as he reddened, turned away and grasping the glass with shaking fingers, gulped down a whisky in one go.

Halby, when they returned home, seemed even more like the back of beyond. However, before they parted, Isabelle was careful to remind Olivia of her debt to her and at the same time extract from her the promise of an invitation to Lindfield Hall.

However, after two months there was still no word from Olivia. Isabelle said some very rude things about her friend under her breath but knew there was absolutely nothing she could do about it. Olivia still had the upper hand and the wrong word could ruin a friendship.

To complete Isabelle's boredom Matilda, who was having what she called her Dower House built and involving herself with architects and builders, had more or less handed over the running of the household to her daughter-in-law. Isabelle had little interest in domesticity. She found it tedious discussing menus with Cook each morning and she'd yawn over the household accounts, which Matilda insisted had to be checked meticulously to see that the servants weren't swindling them.

But the sun began to shine in Isabelle's life again when one morning, a letter arrived from Derbyshire. Smiling in anticipation, Isabelle broke the seal.

'How kind, Olivia's invited us to Lindfield Hall for the weekend.' Isabelle passed the letter to Adam, who looked at it briefly then cast it aside.

'I can't keep perpetually gadding off to Derbyshire, Isabelle. I do have an estate to run, you know.'

Isabelle's voice took on a wheedling tone which Adam detested. 'Please Adam, it's not just any old weekend, Olivia and Max are having a ball to celebrate their wedding anniversary. Not to go would seem extremely rude and churlish.'

'Yes, you should go, Adam,' said Matilda, 'You've seemed out of spirits these past weeks and a little entertainment would be a tonic to you. I'm quite capable of managing here on my own. After all, I've done it for years.'

Isabelle clapped her hands as if it were already decided. 'Oh, good, I'll be able to wear that lovely pink silk gown I had made in London.' In fact it was one that Sir Austin had told her she looked particularly charming in.

When she first walked into the ballroom at Lindfield Hall and gazed about her, Isabelle tried to appear blasé, but even she found it difficult not be impressed by the opulence of it all. With its huge mirrors the room appeared to be lit by a thousand candles, cut-glass chandeliers hung from the ceiling and the air was heavy with scent of white hot-house lilies, carefully nurtured by the head gardener. The musicians sawing away at their instruments made Isabelle's toes twitch. The smooth wooden floor was spread with french chalk and she wanted to get up and dance and remind herself that she really was part of it all.

Briefly, Isabelle remembered what she'd had to do to get here and shuddered. *Don't look back,* she recited to herself firmly. Only look forward and never nurse any regrets. Sometimes, though, she did pause to wonder how she'd achieved so much. By sheer iron will, of course. Isabelle smiled behind her fan and gazed across at Adam, who'd gone to fetch her a fruit cup, but had been waylaid by Max. And a strain of ruthlessness that now had her a guest in one of the grandest houses in Derbyshire. It wouldn't end there either, for she intended, eventually, to be mistress of an even grander pile somewhere nearby.

The musicians struck up a waltz and Sir Austin, who'd been continually glancing in her direction, approached her across the floor. He bowed and held out his hand. 'Would you grant me the pleasure, Mrs Bennett?'

Isabelle lowered her eyes modestly. 'Why, of course, Sir Austin.' Knowing her accent entranced him, her voice became pure deep south for his benefit.

Resigned to him being graceless and clumsy footed with no ear for the rhythm of the music, Isabelle allowed herself to be led onto the floor. But as soon as he slipped his arm around her waist and swung her to the middle of the floor,

Isabelle experienced the pure pleasure of a perfectly matched partner. 'Oh, I do love to dance,' she exclaimed, aware of the fleeting perfection of the moment.

'And you're as light as a feather in my arms,' Sir Austin murmured in her ear.

'Why, thank you.' Isabelle smiled engagingly and, at the same time, offered up a brief thanks to her father. Although, he'd done precious little else for her, having run off with another woman and left her and her mother destitute, it was from him she'd inherited her lightness of foot.

Adam was standing at the edge of the dance floor, glowering at the dancers and as they swung past him, Isabelle made a point of laughing gaily at one of Sir Austin's rather laboured jokes. She didn't care one jot about her husband, she was in her true environment here, and his moods wouldn't spoil her evening, or her plans.

The next dance was a quadrille and Adam wasn't able to wriggle out of this because Olivia insisted he make up the four. Even then though, she had to almost drag him onto the floor.

'Whatever is wrong with Adam?' Olivia asked Isabelle later, during the supper break. 'I've never known him in such a foul mood.'

'I'm sure I have no idea.'

'Is he ill?'

185

'Why do you say that?'

'He looks a trifle pale.'

Isabelle looked across at her husband with a special interest. 'Do you think so? Look, he's coming over,' she added when Adam separated himself from a group of men and moved towards them.

'I'm sorry, Olivia but I'll have to ask you to excuse me for the rest of the evening, I feel a trifle unwell.'

'Oh, dearest, can I get you anything?' The epitome of caring wife, Isabelle moved towards him and placed her fingers on his forehead. 'You do feel a bit hot.'

Adam brushed her hand aside. He knew the cause of his sickness all right: Emily. He pined for her day and night and there would be no cure until he had her. 'I shall be fine, but I need to lie down.'

'Perhaps you are sickening for something?' suggested Olivia, hoping it wasn't infectious for that would certainly spoil her carefully organised weekend.

'I doubt it, and I shall be fine in the morning. I promise you, Olivia, that I shall eat a hearty breakfast.'

'Would you like me to come up with you?' asked Isabelle, still straining to show a wifely concern.

'No, I can manage quite well on my own. And Beauchamp will look after you very well, won't you, old chap?'

186

'It would be a privilege,' answered Sir Austin.

Isabelle knew it would show a careless disregard for etiquette if she were to be seen dancing with Sir Austin too often during the evening, so she made a point of mixing freely, dancing with Max and Gregory as well as Theo Bartlett, who Olivia had sworn she was giving up forever. By one o'clock some of the guests were beginning to leave. For the younger element, though, the night had hardly begun and they lingered on, playing cards or billiards. However, Sir Austin who was a guest for the weekend, came and wished Isabelle good-night.

'Won't you stay and play a hand or two of whist?' Isabelle pleaded.

'No, I plan to go out with the Hunt in the morning and I want to be fresh for that. Shall you go, Mrs Bennett?'

Isabelle, who saw little point in careering over a field and being splattered with mud, shook her head. 'No.'

'I shall see you tomorrow evening, then. Good-night.'

Isabelle waited until Sir Austin had gone, looked around to check she wouldn't be noticed leaving, then slipped out of the ballroom and followed him up the stairs. The long corridor was lit down its length with candles, now burnt so low they cast deep shadows over the large paintings and heavy furniture. Sir Austin had reached his bedroom and was about to enter when he heard the light tip-tap of Isabelle's heels and turned.

'I came up for my shawl,' she lied as she caught up with him. 'It is a trifle draughty downstairs.'

The bedroom door was half open and through it Isabelle caught a glimpse of a large, four poster bed with the covers turned down and a good fire burning. She'd come after him without any particular plan but now she shivered and rubbed her arms. 'It looks warm in there, though,' she said pointedly and taking a huge gamble, moved on past him into the bedroom.

Sir Austin cleared his throat nervously, glanced over his shoulder to check no one had seen them, then closed the door and turned the key.

'Warm me, Austin,' Isabelle murmured, and moved towards him.

At this invitation, he grabbed her and began to kiss her with a violent hunger, while Isabelle concentrated on guiding him in the direction of the bed. When they reached it she fell onto it, pulling Austin on top of her. It was obvious he'd been without a woman for a long time because he was so frantic he hardly seemed to know what he was doing, or where to touch her. To assist him, she took his hand and guided it down the neck of her low-cut gown. 'Touch me, there,' she ordered. 'Do you like doing that?' she whispered as he plunged his hand in and rather ineptly caressed her small breasts.

'Oh, yes,' he moaned into her hair.

Taking his hand again she moved it down between her legs. 'What about there?'

'Darling, you are killing me,' he gasped.

Isabelle gave a small secret smile. It couldn't be going better. 'Would you like me to take my clothes off so that you can do other things to me?' she teased.

Austin gulped. 'Oh ... oh ... yes.'

Becoming businesslike, Isabelle knelt on the bed. 'Unhook me at the back, then.'

In a state of some agitation, Austin fumbled with the hooks and eyes. It took him an age but eventually Isabelle stood up and let the lovely pink silk gown slide to the floor, then with her toe she lifted it and tossed it carelessly onto a chair. She removed her undergarments then, standing naked in front of Austin, she slowly and skilfully undressed him. His skin was pale, the muscles losing their tautness. But she'd seen worse. Far, far worse. Just for the fun of it, she would liked to have practised some of her other skills on him, but she knew it wouldn't do to appear too experienced. And anyway, she didn't want it to be all over before he'd even entered her.

Sprawled invitingly on the the bed, she waited. 'Oh, you are so lovely, Isabelle. And your skin is like silk,' Austin murmured, stroking her body reverently. But he was a man with scruples and Isabelle saw signs of doubt flicker across his face, which wouldn't do at all. Gripping his buttocks in a vice-like grip with her legs, she pulled him down and kissed him, flicking her tongue in and out of his mouth so suggestively that lust finally overcame conscience and he pushed himself into her with a groan, almost of despair. 'This is wrong, oh, so wrong,' he murmured against her throat.

'Not if you truly love me, Austin, it isn't, and you do, don't you?'

'Oh, I do, I do, I do.'

'And I love you,' she whispered in a husky voice. Her declaration satisfied him enough to get on with the job but he was an awkward, unskilled lover, and he aroused not a squeak of desire in her. But Isabelle was a mistress of pretence and she moaned and gasped and arched her back as if in a paroxysm of desire, and when he climaxed she cried out, 'Oh, my God, don't stop, that was wonderful.'

Austin kissed her. 'You enjoyed that, didn't you, my kitten?' he said with a touch of manly pride.

'It was the best ever,' Isabelle murmured, her head resting on his chest.

'Better than with your husband?' he dared to ask.

'A hundred times better.'

'Do you ... you ... love him?' he ventured.

'No.'

'Oh, my dear, why not?'

Isabelle began to weep quietly. 'I can't say.'

'Is he cruel to you?'

'Yes, he lashes me with his tongue.' Isabelle lifted her head from his chest and gazed at him with an adoring expression. 'But I have you now, Austin, so nothing else matters. But we must be discreet, which means shortly I will have to leave you.'

'I understand, dearest. Although I can hardly bear to be parted from you for a single minute. Can you come here tomorrow night?'

'It might be difficult. My husband ... you see.

'Of course.'

Austin lay on the bed and watched Isabelle dress. She kissed him passionately before leaving, hoping, as she did, that he'd considered tonight worthy of a small but expensive gift, a piece of jewellery perhaps, for she had never believed in distributing her favours for nothing. Creeping to the door, Isabelle opened it an inch, checked there was no one about, then blew him a final kiss. 'Good-night my beloved,' she said quietly then slipped out into the corridor and back down the stairs.

Isabelle joined a small group of men and began flirting with them as if she'd never been away. Unfortunately Olivia, who missed very little, had noticed her rather extended absence. If there was the likelihood of liaison between her guests, she considered it her right, as hostess, to be fully in the picture.

'Where have you been?' Olivia asked, studying her friend with a keen eye.

'I went up to check that Adam was all right and stayed with him a while. But he's asleep now.'

Isabelle's explanation sounded so plausible Olivia had no choice but to accept it. 'Well, you've come back in time. I've sent the musicians home and the fun is really about to begin.' Drawing Isabelle over to a card table, she sat her down.

The tired servants, knowing they were in for a long night, hid their yawns behind their hands and replenished the candles. Someone filled Isabelle's glass with champagne, good natured banter quickly lapsed into risqué jokes, which soon became coarse, then downright obscene. But Isabelle concentrated on her cards and didn't blink an eyelid. She'd heard far worse, some, which if repeated, would probably even shock the young gentlemen sitting round the table.

When the party finally broke up, very few of the men could stand and it was left to their weary servants to carry them off to bed.

Although quite sober, it had been a long and rather energetic night, so Isabelle counted her winnings, pulled off her dancing slippers and crept up to her room. Hattie, who'd waited up for her, was asleep in a chair.

Isabelle shook her and the maid started up, yawned and rubbed her eyes. Her mistress threw a handful of sovereigns on to a table, then snapped, 'Undress me, Hattie, and be quick about it, I'm tired.'

Hattie jumped to her feet. 'Yes, Madam. Did you have a good evening?' she asked, as she unhooked the dress.

Isabelle gave a quiet smile. 'In every possible way.'

Yes, Hattie thought slyly, *I bet you did.* Because what Isabelle, for all her cleverness, couldn't possibly know was that on her way down to the kitchens for a drink earlier in the evening, Hattie had seen her come along the corridor and enter Sir Austin's room. She made a careful note of the time then kept watch to see when she left, which she was gratified to find, was well over an hour later.

Chapter Thirteen

To Mary, the wall looked as thick and as impregnable as a fortress. But then, reminding herself that she had scaled greater heights, she stood back and scanned it with a true professional's eye. Her Pa couldn't 'ave been all that clever or 'e wouldn't have gotten 'imself topped, but he had given her one good piece of advice, which she'd never forgotten: *'The rich'*, he'd counselled in one of his rare moments of sobriety, *'build 'igh walls to keep out the like's of us, but always remember this, Mary, walls, like folk, have their weak points, you just 'ave to look for 'em'.*

So she did, and she soon noticed some ivy draped conveniently over the wall and raised her eyes heavenwards. 'Thank you, Pa, if you're up there, it's just what I need.'

Confident in her task now, Mary squared her shoulders, spat on the palms of both hands, then took several steps backwards. Calling up every ounce of strength she bounded towards the wall, found a foothold in a broken piece of brickwork, grabbed the ivy and panting violently, hauled herself up. Astride the wall, her bony behind cushioned by the thick pad of ivy, Mary drew air deep into her lungs and took stock of her surroundings.

The house, she saw, was old, the grounds large, with conveniently mature trees and the whole place stank of money. Although Mary didn't have the vocabulary to articulate her thoughts, there smouldered in her a deep sense of injustice about the way the world was organised. These were folk who had so much tin they deserved to be parted from some of it, she concluded, not that she ever had any scruples about who she thieved from. Rich or poor, it wa' all the same to her. Oh, it was easy for Christian folk like the Reverend to preach, 'Thou Shalt Not Steal', when they'd never gone days—like she and Joe often did—without a crust of bread passing their lips. What did they expect 'em to do, she wondered self-righteously, starve to death in the gutter? Besides, she couldn't bear it no longer, the way her mam treated the little chap. She'd caught her just in time a day or two back, pissed as a newt, beating all hell out of Joe with a stick and screaming at him, 'Speak! Say somethin', you dummy, for Christ's sake!'

'Leave 'im you stupid cow, 'e can't talk!' Her stomach churning with bile, Mary grabbed the stick and swiped her mother across the face with such force, she left a line of bloody weals down both cheeks.

Mouthing every obscenity in the English language, her mam advanced on her with staring madwoman's eyes. 'I'll kill you,' she spat out and, looking as if she meant it, grabbed Mary by the hair and started to slam her head hard against the wall. Mary fought and kicked and scratched but her mother was bigger and stronger. 'I'll teach you,' she snarled in time to each vicious blow. Mary grew dazed and knew her head was about to crack in two and her brains spill on the ground, when she became dimly aware of little Joe pushing between them, making agitated quacking noises. Somehow, for he was a skinny little beggar, he managed to get the old lady off her. She staggered drunkenly, threatened, 'I'll get you, too, you little sod,' then to their relief slumped to the ground.

Mary touched her head gingerly and felt her hair sticky with blood. She gave herself a minute or two to collect herself then grabbed Joe. 'Come on let's get outta here.' But, of course, they'd had to go back. It was either that or walk the streets all night in the pouring rain. But not for much longer, Mary thought and spat contemptuously into a flowerbed. From now on the old woman could rot in hell because, by hook or by crook, she was going to get Joe away from her and find a place where they could be together for the rest of their lives.

Although Mary hadn't come with any clear idea of what she would lift, she'd been careful to choose the dinner hour for her foray, because at this time of day there were always less people about. Swivelling her head, she made a more detailed survey of the grounds and over her left shoulder, saw a line of washing with several pairs of drawers and white linen sheets billowing in the wind. Mary gave a satisfied click of her tongue. Just the ticket, she thought, swung over the wall and dropped with a soft thud on to the flowerbed below.

Concealed behind a large evergreen bush, but poised to make a dash for it, Mary made a further survey of the garden. This was always a tense few minutes, for her one great terror was that snarling hounds, their teeth bared, would leap upon her and rip half her face away. But although no fierce brutes shot from kennels, Mary knew there were other traps for the unwary. For instance, the potting shed on the far side of the garden. There was bound to be a gardener inside, chomping away on his midday bread and cheese.

So best keep well out of his view, she thought, dodged from the shelter of the bush and pressed herself hard against the trunk of a tree. Peeping cautiously out, she saw that the washing was now within snatching distance. Unfortunately it was also in full view of the kitchen window.

But Mary had overcome greater obstacles than that in the past. Also, at this time of the day, most of the servants would be running around at the beck and call of the family. They in turn would be concentrating on stuffing as much food as possible into their fat, overfed faces.

Everything was in her favour as long as she didn't get careless and bugger it up. But she would only have about a second to dive out, grab one item then make a run for it. Entirely focused, the only sound Mary could hear was a pounding in her ears like galloping horses, Well, it's now or never, she told herself, licked her dry lips and eased herself out from her hiding place. Edging, with extreme caution, along the path, she drew breath then shot forward, tugged at a sheet, smelt its cold freshness as it fell into her arms then found she was staring straight into the astonished face of a large, white-aproned woman whose whole bearing said 'Cook'. Mary froze momentarily, muttered, 'Goddle mighty,' then gathering her wits and the sheet together, she bolted.

Somewhere behind her, Mary heard the woman bawl, 'Stop thief!' then blow furiously on a whistle. But she was an old hand at such games and the tough stems of the ivy made her getaway a simple matter. Scrambling over the wall, Mary hit the ground running and was off, swift as a hare and stuffing the sheet up inside her jacket as she went, and feeling rather chuffed with herself and her booty.

Mary's small crime had been committed in a house on the edge of the Newarke, and since she wasn't familiar with the Christian calendar, and hadn't seen the stalls laden with oranges and gingerbread, she had no idea it was Shrove Tuesday until she ran smack bang into a double line of hefty men in blue smocks, wielding cart-whips.

Mary stopped with a dismayed 'Oh,' and looked around for a means of escape. The yearly pre-lenten rough and tumble of wrestling, ball games and shinty was something most of the town's citizens came to participate in and in the past, with her deft fingers, Mary had reaped some rich harvests.

But at two o'clock a bell was rung

and the Whipping Toms arrived to clear the area. The rules said that the Toms shouldn't whip above the knee, although those with any sense still got well out of their way. However, some of the braver—or more foolhardy—youths, their legs protected with strong boots or straw stuffed into gaiters, and fortified with several pots of ale, were always eager to join in a bit of horseplay. Armed with cudgels and an air of bravado, they would regularly run the gauntlet of the Whipping Toms. But these men enjoyed their power and soon the whips were falling on bare flesh, and what had started off as good natured fun, often degenerated into a bad-tempered brawl, to the delight of the crowd.

Mary put up with enough beatings at home and she had no intention of having her unprotected legs whipped raw to provide entertainment for the crowd. She backed away and got ready to run but it was already too late, the men were closing in on her, jovial and sinister at the same time.

'What have we here then?' asked one great bruiser, and tickled her skinny legs with his cart-whip.

'Don't, please, it 'urts,' Mary appealed.

'We'll let you off for a forfeit, won't we chaps?'

'Yeah, a penny will do.'

'I in't got a penny ... Ouch,' Mary screamed as another whip bit spitefully into her flesh.

But the men didn't often get an opportunity like this, someone female, unarmed and too small to retaliate. A real victim. To show who was in charge, one of them gave her a shove, and she was pushed, like a parcel, from one man to another down the line, while they exercised their ancient right to use their whips on her.

Her legs now red raw, Mary began to sob with the pain. Snot and tears running down her face, she stumbled against one of the men, and he pushed her away in disgust. 'Don't come near me, you snot-nosed guttersnipe.' He cracked the whip in warning and she felt a stinging pain curl round her neck.

Crouching down, and covering her head with her hands, Mary whimpered, 'Someone 'elp me, please!' But she could hear the cruel jests of the crowd egging the men on and knew they were as indifferent to her pain as the cockerels they clubbed to death for sport.

Then she spied an opening through the men's legs. Not wasting a second, Mary made a dive for it and was free. Scrambling to her feet, she fled, almost tripping over the sheet that was now trailing after her in the dirt.

'Gotcha! Red 'anded this time.' Mary knew the voice, without looking up. It was her old adversary, Police Constable Pegg, sounding rather pleased with himself. Her booty, no longer pristine white, was evidence of her guilt and, too tired even to struggle, Mary accepted defeat and hung her head.

'Do y'know, I can sniff out thieving little 'ounds like you a mile off. You've gotta specially nasty smell. So it's the clink for you tonight, missy, and then transportation like them brothers of yourn. Best place for you, too, Australia. We don't want scum like you cluttering up this country. Come along now,' the upholder of law and order commanded then, twisting her arm spitefully behind her back, he frog-marched her off in the direction of the Borough Gaol.

'She'll be sent to prison you know.'

'How long do you think she'll get?'

William Jackson sighed. 'A year, maybe two.'

'But she's hardly more than a child!' At the injustice of the situation, Emily began to stride angrily backwards and forwards.

'But nevertheless, an accomplished thief.' Emily's head swung round and the gesture was accusing. 'It is quite likely we would steal, too, if it meant the difference between staying alive or starving to death.'

'The theft of someone else's property is a serious matter,' answered William piously.

'Yes, property has always taken precedence over people, hasn't it?'

William turned away from her question. Emily's voice had taken on a shrill note, which he found rather disturbing. Women, in his opinion, should never raise their voices. Neither did he care for the radical language issuing from those soft lips. William liked certainty in his life, and he was a great believer in the doctrine of everyone knowing their place in the great scheme of things. Order brought happiness, change chaos.

'It was a sheet, that's all. I know the Pomfrets, they've got so much money they could go out and buy ten more and not notice the difference,' Emily went on.

'That doesn't mean we should condone Mary's crime. She has to be taught a lesson.'

'Can you do something for her, William?' Emily's voice had lost its shrillness and become soft and pleading. It was also the first time she had used his Christian name. Taking it as a sign that their relationship had moved on to a deeper intimacy, he weakened slightly.

'I'll do what I can, E-Emily ...' he stumbled slightly, uneasy with such familiarity. 'When she comes up before the magistrate, I'll put in a good word for her.'

'Tell him she attends our Sunday School, that will make a good impression.'

'I think she's been once.'

'Well, at least you won't have to lie, will you?'

'I can't promise anything I say will have any effect.'

'I hate all the unfairness in this world. Don't you ever ask yourself, William, why God allows so many people to suffer?'

'His will be done,' William intoned. 'We mustn't question that.' To tell the truth, William was rather disappointed in Mary after all he'd tried to do for her, and at the moment, if he were the magistrate passing sentence, he wouldn't be inclined to be lenient.

'Oh, poppycock!' Emily snapped, and strode off in high fury, questioning for the first time in her life whether she believed in the Almighty and whether she would ever set foot in a church again. Of course, if she did decide to abandon religion, it would certainly delight her father. Emily paused. Yes, and on the other hand, probably break her mother's heart.

Chapter Fourteen

Adam was weighed down by a terrible desolation, a darkness of the soul to which he could see no possible end. It didn't help, either, that for most of the time, he felt vaguely unwell and was often troubled by stomach pains. The English spring, with its unpredictable weather patterns; the skeletal brownness of winter slowly succumbing to a thrusting green beauty, was what he'd missed most in America. Today though, as he rode about the estate, visiting a tenant farmer, having a word with the shepherd about the new season's lambs, checking on the spring wheat, he was blind to the great spume-white waves of hawthorn rolling across the Leicestershire countryside. He knew what was at the root of his misery, of course: the messy state of his emotional life for which, Adam was prepared to concede, he was more than partly to blame.

Emily had rejected him, and he and Isabelle hardly had a loving relationship. She had quickly lost her sexual attraction, but Adam was aware that he had a duty to produce a son and to arouse himself, he had to fantasise that it was Emily lying beneath him in the dark. His mother didn't say anything but he knew she kept a keen eye on Isabelle's waistline and he waited every month for her to tell him she was with child. However, since her miscarriage, there had been no further indication that Isabelle was pregnant.

Adam wasn't unaware of what was going on around him, had noticed Sir Austin's infatuation for Isabelle, and her response. Sir Austin was a man of honour, so he trusted him, but he would not tolerate any infidelity until Isabelle had given him an heir, for he had no intention of someone else's bastard inheriting his estate. After that they could then go their separate ways, and Isabelle could indulge in as many affairs as she wished. In the meantime he would keep a close eye on her.

Adam had left the house early and he found a morning riding round the estate had sapped his energy. He'd never had this problem before and it troubled him, so as soon as he'd handed over his horse, he went straight to the kitchen for a tankard of Mrs White's home-brewed beer, hoping it would act as a pick-me-up. Instead of the usual noise and bustling activity, to Adam's surprise the kitchen was empty except for Hattie, who was sitting in Cook's rocker, crooning to a small kitten curled up on her lap.

'Where's Cook, Hattie?' Adam asked.

When she heard Adam's voice, Hattie pushed the kitten off and leapt to her feet. Her heart started to throb with a violent passion and she stared at Adam with hungry eyes. He was so 'andsome, she would have done anything for 'im, absolutely anything, and after all, it weren't unknown for a maid and master to get together. There wa' plenty enough bastards littered around the county to prove that. She wa' prettier than that skinny, anaemic-lookin' missus of his, too; pink-cheeked, plump and a man liked something to grab 'old of on a cold night. And Madam weren't up to no good neither, not from what she'd seen, although she'd keep that to herself for the time being, for when the time came, Madam would pay her 'andsomely to keep her trap shut.

'Did you hear me, Hattie? I asked you where Cook was?'

'Oh sorry, Sir. She's gone to have a word wi' Mrs Bennett.'

'Will you get me a tankard of ale, then?' Adam smiled winningly, a blush crept up Hattie's neck like sunrise, and she fled to the ice-cold pantry. She came out carrying an overflowing tankard and as she handed it to Adam, she allowed her fingers to brush against his. A great charge of lust shot through her and she watched him mesmerised, as he arched his strong neck and downed the beer in thirsty gulps.

With her bold, come-hither eyes and other provocative body gestures, Hattie made it quite plain to Adam that she was freely available to him; would even, he didn't doubt, oblige him by lifting her skirts there and then, if he suggested it. And she was a comely wench, he ruminated, studying her over the rim of the tankard. Her body had no hard angular edges and he'd sink into her like a soft feather mattress. And with serving girls, like whores, it was raw sex, not complicated by emotions. Adam's senses titillated by these thoughts, his loins stirred. A quick coupling in the hay, what was the harm in it? he asked himself. The girl was like a bitch on heat, and it might lift him out of his depression. Knowing he was playing with fire, but too aroused now to stop himself, Adam moved closer to Hattie. Handing her the empty tankard, as if by accident, he touched her breast. He heard Hattie's small indrawing of breath, watched her pupils dilate and her rosebud mouth slacken with desire. He was about to slip his arm around her waist when Cook's voice just outside the door made them leap guiltily apart. Hattie, not knowing what else to do, rushed to hide in the pantry, while

Adam moved quickly to the back door.

'Can I get you something, Mr Adam?' Cook enquired, coming into the kitchen.

Adam's arousal was so obvious, he didn't dare turn round. Instead, he smiled over his shoulder. 'No thanks, Cook, I was just quenching my thirst on your delicious beer. Must go now.'

With as much dignity as he could muster Adam somehow got himself out of the kitchen. Round the side of the house he stopped, leaned against the wall, closed his eyes and exhaled noisily. By God, that was a close one. A moment later and Cook might have found them going at it hammer and tongs on the kitchen floor. It was that little hussy's fault, she'd led him on, but he'd been a damned fool to even allow himself to be tempted. It was too close to home and his life was complicated enough. Still, there was nothing to say he couldn't use use young Hattie in other ways. She would be compliant and as Isabelle's personal maid, she would be party to all her confidences, would know exactly what she was up to. There would have to be some financial inducement, but definitely not a sexual one, Adam told himself firmly and, pushing images of Hattie's rounded, naked body firmly from his mind, he strode round to the front of the house and up the steps. He pushed open the door to find Hattie standing in the hall. She gave a small bob. 'Had a good morning, 'ave you, Sir?' she asked with a knowing smile.

Unnerved, Adam didn't reply and brushed past the maid as if she weren't there.

The door was flung open with great energy and Jed strode into the shop with Rory a step behind him. Ignoring the startled customers, he announced, 'Good news, Rory's been offered the job of running our Chartist paper here in Leicester.'

At the dreaded word 'Chartist', the customers took one look at Rory and went scuttling from the shop, away from such a dangerous looking radical.

Emily watched their morning's business seep away with a frown of annoyance. 'Now look what you've done, Papa, lost us customers. And one of them was on the point of buying several books.' Looking past her father, she glared at the real culprit.

'My fault, I apologise.' Rory moved forward and lifted his hands placatingly.

'Do you intend to take the job, Mr Aherne?'

'I certainly do.'

'I imagined that after London you might find Leicester a dull town.'

'Beggars can't be choosers. Financially,

I'm at a low watermark and money is a necessary commodity, Miss Fairfax. I would find any town agreeable for thirty shillings a week.'

'We've just been to look at a room in the High Street, which Rory will be able to use as an office for the paper,' her father added. 'Now, come on, old chap, let's go upstairs and celebrate the successful conclusion of our business with a pot of ale.'

'Are you joining us, Miss Fairfax?'

'No, we've lost enough business this morning. I can't close until one o'clock.' As Emily spoke, William Jackson came through the door. His glum expression told her he wasn't the bearer of good news. 'I've just come from the Town Hall. Mary has been given three months' hard labour.'

Emily's face drained of its colour. 'But that's so unfair! She's only a child. Didn't you speak up for her, vouch for her good character?' she badgered him.

'Come Emily, I could hardly do that without perjuring myself. I did what I could, but she comes from a criminal background. Badness is bred in her. The police know that, so do the magistrates.'

'Circumstances have made her bad. And I thought the church believed in the possibility of redemption.'

'We-ll er ...'

Rory had no time for priests and as far as he was concerned, all religion was humbug: oppression by another name. But watching the young man floundering, he felt a slight pity for him. 'This girl you're talking about. Is she the one with the cut arm I met here?'

Emily nodded, imagining Mary in a fetid dungeon. Her father had spent time in jail and she knew something of the conditions prisoners endured.

Until now, married or single, Rory's failure rate at getting a woman into bed was nil. Emily remained the exception and her unremitting hostility irked, which made him doubly determined to have her. Rory's instinct told him that the cleric was no threat as a potential suitor, but it puzzled him that a comely woman like Emily could still be single. He'd said as much to Jed, but his friend had gone all tight-lipped, which made Rory suspect there was something in Emily's past that made her less than lily-white. A liaison with a married man, perhaps, or even a bastard child farmed out to a wet nurse in the country. Such lapses would certainly render her unmarriageable in a town like Leicester, Rory decided. But he wasn't looking for a wife, or a virgin, and a woman's past was no concern of his. What he was looking to do was to bed her, and this girl Mary was the chink in her armour. If he could do something for her and earn Emily's gratitude, then he'd be almost there. As this idea occurred to him, so another one, brilliant in its simplicity, floated into his head.

'Well, the first editorial in my paper will be a plea for clemency for the girl and a demand for her release.'

The change in Emily's attitude towards him was nothing short of a miracle. In fact she was almost in danger of smiling. 'Do you mean it?'

'I do,' answered Rory, asking himself why this haughty beauty's goodwill was so important to him. Possibly it was her unavailability. 'And I'll keep up the campaign until she's released,' he went on, his promises becoming more extravagant by the second. Not that it would do his reputation any harm. People liked grand gestures, causes they could embrace and by the end of the campaign his name was bound to be on the lips of everyone in town.

Rory sat down at his desk, took up his pen, dipped it in ink and without a pause, started to write, for this was what he loved doing above all else; framing letters into words, words into sentences:

Citizen's Awake! Why, in a civilised society, is a girl by the name of Mary Todd, who is hardly more than a child, locked away behind bars for three months and forced into hard labour for a minor offence? Is she a hardened criminal? No. Is she starving? Yes. And why is she starving? Because no one cares enough about the degraded conditions in which more than three quarters of the population in this town exist. And yet Leicester, recognising it as an evil, was at the vanguard of the anti-slavery movement. Strange then that the good burghers of this town should fail to see the slavery here on their own doorsteps: the SLAVERY OF POVERTY.

Rory paused to underline the words then continued:

And this is what forces people into a life of crime and why Mary Todd will be sleeping tonight on a bag of straw in a prison cell running with water. I beg of you, all good people, campaign for this girl's release. Give her a chance in life, PLEASE.

With a flourish, Rory added the last full stop to his first editorial piece for the *Chartist Trumpeter* then, chewing his pen, swung back on his chair and read it through with a sense of pride. Although,

214

initially, his reason for doing it might have been to impress Emily, it had been written in the heat of genuine moral outrage, and it showed. Undoubtedly his lambasting would ruffle more than a few feathers in the town. However, that was the point of the exercise and Rory was banking on guilt seeping into the hearts of the more pious and shaming them into action. Questions would be asked. Within a week, Mary would be free, or he'd eat his hat.

Chapter Fifteen

Slipping a shawl around her shoulders, Isabelle walked to the bedroom door. 'I have another of my headaches, Hattie, I'm going to take a walk round the grounds.'

'These headaches seem to be becoming quite regular, Madam, shouldn't you see the doctor?' said Hattie, showing an appropriate concern.

'Perhaps, but I find fresh air helps ease them.'

'Of course, Madam.' And not only fresh air, thought Hattie, who went on picking up the various dresses Isabelle had discarded as unsuitable for her short walk. She gave her mistress five minutes then raced to the window. Craning her neck, Hattie saw the direction she was taking and gave a knowing little smile. Some headache, she's off to see *him* again.

Isabelle imagined her secret was safe, that no one had an inkling of what she was up to, but since she'd caught her going into Sir Austin's room that night, Hattie had kept a close eye on her mistress's movements. At first it had been because it added spice to her rather dull life, but gradually she came to see that the incriminating evidence she was building up on the lovers could provide her with a nice little nest egg.

As Hattie imagined the weight of gold sovereigns in her palm, and heard their satisfying clink, the first flicker of ambition started to take shape in her mind, and she saw herself as the owner of a smart dress shop in Gallowtree Gate. Fired by a new goal in her life, Hattie now began to watch for any change in her mistress's routine and one day, out of curiosity, she'd followed Isabelle on one of her so-called walks round the grounds.

She was up to something, Hattie could tell, by the covert backwards glances, then the change of direction, once Isabelle knew she was out of view of the house. Hattie followed her as she climbed a stile then took the footpath that led to Blackthorn

Lane. Squeezing through a gap in a hedge Isabelle skirted the field, making for Rooks Spinney, a secluded spot ideal for clandestine meetings.

So that's it. Hattie didn't try to follow her any further. She had a pretty shrewd idea who she was meeting and she wanted to get back to the house before she was missed. In her room, Hattie, who'd been one of Christopher's brighter pupils, drew out an old school jotter and carefully wrote in the date. She paused, then added: *'Half past two, followed Madam as far as Blackthorn Lane. She was making for Rooks Spinney'.* The information looked a bit sparse on the page, and was hardly likely to damage Isabelle's reputation so, as she closed the book and slipped it under her mattress, Hattie decided that further investigations were going to be necessary.

The following day she made an excursion to Rooks Spinney, did a reconnaissance of the small wood and finally found the perfect hiding place: a thick bush that had formed itself into a natural arbour.

After this, it was a question of being patient and waiting for the appropriate moment. It came, fortuitously, on her afternoon off. Isabelle, on her way out, was delayed by her mother-in-law. This gave Hattie her chance and, taking a gamble on it being Isabelle's destination, she tore out of the house and across the fields to the lovers' trysting place.

Hattie arrived at her lair hot and out of breath. She crept inside and settled down, pulling branches around her as a camouflage. She didn't know how long the two of them would be but she was quite happy to wait, for the air was balmy and she had a large bag of toffee in her pocket. Sitting cross-legged, she popped a piece into her mouth. The elms were in full leaf now but after about a quarter of an hour, Hattie heard twigs cracking under heavy feet. She sat up straight, every sense alert. A moment later Sir Austin came into view. His brow was furrowed and he looked edgy. As if not sure what to do with himself, he leaned against a tree for a moment, then began to pace up and down.

Unseen, Hattie chewed thoughtfully and studied him at her leisure. What does Madam see in 'im? she wondered. For a start he was getting on a bit, you could tell by his jowl, and his hair was wispy and greying. He weren't half as handsome as Mr Adam, neither, so why was she playing fast and loose with such an old chap? It didn't make sense, somehow. Personally, she'd give anything to be warming Mr Adam's bed and she would, in time. He wa' acting all cold towards her at the moment, but that was all put on and didn't worry her one jot, not after the way he'd acted in the kitchen.

There was a rustle of branches, Sir Austin straightened and his expression lightened. 'My precious,' he cooed, held out his arms and Isabelle fell into them.

Hattie, who felt an intense desire to giggle, clapped her hand over her mouth, but it fell away as the lovers, kissing passionately, sank slowly to the ground. Making strange groaning noises, Austin fumbled with Isabelle's clothes. Hattie's eyes popped and she found her own excitement growing. Lord, they were going to do it here, right in front of her! Disappointingly, after allowing him a few fumbles, Isabelle pushed him away. Sitting up she brushed twigs from her hair. 'I'm sorry, Austin but I can't allow you, not today.'

'Why is that, dearest?'

Isabelle hung her head modestly. 'Well ... you see, I ... I fear I have my woman's trouble.'

'Oh, my poor little kitten, what a thoughtless oaf I am. Please forgive me, sweetest.'

She's having you on, don't believe a word of it, you great sap, Hattie longed to shout, for didn't she know every intimate detail of her mistress's life? Didn't she wash her

219

cloths each month? Didn't she know the exact hour she started and the day she finished?—which, as it happened, was the day before yesterday.

'But look, I've brought you a small gift,' said Sir Austin by way of recompense for his brutish behaviour and, drawing a square box covered with dark blue velvet from his pocket, he handed it to Isabelle.

Even from a distance, Hattie could see the greed and triumph in her witch-like eyes. 'Oh, it's exquisite!' Isabelle exclaimed, as she opened the box and lifted a heavy, jewel-encrusted necklace from its white satin cushion. Held between her fingers, filtered rays of sunshine caught the diamonds and small beams of light danced around the woods like fire-flies.

'But I can't take it.' Isabelle pretended to push the necklace back at him.

'You must. This necklace has been in the family for generations, but you've brought joy back into my life, Isabelle, something I doubted I'd ever experience again, and that's worth more than a few diamonds. So, I want you to have it as a token of my deep, deep gratitude and undying love for you.'

As Austin leaned over and kissed Isabelle, she gave a tremulous sigh, then in a voice quavering with emotion, she murmured, 'Oh, Austin, you are the sweetest man. And if you're quite, quite sure ...?' Although her voice sounded uncertain, Hattie noticed that her mistress had wasted no time in pocketing the necklace.

'Tell me, what time is it, Austin?' Isabelle asked, after a pause for a few more kisses, sighs and declarations of love.

Austin consulted his pocket watch. 'Half past three.'

'Oh, dear, is it? I must fly. Mother-in-law has guests coming for tea, and dull though it will be compared with being with you, my darling, I am expected to be there.'

Ooh, and that's another whopper! It astonished Hattie how easily the lies tripped off her mistress's tongue, in fact she seemed to find it easy as breathing. And considering she was supposed to love him, it was funny she was making excuses to get away. If it wa' her and Mr Adam ... Hattie gave a sigh of longing and allowed her thoughts to linger on the many pleasures that might delay them.

The lovers stood up and moved away. Hattie strained her ears but all she could hear was mumble, mumble, mumble, although she guessed they were making plans for another assignation. After one final kiss they separated, walking off hurriedly in different directions. But Hattie stayed put and, hooking a toffee from between her teeth, decided she could count the afternoon a success. The details of their rendezvous would fill several pages of her notebook and bring her ambitions a shade closer to reality.

Fortunately Rory wasn't required to eat his hat because, as he'd predicted, seven days after the publication of the *Chartist Trumpeter*, Mary was released. His piece caused a tremendous furore in the town, so much so that the first run of the paper sold out within hours and had to be reprinted. Rory was applauded and vilified in turn for the outspoken tone of his article, but it stirred people to action and put his name on everyone's lips, which was exactly what he wanted. Rory expanded in the glow of recognition, for notoriety was oil to the wheel of his life and he liked to know he was being discussed over dinner tables. He also loved to be in the thick of any political argument. The small room he rented as an office quickly became a meeting place for Radicals, Tories, Whigs, Quakers and Nonconformists alike, and people and discussions, often heated, overflowed into the street. But best of all, his article had kicked the well-heeled of the town out of their complacency; people with influence were speaking up on the girl's behalf and the wheels of justice were quietly turning.

Whenever she could spare a moment, Emily would slip out of the shop and down the road to Rory's office. 'Have you heard anything?' she would ask him at least twice a day, for she didn't share Rory's conviction that Mary would soon be released.

'Everything is in hand, don't worry,' he would assure her, keeping any suggestion of condescension from his voice, which, he suspected, was the start of Emily's chilliness towards him. She was Jed's daughter, she had his nature, his fire and compassion and she had the right to be taken seriously. In fact, if he were the marrying kind which, thank heaven, he wasn't, for the ideal wife he need look no further than Emily. Except that at the moment it was unlikely she'd have him. Some of that straight-backed frigidity might have gone, but he couldn't in all honesty say she'd warmed that much towards him. Still, as long as he didn't go and put his big foot in it again, the thaw might continue.

Quite by chance, Emily called in to the newspaper office at the very moment a messenger arrived with a letter bearing an official-looking seal. Rory glanced at Emily, and realised their relationship hung on the contents of the letter. It was an anxious moment, undoing the envelope, and his mouth was dry. If his crusade failed he would have to do the equivalent of falling on his sword and leave Leicester, and Emily. 'Well, this is it,' he said and broke the seal.

Emily held her breath and watched Rory's expression intently as he read the letter that would decide Mary's fate. 'Well?' she asked impatiently.

Slowly Rory's face broke into a smile then, waving the letter above his head like a flag, he shouted, 'We've done it! Mary will be released at eight o'clock tomorrow morning.'

'Oh!' Emily's hands flew to her mouth. 'Let me see.' She snatched the letter from him, read it through, then all the pent up emotion of the past weeks was released in a deluge of tears.

'Hey, don't cry.'

'No, I'm all right.' Emily wiped her eyes, feeling foolish. 'It's just that I didn't really think it would happen.'

'So, you didn't have any faith in me, then?'

Emily realised she'd made a blunder, 'That's not what I'm saying, it ... it's just that ...'

'Just what?'

'Oh, never mind.'

'You could thank me.' Rory tapped his

cheek and Emily leaned forward and rather shyly kissed him.

'Thank you. Very much.'

'It was a pleasure,' Rory answered, then not being a man to miss an opportunity, he returned her kiss, but his was full on the mouth. He felt her lips soften and respond but then she jerked her head away and Rory half expected a stinging slap across his cheek. Instead, she studied him intently for a moment, then said quietly, 'I suggest we both forget what just happened.'

'But why, Emily?' Rory grasped her hand.

'Because I don't care to be trifled with.'

'But I'm not trifling with you, Emily, I truly admire you.'

'Men, I've discovered, are rather unscrupulous in their dealings with women, and I've learnt not to set much store by what they say.'

So I was right, Rory thought, she has been badly hurt.

'And it would be wise of me to continue to suspect their motives,' Emily went on, regarding him with a cool eye. She straightened her jacket and went to the door. Pausing there, she said, 'I'll see you outside the prison at ten to eight tomorrow morning. And thank you again for all your help, Rory. It's because of you, Mary is being released.'

Rubbing his chin thoughtfully, Rory watched her go. Had she heard gossip about him? he wondered, or perhaps Jed had warned her off. He'd spent years sowing his wild oats and word got around. She wasn't repelled by him, though, so that was a start, but he was going to have to re-think his strategy. Some man had obviously let her down her badly and she wasn't going to fall, willy-nilly, into anyone's arms. But who was he? And did she still love him? Rory felt a surge of dislike against this unknown man, who was keeping her from him. But the taste of her was still on his lips and the sweet womanly essence of her lingered in his nostrils in an unsettling way.

Orphaned young he'd led a Romany existence since early manhood and marriage had never attracted him. But perhaps the time had come to settle down. After all, he was thirty-eight and their union could be the beginning of a great political dynasty. Politics would run through the veins of any child of theirs, Rory mused, with perhaps a grandson in the Cabinet or even holding that highest office of all: Prime Minister. Rory shook himself. *Stop daydreaming, man.* What can you offer Emily? You haven't a penny to your name, in fact you've hardly even got a proper job. No woman would put up with that, and it was daft to imagine that an independent-minded girl like Emily would accept him anyway. So, best forget it.

By the time Jed, Rory and Emily arrived outside the prison gates the following morning, a crowd of well-wishers had already gathered. They carried with them bundles of clothes and loaves of bread and when the gates opened, there was a simultaneous, 'Here she comes!' and the crowd pressed forward.

An unseen hand gave Mary a push and she stepped out into freedom, blinking in the unaccustomed daylight. She was even dirtier than Emily remembered, and her clothes, little more than strips of rag, hung from her half-starved frame. 'Look at her, the poor child,' Emily exclaimed to Jed and Rory, her soft heart hardening in anger at the people who'd locked her away. 'Mary, it's me, Emily Fairfax, I've come to take you home,' she called, and tried to elbow her way through. But Mary was completely surrounded by people pushing gifts into her arms, while she, unaware that she'd acquired a certain fame, cringed like a terrified dog.

Too bewildered to understand anything, Mary allowed the gifts to fall from her arms and Emily was certain that if the prison gates had still been open, the girl would have dived back inside for safety.

Emily could see that Mary was now casting around frantically for a means of escape. 'Mary, wait, it's me,' she called again, but Mary chose not to hear and when she saw a break in the crowd, she dropped everything and flew from her unwanted fame.

Chapter Sixteen

During all her waking hours, right up until she was drifting off to sleep, Hattie's thoughts swung between her growing obsession with Adam and the mystery of the disappearing diamond necklace. She'd searched high and low, almost pulling the bedroom apart on one occasion when she was sure she wouldn't be interrupted. So far, though, there wasn't a twinkle of a diamond. It did cross Hattie's mind that Isabelle might have buried the necklace or hidden it in any of the outbuildings, but she quickly dismissed the idea; asking herself if she would let such a priceless piece far from her sight. Hattie's philosophy was that it was everyone for themselves in this life and there was no harm in greed. In fact, she recognised in her mistress traits similar to her own. Two of a kind who would pursue their ambitions single-mindedly. And she had no trouble imagining Isabelle alone, taking the necklace from its hiding place, counting each precious stone, running it through her fingers, then trying it on and drooling over its worth; because it was exactly what she would do in a similar situation.

Tonight, as she brushed Isabelle's hair and tied it up in rag curls before she retired, Hattie stared hard at her mistress's reflection, trying to will the secret out of her. Irritated by what she saw as her wilful lack of cooperation, Hattie secured one curl extra-tight against Isabelle's skull.

'Ouch, that hurts, you stupid girl!' Isabelle yelped.

'Sorry, Madam.'

'And so you should be. I'm going into Leicester on a shopping trip with my mother-in-law tomorrow, and I don't want to go with half my scalp missing.'

'Of course not, Madam.'

'And don't think you can laze about while I'm gone. I want you to go through all of my dresses and undergarments, check for any loose buttons or slight tears, and repair them.'

'Certainly, Madam.' Hattie's tone was servile but she had to lower her eyes to veil the excitement in them. It couldn't be better. A whole day to rummage around. She was bound to ferret out the necklace. Although she was pretty sure Adam was being cuckolded, Hattie hadn't actually seen Sir Austin and Isabelle 'doing it'. Nevertheless, she was slowly building up the evidence and when she had enough to incriminate her mistress, she could name her price. *And you'll be dancing to a different tune then, Madam,* Hattie silently promised and unaccountably, the word 'blackmail' floated into her mind. Wasn't that something you could go to prison for? Well, maybe if you were stupid, but she was clever. Mr Harcourt was always telling her so when she was at school. Hattie finished attending to her mistress's hair, then guilelessly, as if butter wouldn't melt in her mouth, she asked, 'Is there anything else you'd like me to do tomorrow, Madam, when you are out?'

The following morning, while she laced Isabelle into her corset, then helped her to step into the numerous petticoats necessary for the wide-skirted dresses that were now becoming so fashionable, Hattie was excessively attentive. She made sure that the shoes Isabelle wore were her most comfortable and, knowing how her mistress responded to flattery, she piled it on as she helped her into them. 'If you don't mind me saying so, Madam, I've never seen such tiny feet as yourn,' she remarked, balancing Isabelle's foot in her own large red hands.

'Do you know, ah had the smallest waist and smallest feet in the whole of Louisiana,' Isabelle confided in that slow speaking way of hers. 'And have you noticed my very high instep? That's a sign of real breeding.'

'I'm sure it is, Madam.' Having done enough toadying for one day and eager to get her mistress out of the house, Hattie stood up and handed Isabelle a parasol and her reticule. There was a tap and from the other side of the door and Matilda called, 'Are you ready, Isabelle?'

'Just coming.'

Hattie held the door open for Isabelle and as she sailed through it, she gave a small bob and said, 'I hope you enjoy your day, Madam.' Isabelle ignored the pleasantry and made some remark instead to her mother-in-law about the weather. Matilda replied that she thought it was going to be hot.

Their voices faded, Hattie closed the door, waited until she heard the crunch of departing coach wheels on gravel then, determined not to waste a minute of the day, she moved quickly to the walk-in cupboard. Dragging out all Isabelle's dresses she piled them on the bed then, balanced on a stool, she made a thorough search of the interior, checking shelves, and pushing her fingers into the furthest dusty corners. When she found nothing more interesting than the corpses of a couple of spiders, she knelt and tested the floorboards, tapping them with her knuckles. Disappointingly, they were all nailed firmly to the joists.

To fulfil her obligations as a ladies' maid, Hattie did a quick check of the dresses, sewed on some loose trimmings and buttons and returned them to the cupboard. Although she knew Isabelle was too smart to hide anything in so obvious a place as her undergarments, Hattie decided that, so as not to leave any element of doubt, she would be systematic in her approach and check everything. Starting at the top, she pulled each drawer out in turn from the tallboy and tipped the contents on the bed. The frilled garments were shaken, folded again and returned to the drawer, except for those needing repairs.

Hattie had finished her search and was about to slot the final drawer into the tallboy when she noticed, stuck to the back of it, a small sealed package. *Hello, what's this?* Intrigued, she felt the package. Whatever it held it was soft, a powder of some sort, she guessed. But it didn't look anything much and Hattie was puzzled why Isabelle should go to so much trouble to hide it. Obviously she had a very good reason, but what? she pondered.

Most of the other maids' lives were ruled by omens and superstition, but Hattie had always dismissed such stuff as nonsense. With her weird transparent eyes, though, and strange way of talking, she often felt there was something witch-like about her mistress. She could almost imagine her muttering incantations, casting evil spells as she boiled up frogs and newts and spiders. *Don't be daft,* she reprimanded herself, yer getting like soft Minnie, the scullery maid. Still, she'd keep an eye on that package, it obviously had something in it which she didn't want the master to know about, and it suddenly crossed Hattie's mind that it could be stuff for getting rid of babies. Hattie tapped the tallboy thoughtfully. Now that would interest any husband, she mused and was giving the drawer a final shove when Mr Adam walked through the door.

'Oh.' Faintly uncomfortable at finding the maid there, Adam went to back out of the door again. 'I was looking for my wife.'

Hattie gave him an inviting smile. 'She's away into town, Mr Adam. All day,' she added pointedly.

'Oh yes, of course, I remember ...' Adam didn't finish. Gripped by a sudden violent pain in his gut, he began to sweat. 'I'm sorry, I'll have to sit down.' Clutching his stomach and feeling nauseous, he sank onto the bed.

'What is it, Sir?' Alarmed, Hattie leant over him. His eyes were closed, the skin leaden, his features crunched up with pain. 'Shall I fetch Cook, get her to make you up a draught?'

'No, it will pass.' Although the attacks, the headaches, the pains in his calves, were becoming more frequent, Adam still hadn't seen a doctor about his symptoms. Initially it was because he was too busy, but latterly he'd become so convinced that he was afflicted with a wasting disease and would soon be dead, that a certain fatality had set in. He was aware of Hattie pulling off his boots, then loosening his necktie. He heard the swish of curtains being pulled across the window, and when she went out of the room, Adam assumed she'd left him to sleep. However she returned a short while later. 'Are you awake, Sir?' she asked quietly.

'Yes, Hattie.' He opened his eyes.

'I've brought you some warm milk, Sir, it's got honey in it.'

'Thank you, Hattie.' The last thing Adam felt like was milk but he forced

234

himself into a sitting position while Hattie plumped up the pillows behind his head. But sipping the sweet mixture, which reminded him of childhood, he felt the pain ease a little. 'I think it's doing me good.' Adam sounded surprised.

Hattie looked wise. 'Cook swears by Holloway's pills, but honey's a real healer.'

'Do you know, I think you're right, Hattie.' With his head resting against the pillows, Adam drank slowly and tried not to think of the recent repeal of The Corn Laws and the prospect of foreign wheat flooding the market, nor of the million tasks that needed attending to around the estate. He was particularly worried about the potato crop, which he feared was going to be diseased for the second year running. If it was, he would need to plant swede turnips quickly as a substitute. Adam sighed and thought it would be quite nice to forget his problems and lie here all morning being pampered by Hattie. But there wasn't the time. Being firm with himself, as soon as he'd finished the drink, and with the pain retreating, Adam swung his legs off the bed. 'Well I'd better be getting on. If the weather holds, we'll be starting the haymaking in a day or two.'

'Are you up to it, Sir? You don't look right.'

'Thank you for your concern, Hattie, I appreciate it. Here.' Adam rifled in his waistcoat pocket then tossed her a sovereign.

As she caught it, Hattie sidled closer to him. 'Would you like helpin' wi' your boots, Mr Adam?"

'No, thank you,' answered Adam, who was already stamping his feet into them.

'Yer necktie, then. Let me do that for you.' The girl's insistent hands reached up, but Adam gripped her wrists to push her away.

'I can see to it myself,' he answered firmly, but Hattie was pushing herself suggestively against him. In the half light he saw her run her tongue seductively around her lips and her eyes invited him to do as he wished. By now Adam was as hard as an iron rod, sex was being offered to him on a plate and his normal young man's appetite had silenced the warning voices in his head. *Well, if that's what you want, young lady, you shall have it.* Scooping Hattie up, he threw her onto the bed and pushed back her cotton working dress. She was wearing drawers but no corsets and without kissing or fondling her, Adam unbuttoned his trousers and rather brutally pushed himself into her. She gave a small squeal of pain, and he thought as he pumped up and down on top of her, *Oh my God, she's a virgin.* There was little pleasure in the act, just a need for release, and he came quickly, withdrew, and buttoned himself up. And with his slackened member there surfaced a deep shame. Unable to look at the serving girl, Adam mumbled, 'This is just between you and me, isn't it Hattie? Our secret.'

Hattie sat up and straightened her dress. 'Our secret, that's right, Sir,' she answered demurely, catching the second coin he flicked in her direction.

After Adam had gone, Hattie pulled up her dress and examined her drawers. There were specks of blood on them and other stuff and it hurt a lot between her legs, but she didn't mind. In fact, she wanted the pain to stay, to treasure it as a reminder that he'd been inside her. Anyway, pain was a part of loving, and she did love him, with all her heart. It wouldn't be so bad the next time neither, nor so quick she hoped. The master had probably told himself 'e wouldn't be back but she knew better, because men couldn't help theirselves. Hattie wriggled her plump behind in anticipation. Although she'd like to, they couldn't do it here again, not on the mistress's bed, it would be too risky. There were other places, though, barns and haylofts which were warm and dry and where no one would interrupt them and the master would be able to take his time.

Hattie lay back on the bed and thought, will he give me money every time, like he would a harlot? Taking the two sovereigns from her pocket she balanced them on each dumpling-rounded breast. Well, she wouldn't complain, not if it made her a woman of means. After all, the only difference between her and the mistress was the value of the gifts they received. But then, who could tell, perhaps one day a man, maybe Adam, would make her a present of some priceless jewels. The master might not care for her now, but he'd change his tune once she had money. For she'd use it well, learn how to talk proper, buy fine clothes and become a real lady.

Indolent as a cat, the maid forgot about the necklace and day-dreamed the rest of the morning away until she saw from the ormolu clock on the mantelpiece that it was time to go down for her dinner. She would sit at the table with the other servants and talk about this and that, and not one of them would guess what she had been up to wi' the master, *and* on his wife's bed.

Hattie stood up, adjusted her cap in the looking glass, checked that there was no blood on her dress, then scrutinised her face, touching her lips, her eyes and nose in turn and searching for some dramatic transformation. Disappointingly, it was no smouldering Jezebel who stared back at her but the same innocent-looking, rosy-cheeked girl. She *ought* to look different, after all she had just 'done it' for the first time, and that was an important event in a girl's life. Still, it just showed, you could never go by looks, thought Hattie. And even if her face remained a blank page, her notebook wouldn't for much longer, because what she was going to record in it would send out such sparks it would scorch the bloomin' pages.

Chapter Seventeen

William Jackson, rather conspicuously, hadn't been amongst the band of well-wishers who'd gone to meet Mary when she came out of prison, neither had he taken the trouble to call since and enquire after her welfare. Emily didn't want to think ill of him, but his absence had forced her to assume that he had washed his hands of the girl, probably for not showing a proper gratitude.

As each day passed, Emily found

herself growing increasingly concerned about Mary's whereabouts and her main worry was that she might be up to her old tricks. For compassion quickly wore thin, and if she were caught thieving again, the good folk of Leicester were unlikely to show as much mercy the second time around.

Although she knew she had to find the girl first, Emily was convinced that with guidance, Mary could be persuaded to stay on the straight and narrow. She had toyed with the idea of going in search of her on her own, but then common sense prevailed. In a notorious area like Sanvey Gate, any reasonably dressed woman venturing down there alone was at risk of being robbed or even murdered for the clothes she stood up in. However, it was clear she could no longer count on William's protection, so after mulling it over in her mind for several days, Emily decided to ask Rory.

And at least she'd feel quite safe with him. No one with an ounce of sense would risk taking on someone of Rory's build, Emily decided, as she stood watching him through his office window. He was writing and totally absorbed. Dipping his pen into the ink he paused, and she could almost see the ideas flowing from his brain to his fingers as he started to write again, the pen skidding over the pages in his haste to get them down. But then he obviously became aware that he was being watched, for he glanced up and when he saw her the corners of his mouth lifted in a smile. Laying down his pen, he came to the door.

'This is a pleasure.' Sounding as if he meant it, Rory held the door open and Emily stepped inside. The small room was made even smaller by the books and pamphlets piled on every available surface and her fingers itched to tidy it up. She doubted if any interference with Rory's way of life would be welcomed, though. Without knowing him long, Emily had found it easy to sum up his character, and she saw him as a man who embraced ideas as easily as he embraced women and was as quickly bored by them. And Leicester, she decided, wouldn't hold him, it was too provincial.

'Have you come on business, or because you enjoy my company?' Rory asked.

'I've come to ask you a favour, actually.'

'Oh, and what would that be?'

'It's Mary, I'm worried about her. She seems to have gone to earth, and I've not seen a glimpse of her since she came out of prison. I want to find her and satisfy myself she's all right. But where she lives isn't the best address in Leicester, so it would be a bit of a risk, me going alone.'

'And you'd like me to go as your

protector, is that the idea?'

'If you wouldn't mind.' Emily glanced round the room. 'Although I'd understand if you said no, because I can see you're extremely busy.'

'I can never refuse a lady, it's one of my weaknesses. But there is a condition.'

Emily gave him a wary look. 'Oh, what's that?'

'You consent to come with me to the cricket ground tomorrow afternoon to watch the aeronaut, Green. I'm interested to see if he can get his balloon off the ground.'

'But I've already promised to go with my parents and Natalie.'

'Well I don't expect they'll object if I join you.'

'No, of course they won't.'

'That's fixed then.' Rory picked up his hat and tapped it into place on his head. 'Now, lead me to this den of iniquity where Mary lives, why don't you?'

There had been very little rain for several weeks now and the day was hot. To avoid looking conspicuous, Emily had chosen to wear a drab brown dress in a heavy material, then as a little vanity, had added a lace collar and cuffs to lighten it. 'Watch where you put your feet,' she warned Rory, holding up her own skirt to prevent it trailing in the dirt.

242

'God, this is depressing,' Rory exclaimed after a few hundred yards.

As if to verify his remark a woman, slumped on a step and as soused as a herring, roused herself and regarded Emily with bleary eyes. 'Christ, will you look at 'er then. Where 'dya think yer going, Lady Muck, to a ball?'

'It's a social call, actually, Madam,' Rory answered with exaggerated politeness, then hooked his arm protectively through Emily's. 'Hulking great Irishmen do have their uses at times, wouldn't you say?'

'They do,' Emily agreed, and smiled as Rory's nose twitched in disgust.

'What's the matter?'

'The smell.'

'It gets far worse, I'm warning you.'

'Mary, mother of God, you're right,' Rory exclaimed, peering down entries into courts of indescribable filth. 'How on earth do people survive in conditions like these?'

'Well, here's some who have, so you can ask them,' Emily replied as they approached a group of women who were standing at an entry to try and catch some fresh air.

Recognising one of the women, Emily paused and smiled. 'Hello. We're looking for Mary Todd. Is she around anywhere?'

'She's done a bunk, miss. Went last

Saturday,' the woman replied.

'Do you know where?'

The woman folded her arms across her breasts. 'Nope.' Emily handed the woman sixpence and she found her tongue again. 'The old lady was gonna sell her brother, Joe—he's a dummy, y'know—to a chimney sweep. Mary got wind of it, said while she had breath in her body the little chap wouldn't be no climbin' boy and scarpered, taking him wi' her.'

'Have you any idea where?'

'Oh, it in't no good askin' me anythin' like that, me dook. She could be anywhere.'

'Thanks for your help anyway. If Mary comes back, could you tell her Miss Emily Fairfax has been looking for her.'

The woman held out a grimy paw, and Emily placed a couple of coppers in it. 'Yeah, awright,' she said. 'Miss Emily Fairfax, I'll not forget a pretty name like that.'

'Well, what are you planning to do now?' asked Rory, as they hurried, as fast as the heat would allow them, from the stench of poverty and cesspits.

Emily gave a dejected shrug. 'I don't know. Look for her in her old haunts, the marketplace, the Newark, I suppose. Try and get to her before the police nab her again.'

'I don't want to sound harsh, Emily, but

244

the stark fact is Mary's not going to settle down, get a job and suddenly transform herself in to a model citizen. It's too late. She's an accomplished thief, but it's her way of surviving, and that's the only life she knows.'

'You sound like William Jackson. It's not *her* we should be blaming, but a society that forces her to live like that.'

'I agree with you entirely, and I'm not condemning her. But I don't think you'll break the mould now.'

'Thanks very much for cheering me up, it's just what I need. Fortunately, I don't take such a pessimistic view as you. All Mary needs is a chance. Some education so that she can learn to read and write.'

'I thought the Reverend Jackson had offered her the chance of some schooling?'

'Well ... yes, I suppose he did.'

'And she didn't take it.'

'She went a couple of times.'

But Rory noticed that Emily's eyes had grown sullen, her manner distant, and he realised she didn't want to hear the brutal truth, particularly from him. And they were on reasonable terms now so it would be pretty stupid to upset the apple-cart. To placate her, he went on, 'Tell you what, in a day or two, we'll do a proper search, visit all her old haunts, walk down by the canal. If she and her brother are sleeping out, it's a place they might choose in this weather. Then we'll see what we can do for the pair of them. The Chartists might be able to help. Find them a room, or something.'

'Do you mean it?'

'Of course.' Rory knew he was making some rash promises, but it was worth it for the smile Emily gave him.

'I'd be really grateful. Perhaps it is a waste of time, but I can't stand by and watch Mary go to perdition, you understand that, don't you?'

Rory flicked her lightly under the chin. 'Of course I do. We're alike in that respect. A foolish pair who hope to put the world to rights.'

They parted outside Rory's office, and walking home Emily remembered how a couple of months previously she could barely bring herself to talk to him. But though she no longer disliked him, she was wary of the aura of sexuality he carried with him, because to her secret shame, she'd enjoyed him kissing her and thought of it frequently with a pleasant tingling sensation down her spine. In fact, Emily decided, she might not even object if he kissed her again.

If possible, by the following afternoon it was even hotter. In her room, Emily washed herself all over with a rose-scented soap, cleaned her teeth, brushed her glossy black hair then stepped into a dress, pale and cool as sliced cucumber. Her shoes were soft white kid, her bonnet a leghorn lined in the same pale green as her dress and decorated with roses and mignonette. Of course, none of this effort was to impress Rory, Emily told herself. Nonetheless, when he joined them in the hackney carriage her father had hired for the afternoon, the open admiration in his grey eyes was extremely flattering. So much so that Emily even found herself responding by twirling her parasol coquettishly.

As the carriage made its way down Humberstone Gate into Wharf Street, the driver was forced to a snail's pace by the crowds pouring off the trains from Derby and Nottingham. 'The good weather's brought on a holiday mood,' Emily remarked, noticing how everyone seemed to be togged up in their Sunday best and obviously planning to make the most of their day off.

'We all need to forget our problems sometimes,' her father answered, 'but if it's too big a crush, we might not see much.'

'I saw some people making for Spinney Hills. They've obviously decided they'll get a better view of the ascent from there.

Perhaps that's where we should have gone,' said Rachel.

Natalie looked dismayed. 'Oh, no, it wouldn't be the same atmosphere at all,' she wailed and since everyone else agreed with her, the horse continued it's slow perambulation along Wharf Street.

The cricket ground, when they finally reached it, was packed, but this didn't deter Jed. 'I'm very interested to see how they inflate this balloon,' he said and started elbowing his way through the throng in his usual determined manner.

'You'll be crushed flat as a haddock in there. I'll wait for you here,' Rachel called, then sank down on a bench and opened a book.

Emily, who had no particular wish to have her shoes trampled on or her pretty dress dirtied, thought her mother's idea a most sensible one. But she also felt honour bound to follow the others. Almost immediately, Emily knew she'd made a mistake. The great crush of people pressed in on her and the claustrophobic atmosphere made her panic. She tried to fight her way out but the heat aggravated the smell of unwashed bodies, the lacing on her corsets seemed to constrict the air to her lungs and the world began to tilt. 'Rory ...' Emily croaked.

Just in time he turned, managing to

grab her before she fell and was trampled underfoot by an indifferent crowd. Lifting her bodily, and pushing his way against the tide of people like a battering ram, Rory eventually found a clear space. 'Take some deep breaths,' he advised, 'you'll feel better then,' and Emily gulped fresh air deep into her lungs.

'Thank you. I thought I was going to suffocate in there, with all those people and that heat,' said Emily when she could breathe easily again.

Rory was still holding her in his arms. 'Are you sure you're all right now?' There was a edge of concern in his voice.

'Absolutely. And I don't want to spoil the day for you. So, if you put me down I can go and find my mother.'

But Rory ignored her request and instead scrutinised her face in close detail. 'You still look pale.'

'I'm not a china doll, Rory.'

'No, but a glass of lemonade wouldn't do any harm. There's a stall over there.' Rory was about to ease Emily to the ground when, behind him, a woman's voice in an accent he recognised as American, complained loudly, 'When is this wretched balloon going to take off, Adam? I'm bored silly and this heat is impossible.'

'Soon, Isabelle,' the man replied and

immediately Emily's head jerked round and she stiffened in his arms.

'Let me go,' she ordered, wriggling from his grasp, and Rory knew she would have fled if he hadn't managed to grab her hand.

'Hey, what's wrong?' Rory asked quietly, although he guessed where the answer lay, for when the man caught sight of Emily, he came to an abrupt halt, his features displaying a variety of emotions, the main one being raw pain.

But he collected himself quickly and raised his hat. 'Good-day to you, Miss Fairfax,' he said, inclining his head, while his wife rewarded them with a pale smile.

Emily didn't acknowledge the man's greeting. Instead, she turned and walked off, but Rory knew she was deeply disturbed by the encounter. *Ah ha, so this is the lucky blighter she loves, and a married one, too,* Rory thought and experienced feelings akin to jealousy.

Sensing that the wisest thing to do in this moment of high drama and unspoken passion was to keep his mouth shut, Rory caught up with Emily and guided her with a gentle hand towards the lemonade stall. He bought drinks for them both, then they found some shade under a tree and sat down.

Neither of them spoke and Rory watched

Emily pull compulsively at a tuft of daisies. At last she looked up. 'I suppose you are wondering who that was?'

'Not particularly,' answered Rory, who was, in fact, itching to know.

'Well, I'll tell you anyway,' she answered a touch defiantly. 'That was Adam Bennett. We once had an understanding. But he went to America and came back married to *that woman.*' She spat the final words out with a venom that surprised Rory.

'And you still love him, don't you?'

'No.' Emily shook her head in denial, but Rory knew she was lying. And such a waste! Here she was, a beautiful young woman, taut-fleshed, curvaceous, in her prime but pining for a useless young man who had betrayed her. Her sexuality was at its peak now but if it wasn't used, it would dry up like a raisin. In fact he felt duty-bound to awaken her to the joys of sex.

Although Rory had always found women extremely accommodating, with Emily's heart elsewhere, he knew this time he was going to have to call on all his powers of persuasion. But half the pleasure was in the seduction; he was in no hurry and already he could imagine Emily's gratitude for releasing her from a such hopeless passion.

A sudden excited gasp from the crowd

diverted Rory's thoughts. Everyone leapt to their feet as a huge red and white striped balloon began to slowly ascend, to sustained cheers and clapping.

It was such a miraculous sight even Emily's misery evaporated. 'Gosh, how does it stay up in the air, and with all those people in the car, too?'

'Gas keeps it up.'

'Oh, I'd love to be in it. Imagine the view, looking down on all the people, and the town, and the fields. You must feel like God.'

'I don't suppose it's much of a novelty for Green. Apparently he's done over three hundred ascents.'

'If it keeps rising, they'll be up to heaven soon. Do you think they ever get frightened?' Emily asked. As she spoke the balloon made a sudden sharp descent and there was a loud gasp from the crowd. But ballast was thrown out and it rose again and drifted off in a south-easterly direction.

'Well, I bet they left their stomachs behind them, then.' Rory laughed.

People stood watching until the balloon was a mere pinprick in the vast blue sky, then, the excitement over, the crowds began to break up and make for home.

The sun was dropping to the west and had lost its fierceness, but although Rory and Emily searched thoroughly, they saw no sign of the rest of the family.

With no eagle-eyed parents around, Rory was wondering if he dare ask Emily back to his room for some tea, when to his left he saw Adam and his wife again. It was clear Emily had caught sight of them, too, because she suddenly linked her arm through his and smiled up at him with an adoring expression.

'Shall we go home, dearest?' she asked, loud enough for the other couple to hear.

'Why, certainly my sweetheart,' Rory answered and, making the most of his opportunity, he bent and kissed her with some passion, full on the mouth.

Chapter Eighteen

During the following weeks the temperature continued its remorseless rise. The drought was beginning to be seriously felt, enormous fissures appeared in the parched earth, grass frizzled to a biscuit brown. People shooks their heads at such un-English weather and scanned the sky, praying for a cooling shower to wash away the town's foul odours and refill the rivers and reservoirs.

Mary alone welcomed the baking heat, for as long as it remained fine she and Joe could continue to camp out in Abbey Meadows. With twigs and branches, they'd put together a hut of sorts under a large tree, and this had been their home for several weeks now. They built fires, washed in the Soar, swung on branches like young monkeys and grew as brown as gypsies. It was a carefree existence, and away from the drink and violence that had dominated their lives, the brother and sister tasted happiness for the first time. A smile was never very far from Joe's face and while he frisked in the early ripening corn, or chased pigeons, Mary would watch over him like a little mother, loving him fiercely and brooding on God's cruelty. Life was bloody 'ard enough. How did He expect the little chap to look after himself if 'e couldn't talk? And the Reverend thought she should actually go to church and pray. Mary gave a snort of derision. Some hopes. He'd done nothing for them. Of course if God performed a miracle, like 'e were supposed to, helped Joe speak, maybe she'd think about it, otherwise she weren't going near no church. And while she had breath in her body, neither wa' Joe going to be shoved up a chimney like a brush, to be suffocated by soot.

But there was so little between them and

starvation that even on the most sunlit days, there lingered at the back of Mary's mind a fear of the future. It wouldn't always be summer. Autumn would come, followed by winter and their crudely-built hut wouldn't give them much protection against icy winds and driving rain. At night in their hideaway Joe would cuddle up to her, and even though he couldn't answer, Mary would chatter away to him, for making plans she'd found helped keep up her spirits. 'I'll always look after you, Joe, cross me heart. And I'm gonna find us somewhere really nice to live.'

Promises were easy to make but harder to keep, and Mary worried where the money would come from. She knew she daren't risk returning to her old ways. If she was caught thieving again she'd be sent down for a long stretch, there'd be no one to look after Joe and they'd probably say he was a barmy and shove him in the loony bin. 'But they won't do that, never, my little chap,' Mary would vow and crush him against her so violently, he would make small protesting quacking noises.

Although her previous attempt at picking up a man had been a disaster, over the months Mary had watched how the streetwalkers in Burley's Lane worked their patch. She saw how they approached prospective clients and bargained with them, saw how they made sure they'd pocketed their money before moving off with the man. Coupla minutes up a dark alley, why it's money for old rope, Mary persuaded herself and, although she was still skinny and unformed, she decided to give it another try.

'Now, you're not to go wandering off while I'm away. I won't be long and I'll bring us back something tasty for our supper, pigs' trotters and mooshy peas,' Mary promised her brother, before setting off on her new career.

Since Mary hadn't any desire to get her eyes scratched out, she checked first that she wasn't on another whore's pitch. Then she took up her position, lounging against a wall in a provocative pose that would tempt some man to try her wares.

She didn't have to wait long. The middle-aged man who sidled up to her had a shifty look about him and was too well dressed to be from the immediate area. 'How much?' he muttered, glancing up and down the street.

'Two bob.'

'A little runt like you in't worth half that.'

'You'd better move on then, hadn't you?' Mary retorted bravely. 'And if you do stay I want ter see the colour of yer money first.'

'You tarts are all the same,' he sneered but handed her two shillings.

'Follow me.' Although Mary sauntered off trying her best to look as if she were an old hand at the game, her heart was pounding and her legs felt as if they'd had the blood sucked out of them. The first time's bound to be the worst, but you'll soon get used to it, she reassured herself, and think of the lolly. The man remained several paces behind her but in a dark, fetid alley he caught up with her. Moving close, he suddenly grabbed her by the throat with one hand and hitched up her skirt with the other. Pinned to the wall, almost choking, she felt his hard thing push into her then a searing pain. 'I hate all women, whores in particular. They should all be dead,' he snarled. As he ground away at her and her behind bumped against the brick, he pressed his thumb against her windpipe and Mary knew he was about to strangle her. But then it was over. The man's hand moved from her throat, he exhaled noisily then, obviously terrified she was going to scream out and reveal his dark secret, he went scuttling off down the street with the sideways motion of a crab.

Mary didn't call for help. The mutilated bodies of whores were always being fished from the Soar and nobody gave a toss.

But she was shaking so violently she couldn't move and she stood in the grim alleyway, touching her bruised throat, the tears streaming down her face. 'I can't never go through that again,' she sobbed, her head rocking to and fro against the wall. Realistically, though, she knew she had little choice, not if she and Joe were to stay together. At the thought of it, Mary's stomach churned with fear and disgust.

No, she couldn't face it, not tonight, Mary decided, and slipped out into the street. She took a quick look round then started to run, through the streets and across the meadows, not stopping until she reached the Soar. Here, Mary pulled off her clothes and plunged into the river, rubbing at her skin obsessively and desperate to wash away all evidence of the man and the disgusting stuff he had squirted into her.

Although he made it clear he didn't share her optimism, Rory did as he'd promised and accompanied Emily on her search for Mary round the streets of Leicester. But after several such fruitless outings, even Emily began to lose hope.

'You know, if she really wanted to make sure her brother was safe from their mother, she might have decided to move on, perhaps to Loughborough or even Nottingham,' Rory said as they dragged their tired feet home after another wasted evening.

'Perhaps you're right,' Emily answered and, her weariness defeating her, she decided she might as well give up. But it had developed into something of a crusade for her and she was soon drawn back to it, except that now she went without Rory, whose heart, she knew wasn't in it.

She stopped and questioned people she thought might know Mary and Joe, but always she came up against a blank wall. Emily often suspected that they knew of their whereabouts but saw her as someone in authority, someone who wasn't to be trusted with such information. Emily was walking home one afternoon, hot and disheartened, when she saw William Jackson emerge from All Saints' Church.

He waited until she reached him then he lifted his hat. 'Good-day to you, Emily.'

'Hello, William. And how was London?' Emily had had to revise her opinion of William and his neglect of Mary when she subsequently heard from another parishioner that he'd been called away suddenly to the capital.

'Hotter even than here,' he answered. 'But that will be nothing compared with where I'm going soon.'

'Are you leaving Leicester, then?'

'I'm being sent out to India to spread the Gospel.'

'Oh.' Emily exclaimed, rather taken aback by this news. 'Is that what you want to do?'

'Yes, I've always felt that was where my true vocation lay, and the church obviously considers me equal to the task.'

'But what about your work here? There's Mary, she's gone missing with her brother and I'm growing increasingly concerned for their safety.'

'I'm sorry about that, Emily, but India needs me more.' William spoke with a deep conviction.

'So when do you leave?'

'I sail at the beginning of August.'

'So soon? India's a long way.' Suddenly aware that she would be losing a good friend, Emily added with a true sincerity, 'I shall miss you, William.'

'Will you, Emily?' William moved closer and gazed at her intently. 'Then come with me.'

Emily laughed. 'But I couldn't possibly.'

'You could, as my wife.'

'As ... y ... yo ... your wife?' Emily stumbled, hardly able to believe that a man of such propriety would propose to her, here, in the middle of the street.

'I'm sorry, I don't know what got into

me.' Red with embarrassment, William took out his handkerchief and wiped his sweating forehead. 'It was my intention to ask you to be my wife, but in the proper manner, and with your father's permission.'

'Well, I'm extremely flattered, William, but I haven't got a strong enough faith to want to go out to India and convert people to Christianity, when they have perfectly acceptable beliefs of their own. Besides, I would die of the heat. I find this enervating enough.' Emily opened a small fan and played it across her face.

'Women and children are sent to the hills in the hottest weather,' William persisted.

Emily reached out and pressed his arm. 'No, William, I am sorry, I cannot marry you. Now, I will have to go. I will see you before you leave and we must keep in touch by letter. I will want to hear all about your life out there.'

To save them both any further embarrassment, Emily moved off, and it was with something like relief that she saw Rory turn the corner and walk towards her with a smile of pleasure on his face.

In his more contemplative moments Adam had a sense that his life was spiralling out of control. After he'd seen Emily in the company of another man at the cricket

261

ground—and kissing him openly—he'd been filled with such a jealous rage that when he arrived home, he'd found Hattie and ordered her to the hayloft. She'd gone willingly, and she continued to be willing as long as a sovereign accompanied the act. At first he used her to still thoughts of Emily, but Hattie's soft body was responsive to him, and gradually he came to take a lusty pleasure in their secret meetings, which were growing more and more frequent. The cooing of pigeons on the roof, the smell of hay, sun filtering through the tiles onto their naked bodies, Hattie's small moans of delight as he moved on top of her, then her gasps of pleasure when she climaxed, were a balm on the open wound of his love for Emily.

But Hattie, as their relationship developed, grew cheeky and started questioning him about matters he considered personal and one evening, she asked outright, 'Does Madam do this to you?'

Adam, who was lying with his hands behind his head and enjoying the sensation of Hattie's tongue moving slowly over his naked body, answered languidly, 'Not very often.'

Hattie wriggled on top of him. 'You don't love 'er, do you?' She stared straight into his eyes. 'And why have you had no babbies?'

'Hattie, I don't intend to be cross-examined by you. My marriage is none of your business.' Adam slapped her behind and tried to push her off, but she hung limpet-like to him.

'Do you love me?' Hattie persisted then, taking the initiative, she grabbed his member, guided it inside her and began to gyrate slowly on top of him.

'When you do that, yes,' he moaned unguardedly, and as they finished and Hattie rolled away, a hint of a smile played round her lips. Maybe, she thought, the time has come for me to start dropping hints about what that wife of his gets up to wi' Sir Austin, and that powder she's got hidden away. It would sort Madam out good and proper and into the bargain, Hattie decided, do her own cause no harm, either.

Chapter Nineteen

Emily remembered how her mother's face had lit up when she'd gone home and told her of William's proposal of marriage. She remembered equally how it had fallen when she went on to say that she had turned him down. And now, Emily thought with a sigh, he was off to a new life in India, and today, as far as her mother was concerned, not only was her daughter saying goodbye to William but also to her last chance of marriage.

And perhaps she was right, perhaps I should have gone to India, thought Emily, for she had to admit that she was sad to see William go. But he was a true soldier of Christ, and he had no doubts about the rightness of his mission. Along with tropical kit and gentleman's relish, his trunks were stuffed with bibles and the book of common prayer. Most of the congregation of All Saints' Church turned up at Campbell Street station and they sent him off with several rousing verses of Psalm 100.

William was obviously deeply touched, particularly by the many gifts pressed on him. Emily's own present was a small leather-bound book of Wordsworth's poetry, 'To remind you of England', she had written on the fly-leaf and imagined him gazing at it and pining for his home and friends.

'I'll write to you from the first port of call,' William promised, and watching the train disappear in a haze of heat and steam, a lump rose in Emily's throat, for she sensed it was unlikely she would ever see him again. They'd become good friends over the months and she was conscious of her eyes growing moist. She also noticed some sympathetic looks and not being at all keen to have her emotions laid bare, she turned and slipped away.

Pretending it was soot, at the entrance of the station Emily paused to dab her eyes and immediately the hot, porridgy air hit her. Raising her parasol she stepped out into a furnace. 'Phew!' she exclaimed, and looked up at the pewter-coloured sky. 'It can't go on like this, the weather must break soon,' she remarked to a dog, which was flopped down on the pavement with its tongue hanging out and didn't even have the energy to wag its tail in reply.

There wasn't a whisper of a breeze and as her skin began to prickle with perspiration, Emily had a sudden vision of Lily's garden. How nice it would be, she reflected, to spend the rest of the afternoon sitting in the cool shade of a tree with the scent of roses and stocks wafting across her nostrils, a lemonade at her elbow and her good friend to gossip with.

Lily wouldn't mind if she turned up unannounced; their friendship went back too far to bother about such formalities. Her house also had the added convenience of only being a short walk from the station. Taking advantage of what shade there was and trying not overexert herself in the sultry heat, Emily set off for Orchard Street.

Already anticipating a warm welcome, Emily pulled the bell. It rang through the house emptily and she noticed how, with the the sun blinds down, the windows presented a blank look to the world. When no one appeared, Emily gave another tug at the bell and Bertha, puffy-faced and obviously roused from an afternoon nap, came yawning to the door.

'Oh, hello, miss. Madam in't in, I'm afraid. The heat was making the children fretful so the lot of them's gone off for a picnic to Bardon Hill.'

'Lucky them,' Emily answered, deeply put out by this news. 'You'll tell her I called, though, won't you, Bertha?'

'I will indeed, miss, and I should be gettin' home if I was you, 'cos I think I just heard a roll of thunder.'

'I think we'd all welcome a storm to clear the air.'

'Yeah, but you still don't want to be out in it, Miss Emily. It could be dangerous.'

'Yes, I suppose so,' Emily replied, turning to walk back down the steps and thinking how, with her clothes sticking to her, she would rather enjoy a good drenching. 'Goodbye, Bertha.'

'Goodbye, miss.' As Bertha closed the door, Emily noticed dense black clouds rolling in from the south-east and by the time she reached Granby Street, she'd also heard several distant growls of thunder. It was hard to move with any speed in such humidity and Emily was cutting through the marketplace when a sudden and violent gust of wind, turned her parasol inside out and sent several stalls crashing over. Vegetables and fruit bounced along the ground and articles of clothing went dancing around in the air like witches without their broomsticks.

Whipped along by the wind, and trying to prevent her dress billowing indecently over her head, Emily was halfway down Loseby Lane when, without warning, the clouds opened. It was as if someone had tipped a bucket of water over her, and in seconds her light summer dress was soaked through. A flash of lightning, then a crash above her head startled Emily almost out of her wits. Remembering Bertha's warning, she tore down Loseby Lane and out into the High Street. She was passing Rory's premises when there was another zigzag of lightning and terrifying clap of thunder, followed with hardly a pause by another, the force of which threw Emily against the window. She gave a squawk of terror then started pounding frantically with both fists on the glass. 'Let me in, Rory! Let me in!'

267

Rory's face appeared, he stared at Emily in astonishment as if not recognising her, opened the door and the wind rushed in, lifting pamphlets and papers and scattering them around the room. 'Inside quickly,' he ordered and forced the door shut with his shoulder. But the wind continued to whine under the door like a wild beast demanding to be let in.

'Whatever are you doing out in this weather?' asked Rory during a brief respite in the storm.

'Seeing William off to India,' Emily answered through chattering teeth.

'Oh yes, of course, I remember now, he's going out to show them the True Way. But you look like a drowned rat,' Rory said bluntly. 'Come on, let's get you dried off.'

Rory led the way into another room with a bed, table, chairs and other signs of domesticity. A fire was laid, he put a match to it, lit a lamp, then turned and studied her. 'You can't stay in those clothes, you know, you'll catch your death.'

Emily wondered what he proposed she should do. Strip and sit there naked? 'I ought to be getting home,' she countered, knowing even as she spoke that it was a silly remark, because the road outside was now a swiftly flowing river.

'You might manage with a rowing boat,

268

in the meantime I'll see what I have that you can change into.' Lifting the lid of a trunk, Rory sorted around in it for a second or two then drew out an extremely large shirt. 'Here, put this on,' he ordered, flinging it over to her, 'then your clothes can dry in front of the fire.'

Emily caught the shirt and gave a disbelieving laugh. 'But I can't wear this.'

'Why ever not?'

'Well ... I'd look ridiculous for a start.' She didn't add that she considered his proposal that she should remove her clothes rather indecent.

'Are you telling me you are so vain you would rather die of pneumonia?'

'It has nothing to do with vanity, It's too big,' Emily bluffed, 'and truly, I'm all right.'

'Why are you shivering then?' Rory accused. 'Do as I say, woman, and put the shirt on.'

There was no denying it, she was chilled to the marrow, the wet clothes also clung unpleasantly to her skin, but his bossiness irritated her. 'I can't change while you are in the room, can I?'

Rory's lips gave a sardonic twitch 'I understand that. And I am a gentleman ... of sorts. So I'll leave you to it. Call me when you're finished.'

Deciding not to take Rory's word for

it, Emily went and turned the key in the lock before removing her dress and undergarments. She had to admit it was a relief to be free of them and she stood for a few minutes, allowing the flames to play on her naked skin. When she felt the blood begin to circulate through her veins she spread her clothes out on the hearth and watched the steam rise. They wouldn't take long to dry, then she could go home, she decided, and slipped Rory's shirt over her head.

It was like being imprisoned inside a large white tent. But at least she wasn't indecently dressed, not an inch of flesh showed, Emily comforted herself and unlocked the door.

'Well, what do you think of the latest Paris fashions?' she laughed, flapping the empty sleeves of the shirt up and down.

Rory, who was watching a fire engine gallop by with clanging bells to some emergency, turned and regarded Emily silently. She was standing at the open door, the lamplight was behind her, he could see the outline of her naked body through the thin cotton and his own body reacted in its normal physical way. 'More nun-like than Parisienne I would say, but quite the most charming sight I have ever seen in my life,' Rory smiled, and it was the absolute truth. Standing there in the voluminous shirt, in his eyes, Emily was the most desirable creature on earth.

'You don't you think I look ridiculous, then?'

'Just the opposite.' He'd wanted her for a long time and there would never be such a heaven-sent opportunity again. Smothering any doubts that he might be taking advantage of her, Rory moved closer. 'But here, let me roll those sleeves back for you.'

Innocently, Emily held out her arm and as she did there was a tremendous crack, and a sound above their heads like exploding cannon-balls. Emily gave a shriek of terror and leapt into Rory's arms and they clung to each other, gazing in awe as roof-slates smashed to the ground, an uprooted tree danced down the road and hailstones beat against the glass.

'God defend us! Look at the size of them, they'll break the windows! We wanted rain, but not this,' Rory exclaimed.

There was now barely a second between each electrical discharge, water was rising at an alarming rate in the street, and the sky was a sheet of flame. The storm's unremitting ferocity frightened Emily half to death and her whole body shook involuntarily. 'D ... do ... you think the world's coming to an end?' she asked, voicing a deep irrational fear.

271

'Well, if it is, I think we should spend our last few minutes on earth fruitfully. And I've got just the remedy for taking our minds off it,' Rory smiled, and lowering his head, he kissed her.

'Don't worry, it'll stop soon, Joe,' Mary promised, as they watched black clouds bank one on top of the other and with the first flash of lightning, turn day into night. And she'd really believed her own words, had imagined that the thick branches of the oak would protect them. But the weather was remorseless; the wind roared in their ears, ripped trees from the earth and flattened the corn. Their makeshift hut offered little protection against the rain and they were soon drenched. Huddled together watching the lightning cleave the sky in two and feeling the earth tremble under them, Mary's small reserve of optimism finally died, and she did wonder then what would become of them.

With an enormous effort of will she fought to control her fears for Joe's sake. 'Cuddle up,' she said, and hugging him tight she tried to soothe his terror away with snatches of song. But it wasn't easy keeping up a brave front and when the hailstones started to fall, large as sixpences and bouncing off the hard ground, it just became too much for Mary. Overwhelmed by the hopelessness of their situation, she began to sob.

But her tears only intensified Joe's distress. 'Shush,' Mary murmured, and patted him gently on the back until he quietened again. 'I always said I'd take care of you, didn't I? That nothing would ever part us? Well it won't, I swear.'

But her assurances sounded hollow when Joe started tugging at her skirt and pointing to the river. She saw the frightening rate at which it was rising. 'Oh, my God,' Mary exclaimed, as the cracks in the earth filled with water, overflowed then poured down the hard-baked clay soil, through their hut and into the Soar. It was obvious that it was only a question of time before the swollen river broke its banks and, if they didn't move, sweep them away with it. But where was there for them to go? *Think, think and don't panic,* she reprimanded herself, banging the side of her head. What about their Mam's? No fear. Suddenly Mary had a brainwave. What about that Reverend bloke who was always on at her to go to church? A Christian gentleman like him wouldn't turn them away in weather like this. He'd take them in, see that they had dry clothes, food and a place to rest their heads.

Mary closed her eyes and tried to imagine what it must feel like to be warm and dry with a full belly. Better tidy meself up before we go, she thought, wiped her hand across her nose, then down her skirt and stood up. 'Joe, things is gonna be all right, take my word for it. I know someone who'll look after us, treat us proper. Come on.'

Her hopes set high for the future, Mary held out her hand. Joe grabbed it and she was pulling him to his feet, when several million volts hit the earth, travelled up through the roots of the oak, split the trunk asunder and killed the brother and sister instantly.

Chapter Twenty

The storm had matched their own passion, rising to a peak then gradually falling away. But neither of them were aware of its diminishing power until, lying sleepy and naked in Rory's arms, the abnormal silence and her own situation hit Emily simultaneously. Stirring, she raised her head and asked in an appalled voice, 'What have we done?'

Rory smiled, then leaned over and kissed her. 'Well, there is a word for it. Otherwise, I'd say passed the time rather enjoyable, as

I hope you'll agree. And although the world might have moved for us, it doesn't appear to have come to an end, so all's well that ends well.'

'For you, maybe.' Emily sat up, pulling a blanket up modestly round her breasts. 'I don't know how this happened. It's a most terrible mistake and I must go home.'

'Emily, calm down,' said Rory gently. 'You don't really regret this evening, do you? You didn't hate every second of it, did you? Because it didn't strike me that way.'

Emily thought about it for a moment. 'No, I suppose not. All the same, it mustn't happen again,' she answered primly.

'Well, that does seem a pity.' He tried to lever her back down on the bed, but she wriggled out of his grasp.

'I must go. My parents will be worried sick.'

Ah, her parents. 'Will you tell them you've been here?' Rory enquired, and thought with a lurch of guilt of Jed, his old friend, whose trust this evening he'd betrayed. Lord, imagine if he found out he'd seduced his daughter. Not only would it be the end of a long friendship, he'd probably run him out of town.

'I don't think that would be sensible. I'll say I was at Lily's.' Rory was ashamed of the sense of relief he felt. 'But as I said, we must both count tonight as something of an aberration. The circumstances were unusual, the storm made us behave irrationally.'

Stung by her remark, Rory lifted himself up on his elbow. 'Is that all I am to you, Emily, an aberration? Listen,' he went on recklessly, 'we could get married.' Even as he spoke, Rory was regretting it. *Jasus, what am I doing?* I haven't two pennies to rub together. It must be the storm, he decided, it's affected my reasoning powers. Before he'd been offered this job he'd been on his uppers and it had reached the stage where he was pawning clothes, although he refused to part with his books. Poverty and hunger had produced an inertia amongst the townspeople and Chartism wasn't exactly flourishing. The *Chartist Trumpeter* hardly paid its way, even though they'd reduced the price and he'd taken a cut in his wages. Rory knew it was only a question of time before it closed down and he moved on. And by and large this was how he'd always lived and it didn't trouble him unduly. But a wife would be an added burden.

Emily smiled down at him. 'Rory, I make no claims on you because of tonight. I shall never marry and besides, I don't love you.'

'Not even a little bit?' Rory asked, his

feathers slightly ruffled.

'No.'

Although Emily been shy with him, there had been no coercion on his part and their coming together had been by mutual consent. He knew how to please a woman and he'd been gentle with her. She had responded in a quiet, rather unsure way at first, but he was surprised how calmly Emily took her deflowering. He'd expected tears at the very least, cries of, 'What if I have a baby now?' and certainly demands to make an honest woman of her. Instead, here she was insisting he meant nothing to her and turning down his proposal into the bargain.

Wrapping the blanket more securely round her Emily slipped off the bed. 'The storm might return, so I'd better get home while there's a chance.'

Rory watched her with a thoughtful expression. 'Who do you love Emily? Is it still Adam?'

'I refuse to answer that question.'

'So, it's yes.'

'Stupid of me, isn't it?'

'Not stupid, we mortals have emotions and can't help ourselves, but pointless I would say.'

'And that's why I will never love a man again. They make false promises then abandon you.'

'What a sad thing to say.'

'But it's the truth, isn't it, Rory? How many women have you abandoned in your time?'

This was blunt questioning. 'A few, I suppose,' he answered uncomfortably. 'But not you, Emily, I'll never leave you.'

'Where have I heard that before?'

'You're being cynical, now.'

Emily, who was searching for various articles of clothing scattered about the room, paused. 'Well you'll be glad to know that your sincerity is never going to be put to the test.'

'Do you know, you're the first woman I've ever asked to marry me.'

'Are you saying I should count myself honoured amongst women?'

'No. But has it really got to end before we've even started?'

Emily didn't answer, instead finding her corset, she said, 'Could you lace me up, please, Rory?'

'It would be a pleasure, Madam.' Rory ran his finger slowly down her spine then kissed each smooth shoulder and the slightly damp tendrils on the nape of her neck before proceeding with this small intimate and domestic task. But with each tug of the lace, his desire for her increased. 'Come here, woman,' he growled finally and tried to drag her back into bed.

But Emily was having none of it and she squirmed away from him. 'No. Think of my worried parents.'

It was the last thing Rory wanted to do at that moment, but he saw Jed's stern face and let go of her. 'You can't walk home on you own, you know. It's late and there's probably been a fair bit of damage done.'

Emily, who was now dressed, secured her hair, found her parasol and once more looked the height of propriety. 'But supposing Papa saw you? If he suspected ...'

Emily didn't finish, but Rory got her point. 'I'll come as far as the corner, and not a step further, I promise,' he answered, pulling his shirt over his head and stepping into his trousers.

They saw how much damage the storm had left in its wake as soon as they stepped out of the door. Uprooted trees and fences were scattered along the street, the torrential rain had flooded cellars and warehouses and an overworked fire service was trying to pump them out.

But people were already out sweeping up tiles and broken glass, boarding up windows and trying to bring order to the chaos.

'Pretty bad, isn't it?' Rory called to a shopkeeper he knew.

The man paused and leaned on his broom. 'Yeah, nature, what can you say about it? It's turned the town into a bloomin' battlefield. I've seen nought like it in all my fifty years, and I don't know where the money's coming from, either, to pay for all the repairs.' His gloom deepened. 'And the lightning got the spire of St George's Church as well, I've heard. Still, must get on,' he said and continued with his sweeping.

'Do you know who I can't help worrying about?' said Emily as they dodged round a large branch. 'Mary and Joe. They've been on my mind all evening. Imagine if they were out in it, poor little blighters.'

'Mary's a street child, she knows what to do to survive, and she would have found shelter for them somewhere, so don't fret.'

'Do you really think so?'

Rory patted her hand reassuringly. 'Yes.'

Emily shivered. 'I don't know. It's just that I feel uneasy about them somehow.'

'Well, you shouldn't.'

'Perhaps not.' And Emily had to concede that it had been a night unlike any other and there had been a touch of madness about the whole evening. How else could she explain why she'd lain naked next to Rory, allowed his hands to explore her body, find its responsive areas, then take advantage of her. She gave a small shiver of delight at the memory, blushed and crept a shy look at Rory striding along beside her, his hand gripping her elbow possessively. There was no question about it, he was handsome with a persuasive Irish charm, but it was Adam she loved, Emily reminded herself. Why then had she given herself so readily to another man? *Because,* another part of her brain answered back, *you wanted to and look at him, even if he is not your real true love, he's a pretty good second-best and pretending it never happened is pointless.* There was no undoing what had happened and if, as seemed likely, she was going to go to her grave a spinster, at least, Emily consoled herself, on her deathbed she wouldn't be wondering what it was all about.

At the corner of High Cross Street, Emily paused and ⋅gave Rory a small shove. 'You'd better turn back now.'

'Please come and see me tomorrow.'

'You are persistent, aren't you?'

'Yes.' Rory moved closer, his body brushing against hers. 'Tell me, Emily, honestly, didn't you like what we did tonight?'

Emily leapt back. 'Ah ... ah ...' she stumbled.

'Well, yes or no?' Rory persisted. 'Perhaps you hated every moment of it. If so, you are a darn good actress, Miss Fairfax.'

'Well, I suppose I quite liked it.'

Rory threw back his head and gave a loud guffaw. 'Dear Mother of God, how can anyone *quite* like sex!'

'Hush!' Emily cast a nervous glance about her, 'There's no need to tell our business to the whole of Leicester.'

'If you don't come and see me tomorrow, I swear I shall stand on this corner and shout at the top of my voice that Miss Emily Fairfax and Mr Rory Aherne did, this evening engage in—'

'Stop it!' Emily giggled and pressed her hand over Rory's mouth, but he grabbed it and kissed it.

'Say you'll come.'

'Oh, all right, but only for a half an hour. At seven.'

'Kiss me good-night, then.'

'No, not here,' and, determined to score on one point, Emily hurried off down the street.

Rory waited, imagining she would pause and wave when she reached the bookshop. But she didn't even glance in his direction and in a strangely despondent mood, he turned and made his way back home. As soon Emily walked into the room her parents leapt to their feet with undisguised expressions of relief on their faces. 'Where have you been, Emily?' they demanded in unison, 'We've been worried out of our minds.'

'I'm sorry, but I went round to Lily's after I'd seen William off and once the storm broke it seemed only sensible to stay put. I never guessed it would last so long.' Emily was well-rehearsed, but even so, she was surprised how easily the lies tripped off her tongue.

'No, I suppose it would have been dangerous if you'd tried to get home,' Rachel agreed. 'But we've been sitting listening to the storm raging and imagining all manner of terrible things.'

'Well, nothing happened to me did it? And I'm here safe and sound,' Emily said brightly. 'Mind you, Lily and I probably drank more tea than was good for us. But we had to do something to keep our courage up.' As she embellished and embroidered, it began to occur to Emily she was digging a deep hole for herself and if she wasn't to fall into it, Lily would have to be put in the picture pretty quickly. And what would her friend make of her tale? Emily wondered. Lap it up, no doubt, like the romantic novels she read so voraciously. At least she wouldn't be censorious, not with her own unconventional marriage and love-life.

'You're home, and that's the main thing,'

said her father, and left it at that. 'Anyway, we've got some glad tidings. Simon's regiment is being posted to Ireland, but he's got a few days leave so he's coming home.'

'Oh, that will be nice, it's ages since we last saw him. When's he arriving?'

'He'll be here tomorrow evening at about seven.'

Jed left early the following day to make a purchase of some second-hand books in Loughborough and, with her mother busy upstairs killing the fatted calf, Emily was left to cope on her own in the shop. Not that this troubled her. Customers came and went all morning and she dealt with them all efficiently. She was glad it had quietened down by three, though, when Lily walked through the door and dumped her library books down on the counter.

'That storm yesterday was a whopper, wasn't it? It's going to take weeks to clear up the damage and poor old St George's looks sad without its spire.'

'To tell the truth, I don't think I've ever been so frightened in my life. Did you get caught in it?' Emily asked.

'No, fortunately we got home from the picnic just in time. Bertha told me you called. Sorry to have missed you,' Lily boomed in a cheerful voice.

'Hush!' Emily put a warning forefinger to her lips and glanced over her shoulder. 'Don't let my mother hear.'

'Why ever not?'

Emily went pink and flicked over the pages of a book. 'I've got a confession to make. I told them I was with you during the storm.'

'And who were you with, Adam?' Emily shook her head. 'Why the secrecy then?'

Emily cleared her throat nervously. 'Well, it was like this, you see. I was on my way home when there were these great flashes of lightning and it got so bad I had to take shelter in Rory Aherne's office.'

'So?'

'Well, think about it. I was on my own with a man for over three hours. If my parents found out they'd imagine the worst.'

'Why should they do that?'

'Rory has a bit of a reputation.'

Lily leaned across the counter, her eyes gleaming. 'This Rory didn't by any chance have his wicked way with you, did he?'

Emily managed to look deeply affronted. 'Certainly not!'

'Methinks the lady doth protest too much.' Lily studied her friend more closely. 'Yes, there's definitely something different about you.'

'Don't talk silly,' Emily huffed.

285

'Come on, you can tell your old friend. I never divulged any of your secrets in the past, so I'm hardly likely to start now.'

'I ... it was the storm and everything, it was all so weird.'

'And you got carried away?'

'Something like that.'

Lily giggled. 'Well, I've heard of some excuses ...'

'But it won't happen again,' Emily insisted.

'Why not? You are both single, both adults, and as I always say, you're a long time dead.'

'Yes, and women have babies.'

'There's nothing to stop you marrying, if the worst happened.'

'But I still love Adam.'

Lily gave a deep sigh. 'You think you do. Listen, Emily, you loved Adam when you were seventeen and hardly more than a child.'

'How can you or anyone else understand how I feel?' Emily wailed.

'Yes, but remember, it was because of him you also wasted nine good years of your life. Do you intend to waste the rest of it? Whatever way you look at it, no matter how many excuses you make for him, in your heart you know that Adam has behaved like a heartless cad.'

'But he explained everything to me.'

'Oh, they always do. Men are very good at explaining away their bad behaviour. I bet it was some scheming woman's fault. Am I right?' Emily nodded miserably. 'Put him behind you, take what Rory has to offer.'

'Financially, Rory has very little to offer. He can barely support himself, let alone a wife.'

'Be a mistress, then, it's much more fun, take my word for it.' Lily patted her friend's hand. 'I must go now. But come and see me soon and tell me what you decide.'

Emily had no intention of taking Lily's advice and when Simon walked in the door at five to seven, she looked at the clock, thought, this is a good way to nip the affair in the bud, and dismissed Rory from her mind.

Her mother had bought a pig's head and made some brawn. There were pickled onions, homemade chutney and one of Simon's favourites: apple pie. Potatoes were in short supply and expensive because of the disease, but Rachel had considered them a worthwhile extravagance with her son coming home. The table was set with a white starched cloth and the rose-patterned crockery Rachel had been buying gradually over the years was given one of its few airings.

A vase of scabious and golden rod stood on a small table and Simon looked about him with a smile of pleasure. 'Gosh, I'd forgotten how nice home was.'

'Oh, it's lovely to see you, Simon,' said Rachel and before she grew weepy and embarrassed her son, she rushed over and embraced him.

Jed shook Simon's hand and slapped him heartily on the back, both his sisters gave him a welcoming kiss, although Natalie, being of that age, did it a bit awkwardly.

'I swear you grow more handsome every time I see you,' Rachel declared, standing back and admiring her son in his soldier's uniform.

'Do you think so?' Simon answered, smoothing his fair moustache. 'And I'm a corporal now,' he said proudly, patting the chevrons on his sleeve.

Neither of the boys had been interested in becoming booksellers but Ben had pleased his father by going into the printing trade and was now in London. Simon, however, had always been set on joining the army, rather against his parents' wishes. But he appeared to enjoy the life, and intended to make it his career, so an understanding had been reached and certain aspects of the army which were hardly to his father's taste, tended to be skirted over for the sake of peace and harmony.

'So, you're going to Ireland?' said Jed, when they were finally seated round the table.

Simon, who'd always been a little too sure of himself, speared a pickled onion and said, 'Yes, we have to keep an eye on the Irish, you never know what the blighters are going to get up to next.'

'Well, since they are dying of starvation in their thousands, I don't imagine many are getting up to anything much at present.'

'No, and don't be rude about the Irish in front of me, please, Simon,' Natalie put in.

'Oh, why not?' Simon gave his younger sister a slightly condescending smile.

'Because I'm Irish.'

'How can you know what you are?' answered Simon, rather bluntly making reference to the manner of her birth.

'Mr Aherne says I must be because of my red hair.'

'Who's this Mr Aherne?'

'An Irishman, a political ally and a good friend of mine,' answered Jed robustly.

Emily kept her head down and said nothing, but she did wonder how long the friendship would survive if her father discovered the truth about her and Rory.

'So you're still dabbling in politics, Father?'

Jed stopped eating and stared coldly at his son. 'Dabbling? What exactly do you mean by dabbling, Simon?'

The relationship between Simon and his father had always been prickly and Rachel, who had no wish for a family dispute tonight, clattered her knife and fork down on the plate. 'Come on, let's talk about other matters. Politics always leads to bad feeling, and I'm not having Simon's few days at home spoilt by rows.'

Chapter Twenty-One

Promising to write more often, Simon went back to his regiment, businesses closed down by the storm re-opened and the town returned to almost normal. Not Emily, though, and as each day passed, she picked over in her mind endlessly her abandonment of good sense on the night of the storm. She even went as far as to persuade herself that Rory had seduced her against her will, although in her more rational moments she knew this was not true.

She went to elaborate lengths to avoid going near his office, but when a week passed and Rory had made no attempt to get in touch with her, it began to irk. Had she been seduced then cast off like all his women? As a sap to her pride, Emily told herself that it was because of his long friendship with her father. If Rory was grappling with feelings of guilt, his instinct would be to stay clear of the shop. Whenever the bell tinkled, though, Emily found herself looking up, hoping to see him framed in the doorway. In the end, it was getting on for two weeks before she saw him again, but not in the circumstances she could have imagined.

She tried hard to prevent it, but as soon as Rory walked into the shop, Emily remembered that this was a man she'd lain naked with, and an embarrassed blush crept up her neck. With her attention focused on him, it was a moment before she realised that Police Constable Pegg was only a step behind. Both wore expressions so grave, Emily guessed right away that something was seriously amiss.

'What is it, Rory?' she asked although she already had an inkling of what it might be.

'I think you had better sit down, my dear,' he answered gently and taking her arm, he led her to a chair. 'Police Constable

Pegg has some bad news, I'm afraid.'

'It's Mary, isn't it?' Rory nodded. Emily glared at the policeman. 'I suppose you're going to lock her up again?'

'No, miss, I in't and I'm sorry to have to tell you this, but Mary Todd is dead. Her brother, Joe, too.'

'Dead? How can that be?' Emily demanded, the terrible words only slowly sinking in.

'It was the lightning, during that storm. It struck a tree and killed them outright. Their bodies were found a few days ago over in Abbey Meadows.'

Emily swung her head back and forth in denial. 'Tell me it's not true, please, Rory.'

'I'm afraid it is, my dear.'

Rory crouched down beside her and took her hand. Emily closed her eyes and saw, in vivid, poignant detail, their small bodies lying together like effigies on a tomb. 'Didn't I say all along something had happened to them?' she accused, lashing out in her misery.

'You did, but no one is to blame, it was a tragic accident. And if it's any consolation, it would have been very quick.'

'If only I'd tried harder to find them.'

'Now come on, you must have walked practically every street in Leicester.'

'But it still wasn't enough. I should have

looked further afield, down by the river, in Abbey Meadows. I could have saved them.'

Rory could see that Emily was turning her grief and anger in on herself and that was not good. 'They are dead because of the storm, one of the worst this century,' he emphasised.

Although Emily had to struggle to come to terms with this idea, she knew Rory was right. Nature in all its rough fury was to blame, not her, not Rory, not even Police Constable Pegg. 'What about their mother, does she know two of her children are dead?' she asked, directing her question at this gentleman.

'The old lady ... Mrs Todd, that is, kicked the bucket ... er, passed on, a while back. The drink finished her off. There in't no other family 'cept her brothers, a coupla bad 'uns I can tell you, who were shipped off to Australia, and good riddance, too. You did your best for the girl, miss, though in my opinion, she weren't always properly grateful. But I thought you'd likely want to know what had happened to them, all the same.'

'Thank you for your trouble, Constable, and at least I can do one last thing and give them a decent funeral.'

'I'm sorry, miss, but it's too late I'm afraid, they've already gone to a pauper's grave. There weren't no money, no family, so it were just assumed ...' The policeman shrugged, stretched his neck as if the collar of his uniform were too tight, then went on, 'Well, duty calls so I must be going.' He hovered, hoping he might be offered something in the way of refreshment for his trouble. But the girl was still too distressed to remember her manners, although for the life of him he couldn't understand why she was wasting her tears on a couple of little guttersnipes. Families like the Todds polluted the earth and were best out of it, in his opinion. Bidding Emily and Rory good-day, PC Clegg set off with a determined tread towards the market, where he knew he was certain to find a stallholder having a brew up.

Rory made sure the policeman had gone, then went and turned the sign on the door to 'Closed', and pulled down the blind.

'Nobody to mourn them and a pauper's grave, which means we ... can't even give them a stone.'

Rory put a comforting arm round Emily and she leaned against him for comfort. 'Yes, poor little blighters, they definitely drew the short straw, in life, and death. But at least they went together.'

A knuckle rattled on the window and when they saw it was Jed, they quickly drew apart. 'Please come and see me tonight, Emily,' Rory murmured, reflecting as he went to let Jed in, that it was as well that he had a fitting excuse for embracing his precious daughter, otherwise he might find himself at the receiving end of a bunch of fives.

When he saw the envelope had an American stamp on it, Adam slipped it, with a deft movement, into his pocket. But not quickly enough for the eagle-eyed Isabelle. 'What was that, dear?' she asked sweetly.

'Another bill,' Adam lied. 'Now, if you'll excuse me I must be off.' He rose from the breakfast table. 'That storm has had dire consequences for the harvest—the fruit crop as well as the wheat—just when we were expecting a bumper one, and good prices, with the failure of the potato crop. I'm going to see what can be rescued from it but we'll all be tightening our belts this winter, Isabelle. Your dress allowance might even have to be cut.'

'Are you telling me I shall have to walk about like some pauper?' Isabelle stared at him with hard-eyed disbelief.

'With the number of dresses you have, I hardly think that's likely. I imagine most of them have at least another season's wear in them. If you're really worried you'll look dowdy, get Hattie to sew some fresh trimmings on them.'

'Hattie is a useless trollop.'

'Come now, those are harsh words.'

'Well, it's true. In fact, I might get rid of her.'

'Who are you planning to have in her place?'

'Not one of the maids here. I would go into Leicester to the employment registry office and get a smart girl from London.'

'You'll do nothing of the sort. I've told you, money is short. Hattie stays.'

'There's been no expense spared on that house your mother's having built, has there? A bathroom, the best in furniture and paper hangings.'

'My mother is using her own money on the house. Hard-earned money at that, and what she does with it is her business.'

Isabelle made a little moue at him but didn't reply, and Adam slammed out in a bad temper. By the time he was striding round the fields inspecting the crops, his anger had lapsed into depression. The jigsaw pattern of cracks had disappeared and the earth was plumped up with water again, but a few days ago the corn had been high and golden. He'd rubbed an ear between his fingers, pronounced that it would be ready for reaping on the Monday and told his foreman to call the harvest gang in. But the storm had beaten him to it and now the corn lay flat as hair on a dog's back. If they were spared another storm some of it might be salvaged, but it was as well, he reflected, that they had a mixture of pasture and arable. Of course, there wasn't only himself to think of, but his tenants as well. This would have hit some of them hard and, come rent day, they would be there pleading poverty and pressing for their rents to be held over, and they already paid in arrears. Or one or two of them might decide they'd had enough of farming and give notice to quit and so would begin the agent's search for a new tenant, who might or might not be hard-working and reliable. If Emily were his wife, she would be at his side now sharing his burden. But Isabelle, selfish woman that she was, showed no interest at all in the running of the estate, only in what it could provide for her in the way of new gowns.

Pausing by a gate to scrape the mud of his boots, Adam spent several minutes brooding on his wife's many faults in contrast to Emily's perfection, until he remembered the letter he'd received that morning from America. Drawing it from his pocket, he tore open the envelope. The letter was dated 10th May, 1846 and he read it through once quickly, then again slowly to absorb the details:

Dear Mr Bennett,

You will be pleased to hear that after many false starts and dead ends I now have information appertaining to your wife, which, I trust, you will find of considerable interest. A Miss Isabelle Dubois, who fits your wife's description, resided in New Orleans with her mother, now deceased, until about 1841. Her father, a Mr Gerard Dubois, was a dancing master, but he deserted his family many years ago, leaving his wife and child totally unsupported and in such dire poverty, his wife was forced to earn her living as a dressmaker.

I would be happy to continue with my investigations on your behalf on receipt of a further advance on our agreed fee.

I am sir,

Your humble servant

Clifford Bones.

So *he'd been right*, there was more to Isabelle than met the eye. Although she never talked about her past unless prompted, he'd caught her out in several inconsistencies and this had led him to decide it might be worth delving more thoroughly into her background. And it seemed his instincts were correct; she was a downright liar. If no plantation had been gambled away, what else might come to light? Adam wondered. It was expensive, this enquiry business, but not wasted if it continued to bear fruit, Adam decided, and resolved to send a money-order to Clifford Bones at the earliest opportunity. Then, in case it occurred to Isabelle to go through his pockets, he put a match to the letter and watched it curl into black tissue, before grinding it into the earth with the heel of his boot.

Hattie was making Isabelle's bed, tucking the sheets into the mattress, when her fingers came into contact with a hard object and she knew straight away she'd found the necklace. 'Now, in't I a daft thing, not looking there before?' she chided herself, and drawing the case from its hiding place, she lifted the lid. The necklace lay on a white satin cushion speckled with the brown marks of age, and though the setting was old-fashioned, even Hattie's untutored eye could see that the diamonds were of a superb quality. 'And much too good for the likes of 'er,' she sniffed, then lifting the necklace from the box, she held it against her neck and studied her reflection in the looking glass. 'Mmm, not bad.' It was surprising what diamonds could do for a girl. Hattie leaned forward, noticing how their fire danced in her eyes and gave a certain refinement to her plump features. There was no doubt about it, in the proper clothes, she could be as ladylike as the next person. Deciding she might as well try it on properly, Hattie was about to clip the necklace round her neck when she heard footsteps approaching. 'God Almighty, I'll be for it if I'm caught,' she panicked, and stuffed the necklace and the box in her pocket. Crimson with guilt, Hattie tucked her chin into her chest and continued with the bedmaking, folding back the blankets then smoothing down the top cover with a deliberate exactitude.

'Finish that later,' Isabelle ordered, sweeping into the room. 'I have letters to write.'

'Yes, Madam,' Hattie answered with a bob and left the room, carrying away with her the priceless necklace. Outside, on the landing, she stopped and put her hand to her mouth. 'What have I got meself into?' she muttered. And supposing Madam starts looking for it? There'll be a right hue and cry then, and I'll be in the clink before you can say Jack Robinson. Her imagination gripped by the terror of a rat-infested dungeon, sweat oozed from Hattie's armpits and marked out two damp crescents on her blue cotton dress. She'd throw it away, that was it! Box, everything. But wait a minute, under the circumstances, Madam was hardly going to report the necklace missing, or pursue her crying, 'Stop! Thief!'

If she left now, no one would miss her for a hour or two, and there'd be ample time to get well away. Adam paid generously for her favours, and she now had about ten pounds saved. If she could get to London and sell the necklace, then she'd be able to set herself up nicely with a dress-shop. Except that it would mean leaving Adam, and she could never do that, she loved him far too much. He'd caught her alone yesterday, and whispered to her to meet him in the hayloft later tonight, and how could she forego such a pleasure, even for a priceless necklace?

But Adam was taken ill late in the afternoon, so ill he took to his bed and a worried Matilda sent for the doctor. The man's name was Arden and he was a bluff, heavy drinking retired naval surgeon, expert in sawing off limbs, but little else. He tapped the patient's back, enquired what his symptoms were, and although Adam struggled to reply it was too much for him and he sank back on his pillows.

'My son is suffering from violent stomach pains and vomiting as well as cramp in his legs,' Matilda informed him, while Isabelle solicitously sponged her husband's forehead with a cold compress.

'Is he now?' Dr Arden scratched his chin reflectively then, having decided on his diagnosis, he said, 'A touch of flatulence, I would say. And that will be one guinea, please.' He held out his hand for his fee.

Matilda was outraged. 'Flatulence? My son is lying there obviously in great pain and you have the nerve to tell me it's flatulence! You'll whistle for your guinea, my man, now be gone with you!'

'I shall be consulting my lawyer,' Dr Arden huffed, when he reached the door.

'Yes, you do that, but I'm not without influence in the County and when I tell everyone around here that you are nothing but a charlatan, you will quickly find yourself without any patients.' But Dr Arden had slammed out and Matilda was now shouting to a closed door. Her face haggard with worry, she went over to her sick son and grasped his hand.

Adam opened his eyes. 'Don't worry, Mother, I've had this before and I'll be right as rain in a day or two.' As he was trying to reassure her, he was gripped by another spasm and his face twisted with pain.

'Oh, what are we going to do, Isabelle?'

Matilda pleaded, wringing her hands in agitation.

Now, Isabelle decided, was time to take on the mantle of ministering angel. 'I know something that might help, I'll go and get it made up in the kitchen right away.' She stood up, pressing her mother-in-law's shoulder reassuringly on the way to the door.

When she'd gone, Matilda sat there listening to Adam's laboured breathing, and trying not to consider the possibility of her son's death. Although it seemed an age, Isabelle, was back in about ten minutes, easing Adam up on his pillow and putting a cup to his mouth. 'Drink this.'

'What is it?'

'Milk and water and a little castor oil.'

'Sounds disgusting.'

'Yes, but it might help.'

Remembering how the milk drink Hattie had given him had helped the cramps in his stomach, Adam sipped the drink obediently, then lay back and closed his eyes.

'I'll sit with him until he's asleep,' said Matilda.

'I will, too,' said Isabelle, although she fumed inwardly at being forced into the role of dutiful wife, and her glance kept straying to the clock. Austin would be waiting for her at Rooks Spinney now, she thought, when the clock chimed three, and with the emerald bracelet he'd promised her. She squirmed in her seat with impatience at the half hour chime. She could catch him if she went now. But Matilda sat on and at four o'clock Isabelle gave up, for their arrangement was that Austin would not wait longer than an hour. Directing all her hatred at him, Isabelle glared at her sick husband. *You spoil everything, so why don't you just hurry up and die?* However, her expression quickly melted into one of tenderness when she caught Matilda studying her.

'Are you all right, Isabelle?'

'No, I'm so worried about, Adam.' Isabelle dropped her head and managed to squeeze out a tear.

Matilda grasped her hand. 'See, he's sleeping now, and that's thanks to you.' She kissed her daughter-in-law with great affection. 'Thank you, dear, you seem to have worked a miracle and I can't tell you how grateful I am. We'll leave him now but if he's not fully recovered by the morning I shall go into Leicester, find the best doctor there is and bring him back here so that he can give Adam a thorough examination and find out what is wrong.'

Chapter Twenty-Two

Knowing that if she were caught with the necklace she would have trouble talking herself out of a prison sentence, Hattie had rushed over to the hayloft in a high of state of panic, and stuffed it under a pile of straw. She'd intended to put it back where it belonged the first chance she got but then Adam had messed up her plans by falling ill. For several anxious days after this she waited for an accusing hand to descend on her shoulder. But then it struck Hattie that she was causing herself a lot of unnecessary worry, because even if Isabelle discovered the necklace had gone missing, she could hardly kick up a fuss without having to do a great deal of explaining to her husband.

When she realised it was unlikely she'd be called to account, Hattie relaxed, and a week later Adam was up and about again. To celebrate his recovery, Isabelle insisted on inviting Olivia, Harry, Clare and Christopher and the odd woman who ran the stables, to luncheon. In the preceding days Isabelle was in the kitchen bullying the staff, changing the menu on a whim and questioning Mrs White's expertise so often, in the end the exasperated cook gave in her notice. With her bags packed, it was only diplomatic intervention by Matilda, and the promise of a pay rise that saved the day—and the luncheon party.

On the morning of the party Isabelle managed to find fault with everything; Hattie didn't lace her corset properly and she hadn't the least idea how to do her hair. 'Look at it, you stupid girl, it's an absolute mess,' Isabelle pouted and threw the hairbrush bad-temperedly across the room. Hattie said nothing and went to pick it up; the black marks against Isabelle were already in double figures and this was another one to add to them. And Hattie could console herself with the thought that when the time came, revenge would be sweet.

Eventually, Isabelle's hair was primped to her satisfaction and she was dressed, all she had to do now was wait for the guests to arrive.

Leaning on the banisters, Hattie watched with a cynical eye as Isabelle, all sweetness and light, flew down the stairs to greet them. Chirruping, 'Dearest,' she planted a fond kiss of each of the ladies' cheeks.

I bet it's all pretence, that lovey-dovey stuff. I bet she doesn't like any of them very much, Hattie sniffed, hopping from one impatient foot to the other as she watched them move into the drawing room. After what seemed an age, luncheon was announced.

Hattie had waited for this moment, for she knew it was one of the few opportunities she'd have to put the necklace back. So, once she was sure that everyone was seated around the table, she dashed, hell-for-leather, down the stairs, across the yard and up the ladder into the hayloft.

Here, arms spreadeagled, she collapsed into the hay. Its sweet summery smell and the dusty afternoon light roused in her thoughts of Adam, and if she closed her eyes he became a solid presence. Her mind drifted to the many stolen hours they'd spent here then to the anticipation of future carnal delights, now that he was well again. Although it was difficult, Hattie tried not to nurse any false hopes, realised Adam was using her body merely for gratification. But she didn't mind, because that way she could hold on to him and her greatest fear was that he would tire of her and that would be worse than dying.

The grumbling voices of two field labourers below jolted Hattie out of her reverie. Diving under the hay she kept still as a dormouse and prayed that neither of them would come up because, although she struggled to think of a valid excuse for being there, her mind remained resolutely blank. But they appeared to find whatever it was they were searching for and moved off. Hattie scrambled to her feet, picked the hay from her hair and clothes, retrieved the box from its carefully marked hiding place, and stuffed it in her apron pocket.

But it was bulky. Terrified of being stopped and questioned, Hattie dashed back to the bedroom. Leaning against the door, she exhaled with noisy relief and decided that the life of a jewel thief probably wasn't for her. 'Still, that don't mean I can't try you on one last time, does it my little beauty?' said Hattie, opening the velvet box and propping it on the tallboy.

The necklace was halfway to her neck when a harsh, voice challenged, 'And what exactly do you think you are you up to?'

Hattie swung round with a gasp, the necklace dangling from her fingers.

'Give me that!' Isabelle moved forward, snatched the necklace from Hattie then gave her a resounding slap across the face. 'Thief!' she screeched.

Tears blurred Hattie's eyes and her hand flew to her stinging cheek. 'No, I in't!'

'What were you doing with it then, if you didn't plan to steal it?'

'Just lookin', that's all.'

'Oh, yes?' Isabelle sneered.

'Well, let me ask you somethin', Madam,' Hattie retaliated. 'Why were you hiding the necklace under the mattress in the first place?'

'I was hiding it from thieves like you.'

'Huh! Mr Adam, more likely.'

Isabelle pushed her face so close to Hattie's, she was convinced her witches' eyes were burning into her soul. 'What exactly do you mean by that?'

The edge of the tallboy dug into Hattie's back, sharpened her senses and reminded her that she had the upper hand. 'Well, I 'appen to know who the certain person was that gave you that necklace, and if it got back to the master, who's a very proud man, that he wa', you know,' here Hattie waggled two hands above her head, 'wearing two horns, he wouldn't like that at all, now would 'e?'

'I'll kill you if you say one word.' Isabelle's saliva dampened Hattie's face like venom, leaving her in no doubt that she was capable of it.

'I'll keep quiet, Madam, don't you fear, but at a price. Twenty pounds in sovereigns will keep my lips sealed for a whole year.'

'Why ... you ... you little trollop!'

'Well, that makes two of us, then, don't it? Ooh, there in't much I don't know about you, Madam, and I've got it all wrote down,' Hattie taunted.

Apoplectic with rage, there was no telling what Isabelle might have done to Hattie if Adam's voice hadn't called up the stairs, 'Isabelle, what is taking you so long? Your guests are growing anxious.'

Anger had made Isabelle's pale skin blotchy, but she pulled herself together and twittered, 'Just coming, dear.' Then, after ordering Hattie out of the way, she stuffed the necklace under some clothes in the top drawer. 'And keep your fingers off it,' she warned.

Hattie didn't reply to this insult, but as Isabelle pushed past her she held out her hand. 'My money, or I go downstairs this minute and tell your guests everything. And I know a good deal.'

'I don't have twenty pounds. Five will have to do until I can get hold of some more.' With an expression of utter contempt, Isabelle flung the coins at her maid's feet and stormed out.

'Well, don't think you can wriggle out of it,' Hattie shouted after her.

Isabelle turned at the door, her mouth a thin line of hatred. 'One day you will regret this,' she threatened through clenched teeth, 'very much.'

Hattie didn't realise until Isabelle had gone that every single part of her body was trembling: her fingers, her toes, her scalp, even her teeth. Nonetheless, it didn't stop her from scrabbling around on the floor for the sovereigns, then counting them into her pocket, one by one. Tension had kept her going, but suddenly the energy seeped out of her. Overcome with exhaustion, she collapsed onto the bed. 'Now, where did I find the nerve to do all that?' Hattie giggled, gave a loud yawn and fell asleep.

Hattie was having a lovely dream. She and Adam were in a meadow of wild flowers, both of them were completely naked and he was chasing her. She wasn't running very fast and Adam had just reached out to grab her when she was shaken roughly and a voice said close to her ear, 'Get off that bed, you slattern and pack my clothes.' Still partially in her dream, Hattie sat up and rubbed her eyes. 'Come on, I'm in a hurry.' Isabelle grabbed Hattie by the arm, yanked her off the bed, then started hurling a variety of clothes in her direction.

'You goin' away, Madam?'

Isabelle, who was pacing the room, paused. 'What does it look like? Now, get on with that packing.'

'Will you be gone long?'

'A week, two weeks, I don't know.' Isabelle was clearly agitated and her hatred was palpable. But more importantly, Hattie knew her mistress feared her and it was from this position of power that she intended to milk the cow dry. 'Go and get the boot boy and tell him to take these boxes downstairs,' Isabelle ordered, when Hattie had finished packing. When she returned with the boy, Isabelle was dressed in outdoor clothes and ready to depart.

But Hattie decided to have one last game with her mistress and she waited until she reached the door then called out, 'Here, don't forget your jewellery, Madam, you might be wanting to wear it.'

Hattie tossed the necklace to Isabelle who caught it, dropped it in her reticule then snarled, 'Bitch!'

'Tut, tut, that's no sort of language for a southern belle to use,' Hattie taunted, but Isabelle had already slammed out of the room.

Hattie went to the window, watched them all pile in the carriage and move off, then she picked up her skirts and did a happy little jig around the room. Things couldn't be going better. She and Adam could dally in the hay to their heart's content, and it looked as if she could go on squeezing money out of Madam indefinitely. She had a proper little goldmine there, in fact.

'What on earth are you up to, Hattie?' Adam stood at the open door with a frown of annoyance on his face for, in spite of their relationship, he never let Hattie forget who he was.

'I were just havin' a little dance, Sir,' Hattie pouted. Not taking him very seriously, she waltzed over to Adam and standing very close, began fondling his crotch.

'Not here, please Hattie,' Adam protested, although he took the precaution of closing the door.

'Why not? Madam has gone.'

And thank God, too, Adam said to himself. She'd acted most strangely over lunch, and had more or less bullied Olivia into inviting her over to Fern Hill. He was more than delighted to see the back of her, though, for he found he could hardly bear to be in the same room as his wife now. He'd stood on the step waving goodbye like a dutiful husband, but as soon as she'd gone it was like a cloud lifting. He felt his old vigour return and Hattie's fingers were working their magic. 'Take your clothes off,' he ordered then, pushing the more worrying aspects of their affair to the back of his mind, Adam turned the key in the lock, and quickly divested himself of his own clothes.

Chapter Twenty-Three

As autumn moved into winter, *The Leicester Chronicle* began to list, weekly, the deaths by starvation in Ireland. For the second year running the potato crop had failed and Rory was so deeply affected by the dreadful famine in his stricken country he spoke continuously of trying to raise money and returning there with food. But times were not good in Leicester, either, and as wages dipped so the price of provisions rose. December was exceedingly cold with snow falling throughout the month and it was not uncommon to see groups of men, many of them destitute stockingers, begging in the street or from door to door.

Rory burned with anger and indignation at the injustice of it all, and since he'd never been given to caution, when he spoke out his tongue tended to run away with him. In the marketplace, balanced on an upturned box, he would pound a fist into the palm of his hand and thunder, 'No work! No bread! No hope! That is our lot in life, and many are dying of want. Is that not wrong, citizens?'

'Yes,' a packed marketplace would yell

back, swinging lanterns accentuating their pinched features.

'And while thousands are trying to maintain their families on tuppence a day, and framework knitters are reduced to starvation, Prince Albert receives daily for his private use the sum of one hundred and four pounds. Is that not wrong, too citizens?' Rory would demand.

'Yes, yes,' they would repeat with growing excitement, stamping their poorly shod feet on the hard-packed snow.

'And I tell you we will continue to suffer these many gross and rampant evils in this so-called Great Britain as long as we are excluded from politics. That is, until the People's Charter passes into law and we have adult male suffrage.'

Their hungry eyes fixed on Rory, the crowd responded with vigorous cheering. In spite of their miserable lives, he somehow managed to light a small flame of hope in their hearts and they gobbled up every word he said.

Emily knew it was Rory's utter disregard for authority, the sense of danger he carried with him that attracted the crowds, but the more inflammatory his message became, the more she began to fear that there might be spies planted in the crowd. There had been a deal of unrest in the town in previous years and the mob was still feared. As a known hot-head and agitator, Rory could ignite it again, so a nervous authority was bound to be keeping a close watch on him.

And so it proved to be, for one night as Emily was about to shut up shop a young man came to the door. He glanced up and down the street, then said hurriedly, 'Can I come in, Miss Fairfax? I have something important to tell you concerning Rory Aherne.'

Emily's heart jumped. 'Why, is something wrong with him?'

'Not yet. But there might be. I can't talk out here, though,' he said.

It wasn't the time of day to let a stranger into the shop, and Emily studied him with a wary expression. He could be one of those tricksters who wheedled his way into shops then robbed people of their day's earnings. But although his topcoat was threadbare, the leather on his boots split, his cheeks cadaverous, he had about him an air of respectability. Deciding to trust her own judgement, Emily held the door open and he stepped inside.

'May I know your name?'

'I'm telling you nought about myself. It's safer that way. But I want you to warn Rory that at the next meeting, fights are going to break out, the Militia will be sent for and Rory will be arrested for aiding a riot. The authorities are determined to stop the Chartists speaking out by putting as many as possible in jail. Tell him a well-wisher says he ought to get out of Leicester until the dust settles or he's likely find himself behind bars on a trumped-up charge.'

'How do you know all this?'

'Never you mind, but there are ways and means,' the young man answered mysteriously.

'How do I know you're speaking the truth?' Emily asked, even though he was confirming what she herself feared.

'You'll just have to trust me, won't you? But believe me, I am risking my neck coming here tonight, that much you can know. Anyway, I'd better not linger and I'd prefer it if you turned out the light before you open the door.'

'Certainly. But here, let me give you something for your trouble.' Emily went to the till, took four shillings from the day's takings and handed the money to the young man.

'Thank you, Miss Fairfax, I'm most grateful. I didn't come here cadging, but I'm out of work, so for my wife and children's sake I won't refuse.' He clinked the coins together in his hand. 'This will buy them milk and bread.'

Emily turned down the light, opened the

door, looked up and down the street then beckoned to him. 'All clear.'

He bid her good-night then, as an afterthought, added, 'I wish Rory well. Conditions for the likes us will never change unless we speak up. There should be more like him, that's why I wanted to help.' He slipped out into the street then, hugging the buildings, became one of the shadows of the night and was gone.

What a strange encounter! thought Emily as she pushed the bolts across the door, then went upstairs and repeated to her parents the young man's warning.

'Do you think he was telling the truth?' asked Rachel.

Jed removed his spectacles and laid aside the newspaper he was reading. 'It seems pretty likely to me.'

'And me,' said Emily. 'I've been half expecting the authorities to take action. Rory doesn't always guard his tongue.'

'The Government are fools if they think they can silence us.'

'But where do you suppose this young man got this information from?' asked Rachel.

'Perhaps he overheard it in an alehouse, Mama. Drink makes people careless. But he obviously wanted to protect himself because he wouldn't even tell me his name.'

Jed stood up. 'I'll think it would be a good idea to go and warn Rory right away. Suggest it might be wise for him to have a spell in Ireland until things quieten down.'

'Ireland? Surely London would be far enough?' Emily couldn't hide her consternation.

'Well, that will be for Rory to decide,' Jed answered, putting on his topcoat, wrapping a muffler several times round his neck, then banging off down the stairs.

It hadn't escaped Jed's notice that there was a growing affection between Rory and Emily and although it took her mind off Adam Bennett, he wasn't altogether happy about where their relationship might be leading. He loved his daughter and wanted the best for her, indeed she deserved it, but he knew Rory pretty well and although he admired him for his courage and ideals—which mirrored his own—he was not husband material. For a start, he hadn't the means to support a wife. He was also by nature a vagabond and a womaniser. Emily, on the other hand, had always led a sheltered existence, and while there wasn't a great deal of money, she had never experienced true want.

It seemed strange to imagine it now, but Emily had really disliked Rory when they first met. But of course, he had such a dynamic personality it never took him long to win a woman over, if he had a mind to. There was also the common interest of politics. But perhaps he was reading too much into their attachment. He couldn't really see Rory abandoning his unfettered existence for domesticity, baby-sick and sleepless nights. As far as Rachel was concerned, her daughter had missed her best chance by not accepting William Jackson's offer of marriage. And he could see her point; the list of marriageable men of Emily's age was shrinking fast.

In his more contemplative moments, Jed held himself, and his pig-headed attitude, responsible for Emily's spinster state. Because of a personal vendetta he had prevented a marriage between two young people in love, and in the process had broken Emily's heart. Sometimes it was a heavy burden to live with, which was why, Jed decided, that whatever his reservations or the trouble she was possibly heaping up for herself, he would not interfere in Emily's life a second time.

Jed reached this conclusion between leaving home, banging on the door of Rory's office, and being let in.

Rory led him through to his living quarters where he was in the middle of a rather meagre supper of dry bread, a piece of cheese and tea. 'Would you like some?' he offered.

'No, I'm not stopping. But I have some information which I felt was too urgent to leave until morning,' Jed replied and repeated the story Emily had told him.

Rory pared the cheese down to the rind, took a final swallow of tea, then asked, 'What do you think I should do? Disappear?'

'It might be a good idea until things cool down.'

'Yes, you're right, I'll go to Ireland.' Rory placed two hands firmly on the table and levered himself up.

'When will you leave?' Jed asked.

'Tomorrow, on the first train. They might try and get me on a faked-up charge, and I don't relish another term in jail. The paper is on its last legs, anyway and I've been wondering what I should do. Now, the powers that be have made the decision for me.' Rory began sorting papers and gathering books together in some haste. 'Can I leave it to you to wind things up here, Jed?'

'Certainly.'

'There's not a lot to do, but you should probably burn the pamphlets. I don't want you incriminated.'

'Have you any money, Rory?' asked Jed.

'Enough to get me to Liverpool, but not to Ireland. I suppose it will mean pawning my books.'

'Let me lend you some.'

Rory paused in his task. 'Well, it would be a great help.'

'Would ten pounds see you all right?' Jed laid the money out on the desk.

'Thank you, Jed. And I'll repay it, once I'm back in employment, every single penny, I promise. If my luck's in, I might be able to do a bit of journalism in Dublin.'

'We won't be seeing you for a while, then?'

'Doesn't look like it.'

'Have you a message for Emily?'

'Say "goodbye" for me and tell her I'll write.'

'Is that all?'

Rory straightened. 'At this precise moment, it is the only message I can afford, Jed.'

'I thought Rory would have at least taken the trouble to come and see me before he left,' Emily complained.

'He sensed his days of freedom were numbered, so very wisely made his escape as soon as he could. But he did ask me to say goodbye to you.'

'Do you think he'll come back here?'

'To England, probably, but I doubt if he'll return to Leicester. There is no work for him here now.'

'Is this the end of Chartism, Papa?'

'No, it's just a lull, my dear.'

'I do hope so. It would be such a waste after all our hard work.'

'People can't give much thought to democracy when they've scarcely enough food in their bellies. Things will look up in the spring.'

Emily smiled. Her father was a real old war-horse, and Rory was a young one, she decided. But although she understood his situation, in the days following Rory's departure Emily did feel she'd been abandoned a second time by a lover. But there wasn't time to sit around and mope. With the numbers of unemployed rising daily, there was much that needed to be done.

The poor dreaded the workhouse and many of them vowed they would rather starve than set foot in the dreaded 'Bastille' as they called it. To try and do a bit to alleviate the suffering, Emily had offered her services to the Ladies' Working Society and at All Saints' Open they prepared huge cauldrons of free soup for the destitute of the town. A relief fund had also been set up and another of their tasks was to hand out dispensary, coal and bread tickets, as well as clothing which the better-off had brought in.

A large sign nailed to the wall read 'DO NOT SPIT', but since most of the shuffling line of scarecrows couldn't read, this request was largely ignored. There was little in the way of conversation but, like musical notations, the rafters rang with the sound of hawking, coughing and spitting, interspersed with the occasional scrape of a chair.

One day towards the end of January, Emily and another woman were ladling out soup when a carriage drew up outside, and a young woman struggled into the hall with a large bundle of clothes and blankets. It wasn't until she dropped them on a chair with an exhausted, 'Phew,' that Emily saw it was Clare.

'Hello, Emily,' she called, 'I've brought some clothes for you.'

'Clare! How marvellous to see you.' Leaving the other woman to cope on her own, Emily moved round the counter to embrace her kinswoman. Then, taking Clare's hand she said, 'Come on, let's talk,' and led her over to a couple of chairs in the corner of the room where they wouldn't be disturbed.

Although she managed to hide it, the utter despair that pervaded the room often got Emily down, so she welcomed the chance to sit and talk about inconsequential matters with Clare. 'It's ages since I last saw you,' she said, 'so tell me absolutely everything. But first of all, how is the school doing?'

'Tremendously well, which is just the opposite to Adam and his wife.'

Emily struggled to appear uninterested, but failed. 'Oh, why is that?'

'I don't know exactly, but when we went to luncheon with them a while back, you could have cut the atmosphere with a knife. Although he has never said so, I suspect one of the deepest regrets of Adam's life is marrying Isabelle.'

'Well, it's too late for regrets. He's tied to her for the rest of his life.'

'He's unhappy, and often ill.' Clare leaned towards Emily. 'It's because he still loves you.'

'Oh, is it?'

'And I can tell you, my dear, I never liked Isabelle, not from the first moment I set eyes on her.'

'Well, I can second that. But are there no children yet? I would have thought an heir was of prime importance to Adam.'

Clare shook her head. 'The dear Lord has not found it in his heart so send us any, either, I'm afraid.'

Emily patted her hand. 'Don't worry,

you are young and there is still time.'

'I fear I am barren.' Clare's mouth wobbled but she quickly collected herself. 'But I mustn't complain, I've got Christopher, the school and Freddie, who is a lovely boy and very bright and it's greedy wanting more when my cup is already brim full. And look at these poor souls, they've got absolutely nothing.' Clare glanced around her at the defeated-looking groups hunched over their bowls of soup, some verminous-looking, some still struggling to keep up appearances and tried not to shudder with disgust. They probably had all sorts of diseases and she didn't know how Emily faced them day after day. But then, she had always been that little bit different from other girls. 'You know, I so admire you, doing all this,' she said. Then, wondering if the good deeds were a compensation for not having a husband, Clare asked, 'Have you a young man, Emily?'

Emily supposed Rory could be classed as a suitor, but a rather distant one at the moment. His letters were infrequent and when they did come they were desolate in their tone: *'Although the Government has sent relief money, I fear it is already too late. It's my belief that there won't be a soul living on this beautiful but benighted island soon, because those who haven't starved to death are leaving while they still have the strength to walk'.*

'I have a friend,' Emily said, in answer to Clare's question, 'but he's in Ireland and likely to remain there for some time.'

'So you won't be inviting us to a wedding in the immediate future?'

'I doubt it.' The line of people waiting to be served was getting longer and Emily could see that the other helper was casting reproachful glances in her direction. 'Look, I must go. But come in again, and whatever you've got, bring it. More clothes. Winter vegetables, milk, cheese—anything.'

'I'll come again next week, same day, same time, so be here.'

'Oh, I will be.' The girls kissed and Emily walked to the door with Clare to wave her off before going back to her place behind the counter.

Ladling soup out to the endless line of people was such an automatic task it left her mind free to ponder on what Clare had told her about Adam. *So, he's unhappy, is he? Well, it serves him right and maybe now he has an inkling of what I went through.* Then, deciding not to waste her pity on him, Emily gave a surprised customer a double helping of cabbage soup.

Chapter Twenty-Four

The following week the carriage pulled up outside All Saints' Open, on the exact day and hour as Clare had promised. Emily, who had been given the job of sorting cast-off clothing into separate bundles for men, women and children, managed not to react when a small mountain of turnips, carrots and onions were tipped onto the table in front of her and Adam's voice said, 'Clare sends her apologies, she has a slight chill, so I've been sent instead.'

'Do tell her I hope she is soon better,' Emily answered and went on smoothing and folding.

'How are you, Emily?' Adam ducked so that he could see her face. 'Well, there is no need to answer that, for you are obviously blooming.'

'Please go, Adam, I don't want people to get the wrong idea and start talking.'

'Now, what is there to gossip about, when I'm the model of propriety?' Adam moved closer and lowered his voice. 'Of course, if I were to kiss you like that fellow did at the cricket ground, that would be a different matter. Then people would be entitled to talk. It might even brighten up their day.'

Emily reddened with annoyance. 'Your generosity doesn't entitle you to be offensive, and what I do ceased to be any business of yours a long time ago. Here, take your turnips and go.' Emily shoved the vegetables back at him with an angry gesture, and several went rolling onto the floor where they were quickly snatched up and stuffed into pockets.

'Sorry, I shouldn't have said that. You're quite right, it was absolutely out of order. Put it down to jealousy.'

Emily paused and stared straight at Adam. 'What right have you to be jealous?'

'None, I admit. But I dread opening a paper and reading that you are married.'

'Since you never had the courtesy to tell me of your own marriage, I can't see why you find it such a problem. But then, men have such double standards, don't they? Or maybe you are suggesting I stay single to avoid hurting you?'

'No, of course not, but I miss you every day of my life. Hang it, Emily, there's no law that says we can't be friends, is there?'

Knowing it was a waste of time, Emily had given up examining her own feelings towards Adam, but, as always, his ardour confused her. 'Your wife might possibly object,' she pointed out.

'That is a matter of total indifference to me.'

'You shouldn't be talking about your wife like that, after less than two years of marriage.'

'I've already told you, the marriage was a mistake. She hoodwinked me into it. She lied to me over various other matters as well, as I've recently discovered.'

But Emily didn't feel inclined to be drawn into a discussion of Isabelle's many faults, and she wondered whether, if she were Adam's wife, he would be listing her many failings to another willing female ear ...?

'Well, you are stuck with her now, "until death us do part", isn't that what you promised?' she taunted.

Adam's dark-lashed eyes gazed at her with a hurt expression. 'Don't please, Emily, this isn't like you.'

'You shouldn't provoke me,' Emily replied then, not caring for the words she heard coming from her mouth, she moved to a less contentious subject. 'How is the estate going?'

'Not well at the moment. The harvest was a disaster and several beasts we were fattening went down with a disease and died. Fortunately, we can cope with setbacks like that. It's these poor blighters

330

I feel sorry for. Look, can I come again next week, Emily? I'll bring more vegetables, and I'll behave myself, I promise.'

'It's a free world, so I can hardly stop you. Besides, these poor hungry souls are more important than my personal feelings.'

'Good. And here.' Emily's tone was a fraction less abrasive, so Adam knew he'd made slight headway. Feeling pleased with himself, and generous, he fumbled in his pocket and handed her a couple of sovereigns. 'Put this towards the relief fund.'

'Bribery' was the word that sprung to Emily's mind when Adam returned the following week with a whole cheese, several fresh crusty loaves and a keg of ale. This was luxurious fare, a mile away from the normal monotonous diet of cabbage soup provided by the centre. If the Angel Gabriel had floated down on celestial wings he wouldn't have received a more enthusiastic reception than Adam did that day from the broken men and women and their sickly children. Briefly, the unrelenting misery of their lives was lightened by the sight of decent food. There was no pushing or shoving, but they watched every move, making sure that there was no sleight of hand and that the bread, Stilton and ale were divided into equal shares.

When everyone was served and tucking in, Miss Hancock, who was in charge of the Working Committee, came over and shook Adam's hand in gratitude. 'Thank you, Mr Bennett, you've done wonders for their morale. We've even had a respite from the coughing and spitting.'

'I'll bring more next week, Miss Hancock,' Adam promised, with a glance at Emily.

'That is kind of you. The lines of unemployed grow longer every day and even with all the charity we receive, it's still never enough.'

So, with a stamp of approval from Miss Hancock, Adam was free to come and go as he pleased. And with his generosity, handsome features and air of breeding, he soon became something of a pet amongst the other ladies.

Emily was quite aware of Adam's motives, knew he was trying to dismantle the wall of self-preservation she'd erected around herself. She was also aware that she had to strike a balance, knew that if she were seen to be too hostile towards him it would draw attention to them, which she didn't want. Little by little, though, by making himself useful, Adam managed to extend his visits until he was stopping for well over an hour.

'Isn't it about time you went?' said Emily one afternoon with a glance at the clock, 'You've been here nearly two hours. And I have to go out, anyway.'

'Oh, where to?'

'The Shambles,' she said unguardedly. 'One of my less pleasant tasks is scrounging bones off butchers for soup.'

Adam picked up his hat and topcoat. 'In that case I will go. But I'll see you next week. Goodbye ... dearest.'

The last word was the merest whisper and Emily buttoned herself into her cloak, pretending she hadn't heard. She also made sure Adam had driven off before she stepped outside herself.

It was well into March now, and although rain had washed away the last vestiges of snow, it was a raw day with wisps of fog that looked set to thicken as the afternoon progressed. Emily shivered and thought of home and a warm fire. And that was where she would be heading once her errand was completed, she decided, setting off towards St Nicholas Street.

The air in Shambles Lane was tainted with the smell of blood and carcasses, and going there strained Emily's charitable instincts to their limits. Endeavouring not to show her disgust, she waited for an obliging butcher to wrap up a bundle of bloody bones in newspaper, thanked him for his generosity and shot out of the shop. Pausing to draw breath she saw the fog was now closing in in earnest. The lamps had been lit but there was a yellow aura around them, footsteps were muffled, figures loomed briefly and disappeared in a way Emily found quite eerie.

Emily set off, heard a tread, deliberate and rather sinister, a short distance behind her and her spine began to tingle with fear. Dirty deeds, rape, murder, were done on nights like these. Her heart racing, Emily hurriedly unwrapped the parcel, grabbed the largest bone and, as the footsteps drew level, held it aloft like a weapon. 'Don ... don't come a step nearer, or you'll get what for,' she threatened.

'What are you doing, Emily?'

'Adam,' she squeaked. Weak with relief, her arm dropped to her side. 'Don't ever frighten me like that again.'

'I'm so sorry, my dear, I didn't realise.'

'You're lucky you didn't feel the weight of this on your skull.' Annoyed with him, Emily waved the knuckle bone under his nose. 'I thought I was about to be attacked.'

'Here, give me that before you do me an injury.' Adam prised the bone from her fingers and threw it in the gutter. Almost as if it had been waiting, a dog shot out of the fog, clamped the bone between its hungry jaws and loped off. Its coming and going was so sudden they both burst out laughing and the final remnants of Emily's fear drained away.

'The last time I saw you, you were on your way home,' Emily commented, as they began to inch their way forward.

'I started off, got a short way then the fog came down like a blanket. Since I had no desire to end up in a ditch, I turned the horse round and booked myself into the Bell Hotel for the night.'

'Won't they be worrying at home?'

'My mother probably will, but there isn't much I can do about that.' As Adam spoke, Emily missed her footing and slipped into the gutter. 'Here, take my arm before you break your ankle.'

Rather glad of his company now, she did as he ordered, although with no landmark to take their bearings from they were soon hopelessly lost. Somewhere in their wanderings, Emily abandoned the parcel of bones and more by luck than judgement, about an hour later they found themselves outside All Saints' Open. But it was in darkness and the doors were closed and bolted.

'Looks as if everyone has gone home,' Adam observed.

'Very sensible of them. I'm going to follow their example, so I'll say good-night to you here,' Emily replied.

'I'll walk with you to your door.'

'That won't be necessary.' To make her point Emily placed an emphatic hand on Adam's chest and pushed him away.

'I can't abandon you here, and nobody will recognise me in this fog if that's what you're worried about.'

Emily had to admit that she didn't feel particularly brave about setting out on her own, so she allowed herself to be swayed by the logic of his argument. Three doors from the shop, however, she said in a determined tone, 'Not a step further, Adam.'

Adam came to an immediate halt and raised his hands in an attitude of surrender. 'See, I'm doing as I'm told and for that, don't you think I deserve a good-night kiss?'

'Adam, please stop it.' Emily marched off, calling over her shoulder, 'You're married, remember?'

'It makes no difference, You haunt me and nothing will stop me loving you, Emily, so please, grant me this one wish.' Almost as if she were being reeled in on a fishing line, Emily back-tracked and when she reached Adam, he gathered her up in his arms. Rocking her backwards and forwards he moaned, 'Oh Emily, what are we to do?'

'There is nothing we can do,' she answered in a small sad voice.

'Loving you has become a sickness and I'm often ill.' It was said almost accusingly. 'But if I could see you, even if only once in a while, it would be enough to keep me going. Oh, say you will,' Adam. beseeched.

'It's not fair of you to ask such things of me, Adam.'

'Don't be cruel and send me away again, I couldn't bear it. If I rented a room somewhere here in town, we could make it our own little secret place.' Adam lifted her hand to his lips and kissed the palm.

Cut off by the fog, in a weird sort of no-man's land, Emily could feel her common sense deserting her. *Why not give in? What was the harm in it, when they loved each other?* Well, there was the pain he'd already caused her, plus the small matter of a wife, the voice of reason reminded her. *Yes, but he wouldn't hurt me so much again and he doesn't love Isabelle, so she hardly counts,* she was explaining to her interfering conscience when nearby someone called, 'Emily is that you?'

'Oh, my Lord!' Emily leapt away from Adam. 'It's my father, now go,' she hissed, pushed him off into the night and managed to answer in a normal voice, 'Yes, Papa, it is me.'

Jed appeared, wraith-like out of the mist. 'Thank heaven, I've been hunting all over for you. Were you talking to someone?'

'No,' Emily lied.

'That's funny, I could have sworn I heard voices.'

'It's the fog, it plays tricks.'

'You're quite right, it does, so let's get out of it, shall we?'

'There's a letter for you, dear,' said Rachel, once she made sure Emily was seated by the fire with a nice fresh cup of tea and some hot buttered toast.

Still with Adam in all but the physical sense, Emily looked up, saw the letter propped against an ornament on the mantelpiece, but made no attempt to reach up for it.

'It's from Ireland,' Rachel said encouragingly.

'Is it?' Emily went on warming her chilled fingers by the fire.

'Then it'll be from Rory,' Jed put in.

'I dare say.'

Jed was growing impatient with his daughter's indifference and he pushed the letter into her hand. 'For heaven's sake open it, girl, and tell us what he says.'

Because of her emotional confusion, Rory's letter seemed like an intrusion

338

and Emily was reluctant to open it. But she was also aware that both her parents were beginning to think her behaviour strange, so to appease them and quieten any suspicions, she broke the seal.

My dearest Emily, she read,
You'll be glad to hear that, for a change, I have extremely good news, something which you'll agree has been in rather short supply in my letters of late. I recently met a London newspaper proprietor who announced himself so impressed with my journalism, he has offered me a position on his paper in London at a salary of three pounds a week. In my dire financial situation it is hardly an offer I can turn down, so I shall be returning to England shortly, although I can't give you an exact date at the moment.

I intend to call on you en route to London, because I have have an important question to put to you. Emily, will you marry me? I don't think you took my first offer seriously, and you've already made it clear that you don't love me, but I also have definite proof that you don't find me repulsive, either. We do share an interest in politics, though, and I think we could have a successful and fulfilling marriage together. I am in a position now to offer you a bit of security,

so think about it carefully, Emily, then give me your answer when I next see you. If your answer is yes, I will speak to your father, then look for lodgings in London and we can be married as soon as you like.
With my deepest affection,
Rory

Emily let the letter fall to her lap. *'With deepest affection'.* So, he was making it clear he didn't love her either, and that this was going to be purely a political union. Not that it mattered, she'd probably turn down his proposal anyway, she decided, folding the letter in two and pushing it into her pocket.

'Well, what does Rory have to say for himself?' asked Jed, who had grown tired of watching his daughter stare into space.

'He's been offered a position in London on a newspaper, so he's returning to England soon and he says he'll call in and see us.'

Jed slapped his leg. 'That is splendid news. I feared at times that Rory might have decided to decamp permanently to Ireland.'

Emily gave a huge yawn and stood up. 'I think I'll go to bed. I'm tired.' She kissed both parents, wished them goodnight and

340

escaped to her bedroom before her father could cross-examine her further on the contents of Rory's letter.

The fog pressed thick and yellow against the windowpane and the bedroom was so cold her breath came out in small condensed puffs. Emily drew the curtains, undressed quickly, put on a thick flannelette nightgown and jumped into bed. Her mother had heated it earlier with a warming pan and some of the heat had been retained. Snuggling down, Emily stared at the ceiling, and recited to herself Rory's letter. Two men were asking her to make momentous decisions: Adam wanted her as his mistress, Rory, his wife, and within the next few weeks she would have to say 'yes' to one and 'no' to the other.

Should she go for the intensity of an illicit love affair with Adam or should she accept Rory's more mundane offer of marriage?

Oh, what am I to do? she asked the ceiling. Finding no answer to her dilemma there, Emily tossed onto her side. She heard her mother creep in to blow out the candle and, left in the darkness, her lids drooped with tiredness. I'll leave it until tomorrow, she decided, pushed her problem aside and allowed sleep to gather her up in its arms.

Chapter Twenty-Five

Catching up with him, Hattie tugged Adam's coat. 'Sir, can I speak with you?' 'Yes, what is it?' With his passion for Emily so intense, his mind so absorbed by her, Hattie was an intrusion—and an unpleasant reminder—and Adam's manner was rather brusque. He frequently felt like a callow youth in the first throes of love; a laughable situation, he knew, for someone of his age. But now that he knew for certain that Emily felt more than a glimmer of love for him, his life had taken on a whole new perspective. The world was a brighter place and best of all, he had hope. But this would be his final chance, so he'd better not muck it up. And he mustn't let his impatience, or his ardour get the better of him, try to hurry things along and frighten her off again. He understood why Emily vacillated. It was an enormous step for her to take: to live a secret life and perhaps never marry. But though their union would not be sanctified by the church, she would be his bride in all but name; pure and untouched.

It was in small acts of charity that Adam

knew he could wear Emily down, so he continued to drive into town each week with his gig piled high with provisions for the bundles of rags she insisted needed her care. And that had been his intention today, until he heard Isabelle and his mother making plans to go into Leicester to purchase linen at Morley's for the Dower House. Deciding it would be unwise to be seen in town by his wife and mother, Adam postponed his trip. Instead, with it coming up to Lady Day when the rents were collected, he thought he would call with a final warning to a troublesome tenant who drank too heavily and neglected his farm.

It was while Adam, was crossing the stable-yard that Hattie caught up with him. Now that his relationship with Emily was entering a more promising phase, and he'd struggled out of his moribund state, he began to view his behaviour towards Hattie with disgust. For him she'd been nothing but a piece of comely flesh, to use as he pleased. He'd taken no account of her emotions, and in the end guilt had staunched his sexual itch. Although he knew the offer was still there, he'd resisted temptation and hadn't touched her for weeks. In fact, he felt quite proud of his iron will.

'Yes, Hattie?' Adam repeated, wondering

if she was going to proposition him, because she was quite a bold young miss.

Hattie smoothed her apron taut over her belly. 'I've got a surprise for you, Mr Adam.'

'Oh, and what is that?' queried Adam, only half listening.

'Look, can't you see something different about me?' Hattie asked pertly.

Her hands were still pressed down over the apron and Adam noticed, with a stirring of unease, that there was a definite curve to her belly. 'No,' he lied.

'Well, I want to tell you, sir, that I'm going to 'ave a babby. Yourn.'

Adam looked quickly round then pushed her inside the stable door. 'What are you talking about? I haven't been near you for weeks.'

'I'm more than two months gone.'

'Well, it's not mine!'

Hattie's eyes filled with tears. 'Oh, it is, sir and you know it. No man's ever touched me 'cept you, and I'd swear that on the bible.'

Adam's head swam with disbelief, his throat filled with bile and he knew he was going to vomit. *Christ, what was happening?* 'Take something! Get rid of it!' he yelled at her in panic.

'No, I will not!' Hattie's voice was shrill and tearful.

'Hush, girl, do you want everyone to hear?'

'Oh, they'll know soon enough anyway. And wait until I tell them you wanted me to kill your own babby, people won't have such a high opinion of you then, will they, Mr Adam?' When Adam didn't answer, Hattie went on, 'And you should be glad I'm carrying your babby, because, mark my words, there willna be another, not if that wife of yourn has anything to do with it.'

'Stop this babbling nonsense!'

'Oh, it in't nonsense. Madam swallows stuff to make sure she don't have one.'

Adam advanced on Hattie and grabbed her shoulders. 'Stop these lies, I say.' He was hardly rational now and in a state of pent-up fury with the girl for her carelessness in getting pregnant and in tempting him in the first place, he shook her so savagely she cried out.

'They in't lies, it's the truth. The stuffs hidden in the bedroom. I'll show you if you like.'

'You do that.'

'Not until you tell what you're going to do about me and 'im. Your son and heir.' Hattie pointed to her bulge.

Adam slumped against the stable wall and covered his eyes with his hands. This was an absolute nightmare, but he must

345

calm down and admit responsibility. Hattie had been a virgin the first time he took her and she was too fond of him to bother about any other man. 'You had better go away somewhere, a long way from here. I'll pay for you to be looked after, then when the child is born I'll buy you a cottage and see that neither of you ever want for anything. But it is on condition you never set foot in Halby again.'

'And supposin' I refuse? I had plans you know, I wanted to buy a dress shop in Leicester.'

'No, not Leicester!' God, if Emily found out about this it would be the end for him. Adam searched around in his mind. 'Birmingham, that's a big place, I'll set you up in a shop if you go there. But you must leave today.'

'How? Am I supposed to walk? In my state, too. Anyway I in't going to Birmingham all on me own. You must come wi' me. Find me a place to stop.'

She was right, no man with a scrap of decency would send a young woman he'd made pregnant off into the unknown. Adam tugged his hair, almost wanting to pull it out in his frustrated anger. 'All right, we'll go tomorrow if it can be managed, but you are not to breathe a word of this to the other servants, because if you do you will not get a penny. And after all, it

346

is your word against mine, isn't Hattie?'

The girl nodded. 'Yes, Master.'

'Right, tomorrow morning, pack and leave the house before anyone is up. Wait on the corner of Halby Lane, but make sure you keep well out of sight. I'll meet you there later.'

'I won't say nought, Mr Adam, I promise.' But even as she spoke, Hattie's mind was working. He thinks I'm just a big soft country bumpkin. Well, he's got another think comin' and I in't finished wi' im yet.

'Good girl.' With some plans made, Adam grew slightly calmer. If they worked out, nobody need be any the wiser about this unfortunate affair. But he would have to be careful. Hattie's disappearance mustn't attach itself to him in any way. During their meetings, discussions of a personal nature hadn't been high on their list but he seemed to remember that both parents were dead, which removed a large inconvenience.

'Do you want me to show you that stuff now?' Hattie asked.

'Yes, but I'll go first. You follow me.'

Adam was pacing backwards and forwards across the bedroom floor when Hattie slid round the door, but he stopped and watched her as she made straight for

347

the tallboy and pulled out a drawer. He continued to watch as she tipped the contents on the bed and pointed to a small paper package stuck to the back of the drawer. 'That's what I'm talkin' about.'

Adam moved closer and poked the package. It was certainly a clever hiding place, where few people would think to look. 'How did you find out about this, Hattie?'

'Well, I wasn't sneaking around spying, if that's what you're hinting,' the maid answered in an injured tone.

'I wasn't suggesting anything. It was a straightforward question, with no double meanings attached to it.'

'That's all right then. If you want to know, I was sorting through Madam's clothes one day, sewing on buttons and things, like she told me to. When I found it I asked meself, now why should she want to hide that there, and put two and two together.'

'And made five?'

'No, sir, two and two makes four.' Hattie corrected him.

'Are you telling me my wife purges herself each month to stop herself becoming pregnant?'

Hattie shrugged. 'Well, I'm not rightly sure. But she in't never had one 'as she?

348

And why is she hiding it from you, if she's so innocent?'

Why indeed? Adam thought, ripped the package off the drawer and unfolded it. Inside was a white substance. He smelt it, went to dip his finger in it but then changed his mind as it hit him. It was arsenic, he would swear to it! They'd once used it in the house for killing rats. He folded the paper carefully. 'Hattie, put that drawer back, and say nothing of this if your mistress returns. I'm going to visit a chemist in Loughborough.'

With his suspicions confirmed by the chemist, Adam rode home in a reckless fury, cursing his wife savagely and taking it out on the horse by spurring it over hedges, gates and streams. When they arrived at Trent Hall, his coat had a dark line of sweat down the back and the exhausted horse was foaming at the mouth. Adam dismounted, flung the reins at the groom, Jenkins, who said nothing, but gave his master a reproachful look before leading the tired animal away.

The blood in Adam's head was at boiling-point from trying to get his mind round not one, but two, devastating disclosures in one day. Firstly, that Hattie was pregnant, by him and secondly, with all the symptoms of his recurring illnesses pointing to it, clear evidence from the chemist that over recent months, his wife had been slowly poisoning him. *But why should she want to? What motive did she have?* There was little love lost between them, but that was hardly a reason for murdering him, particularly when he was her bread and butter. Well, he would soon deal with her and she'd live to rue the day she ever set eyes on him, let alone tried to kill him.

Propelled up the front steps by his need for revenge, Adam swept past the parcels piled in the hall, evidence of an expensive day's shopping by the two women, and went straight into the office. He sat down, pulled out paper, pen and ink, scratched a note at frantic speed, signed and sealed it, then addressed it to Police Superintendent Sibson, Town Hall, Leicester. He waited until the ink dried, went up to the stables and shouted, 'Jenkins. Where are you?'

When the groom came running, Adam handed him the letter. 'Take this into Leicester and deliver it into the hands of the Police Superintendent, and no one else. It is a very grave matter and he is to come back with you, is that clear?'

'Yes, Mr Adam,' The groom touched his forelock, noticing at the same time that the master's jaw muscles were knotted with tension. He wasn't himself at all and something serious must have happened for it to warrant a visit from the police. Had one of the servants run off with the silver, maybe? Well, he wasn't going to be told, although he'd find out soon enough ...

Adam stood and watched Jenkins drive off, then strode back to the house. With a grim expression he mounted the stairs two at a time and flung open the bedroom door with such force it slammed against the wall and a lump of plaster fell to the floor.

A charming scene met him. Isabelle was standing in front of the cheval glass, while Hattie draped a newly purchased Paisley shawl around her shoulders. But the noise startled them both and Isabelle spun round with her hand pressed against her breast. 'For goodness sake, Adam, you nearly gave me a heart attack.'

'What a pity I didn't,' he snarled. 'It would have solved all your problems, and mine.' Adam advanced on her and his expression was so murderous, Isabelle had the good sense to take a step backwards.

'What's ... wrong?'

'This.' Adam held out his hand. The package lay in his palm. 'Explain yourself.'

'Where d ... did you get that from?'

'From where you so carefully concealed it. I've also been to a chemist in Loughborough, who confirmed that it is arsenic.'

'Yes, but I take it for my blood. I'm anaemic, you know it,' Isabelle blustered.

'In that case, why go to so much trouble to make sure I didn't find it? And why am I so often ill, when I never was before I married you? Anyway, I've sent for Police Superintendent Sibson. He'll get to the bottom of it. Poisoning your husband is a rather serious crime, my dear, so expect to spend the next few years in prison.'

'No!' Isabelle screeched and made a run for the door. But Adam blocked her path.

'You're are not going anywhere, my dear. The only thing that puzzles me is why you should want to kill me?'

'Ask 'er about Sir Austin Beauchamp,' Hattie piped up.

Adam glanced at Hattie. 'Now, why should I do that?'

'Because she fancies 'erself as Lady Beauchamp.'

'Keep your mouth shut!' Isabelle swung round and slapped the maid hard across the face.

But there was no stopping Hattie now. Clasping her stinging cheek, the secrets came pouring out. 'And while your at it, ask 'er about the jewels he gave her. And she didn't get them for nothing, I can tell you. I've got it all wrote down in a book if you don't believe me.'

'Cow! Bitch!' In her fury, Isabelle began pummelling Hattle with her fists, but the girl fought back.

'Stop it,' she screamed, 'you'll harm the babby!'

Isabelle paused. 'The baby? What baby?'

'Hattie, *leave*. This minute!' Adam roared, moving over to part the two women.

Hattie ignored him, adjusted her dress and cap, glanced at the warring pair and decided this was as good a time as any to repay them for the callous way in which they had both treated her in the past. 'Mr Adam's baby,' she smirked.

'It's not true, don't listen to her.'

'Adam, what on earth is going on here? I've never heard such a noise in my life. I thought murder was being done.'

Adam turned slowly. Standing in the open doorway was his mother, Clare, Christopher and an assortment of servants. All of them were staring open-mouthed at the scene before them.

'You couldn't have come at a more opportune moment, mother-in-law. Let me congratulate you, you're going to be a grandmother. But sadly, it's not me,' said Isabelle, when Matilda's expression brightened. 'Your precious son has made this whore, this ... piece of dog dirt, pregnant.' Isabelle gave Hattie a look of

353

disgust. 'Not exactly class, is she?'

'And tell her while you're at it how you've been trying to poison me,' Adam yelled.

Matilda put her hands to her ears. 'I can't believe this,' she wailed, then had the good sense to move into the bedroom and close the door. 'Now, please explain calmly what is going on.'

Adam flung himself down in a chair and covered his face with his hands. His whole world was collapsing about his ears and he wanted to run away from it all and curl up safely in Emily's arms.

'Adam,' Matilda repeated, 'I want an explanation.'

When Adam lifted his face, his blue eyes, so like Harry's, had the sullen, cagey, expression of a small boy who knows he's been naughty and is about to be reprimanded. Matilda also reminded herself that Adam had more than a little of his father's character and Harry had been a philanderer *par excellence*. 'Hattie is going to have my child,' he admitted, then hung his head with shame.

'Are you pregnant by my son, Hattie?' Matilda asked, still nursing a faint hope that she would deny it.

Pleased with her achievement, Hattie grinned and patted her stomach. 'Yes, in here is the heir to Trent Hall, which is more than Madam could manage. All she's ever done is try and bump the master off.'

There was such total unreality about the situation, Matilda hoped she was dreaming. 'Bump him off?' she repeated.

'My dear wife has been trying to poison me with arsenic. It's why I kept having those mysterious illnesses.'

'I told you, the arsenic was for my anaemia.'

Matilda glanced at her daughter-in-law, of whom she'd always been extremely fond. 'But what possible reason could Isabelle have for wanting to murder you?'

'She's been making a fool of me with that chap, Beauchamp. She obviously fancies herself with a title. Anyway, we'll have to wait for the police to prove it.' Adam stood up and took the key from the door. 'Come on Mother, Hattie. No, you are not going anywhere.' Isabelle darted forward but Adam pushed her back, ushered the maid and his mother from the room, turned the key in the lock and placed it in his pocket.

'Can we discuss this please, Adam?'' said Matilda, once they were back downstairs. She felt sure that if she could sit down somewhere quiet with her son and discuss the situation in a rational manner, she could unravel the whole sorry mess.

But Adam turned on her angrily. 'No. If Emily and I had been allowed to marry, none of this would have happened,' he accused, then strode off to the office.

She followed after him, calling through the door, 'Adam be reasonable, please,' but he refused to answer and when she tried the handle she found he had locked himself in. Matilda gave up and with a weary sigh turned to her next problem, the maidservant. 'Hattie, go to your room, and don't speak to anyone about this until the police come. As to the other business, y ... your pregnancy, you have my word you will be supported throughout.'

Hattie curtsied. 'Thank you, Ma'am. I won't say a word, I promise.'

But Matilda knew that by morning, the whole sordid business would have ripped through the village like a forest fire, spread out into the County until it finally reached Leicester. Trying to stop it was as useless as Canute attempting to turn the tide back. The gossip would roll on remorselessly, swelling with rumour and innuendo on its journey.

Sitting alone in the twilight listening to the house echo with whispers, Matilda rubbed her forehead wearily and railed at the fates for giving her no warning. How could a day which had started so normally, end so disastrously? she asked herself. As for Isabelle poisoning her son, it sounded absolutely ludicrous. And this business with the maid. How could Adam behave like a common farm labourer?

It was a nightmare situation and she was desperate for someone to confide in, but just when she needed him most, Harry was in London and likely to remain there for a week or more. And she could hardly believe the way Adam had turned on her. She hadn't prevented his marriage to Emily, just not encouraged it, and he'd certainly married Isabelle of his own free will.

Matilda was aware of someone bringing her tea but she left it untasted. The clock ticked and chimed a few more hours of her life away, then at about nine, she saw carriage lights.

As the gig pulled up outside, Matilda went to the office and banged on the door. 'Adam, the police are here,' she called, then opened the door to the gentleman walking up the front steps. Matilda had met Police Superintendent Sibson socially on a number of occasions, so he greeted her in a friendly manner. 'How are you, Mrs Bennett?'

'Not at my best at the moment.'

'That is understandable, for your son is making some grave accusations.'

'Come into the drawing room, Adam is there and since he sent for you, he'd better do the explaining.'

Adam was standing in the middle of the room looking deeply unhappy and at the same time, vulnerable. His hair and clothes were rumpled, his eyes bloodshot as if he'd been weeping, and Matilda had a tremendous urge to sweep him up in her arms and kiss away the raw pain in his eyes.

The policeman introduced himself then, getting down to business without delay, he drew out a notebook and pencil and reading from Adam's letter, said, 'You claim your wife has been trying to poison you, Mr Bennett?'

'That's right, with arsenic.'

'What evidence do you have?'

Adam handed the small package to the policeman. 'She had this hidden in her room. I've also suffered from bouts of illness over the past months that really laid me low, as my mother will verify. When I found the package my suspicions were aroused so I took it to a chemist, who confirmed it was arsenic. He also told me, when I described the symptoms of my illness that, in his opinion, I was suffering from arsenic poisoning.'

The policeman, who had been writing steadily, looked up. 'Is there any reason why your wife would want to commit such a dastardly crime, Mr Bennett?'

'I discovered from her personal maid today that's she's been carrying on with Sir Austin Beauchamp. I think she fancies herself as a "lady", although she'll never be that,' Adam finished bitterly.

'Am I to infer from your comments that you and Mrs Bennett do not have a close relationship?'

Adam stared at the carpet. 'Yes.'

'You know this might be hard to prove. Your wife has grains of arsenic in her room, but what are we to deduce from that? As you know, young women use it for various reasons; their complexions, anaemia. Where is Mrs Bennett?'

'Locked in the bedroom.'

'I'd like to speak with her, if you wouldn't mind, so that I can get her version of events.' The superintendent stood up. 'So, if you'd take me to her, Mr Bennett, it would be very helpful.'

'Yes, of course. Follow me.' Adam led the way with the policeman a step behind, but Matilda remained at the bottom of the stairs. She knew she'd find it impossible to behave civilly towards a woman she had welcomed into her house, but who, all this time, had been cuckolding her son and possibly trying to murder him. How could she have so completely misjudged a person? It was an uncomfortable truth to accept, but she knew it was because Isabelle had spared her having Emily as a daughter-in-law. For that reason alone, she'd been prepared to overlook certain less attractive aspects of her character. But a murderess in their midst ...? Matilda shuddered.

In a moment there would be counter-accusations from Isabelle and Mr Sibson would uncover a few more family skeletons. Certainly, the fact that Adam had made one of the maids pregnant, was going to introduce a whole new perspective to an already tangled plot. But what if Isabelle was accused and put on trial? A lot of dirty linen would be washed in public, which would then be reported in all the papers, perhaps even the London ones. Matilda felt sick. Oh, God, how was she going to face the humiliation of it? The curious glances, tongues wagging behind fans and cruel laughter.

'She's gone!' Adam's voice broke into Matilda's morbid thoughts and she tore up the stairs.

The two men were standing in the middle of the room, Adam was staring at the wide-open window and the knotted sheets that disappeared out of it, while the superintendent scribbled busily.

Adam turned as Matilda entered. 'The

bird has flown,' he said grimly.

'So it seems.' Matilda gazed about her at the hastily emptied drawers, then walked over to the window and peered out. 'Did Isabelle really climb down all that way?'

'It would appear so, Mrs Bennett,' said Superintendent Sibson.

Matilda felt strangely relieved and hoped Isabelle had got well away. That way, they'd be spared the upheaval of a trial and of having their lives subjected to public scrutiny.

'If you need proof of my wife's guilt, this is it, wouldn't you say, Superintendent?' Adam queried. 'If she was innocent, surely she'd want to stay and prove it.'

'Mr Bennett,' the policeman replied rather censoriously, 'in English law, *everyone* is innocent until proven guilty.'

Chapter Twenty-Six

It was a typical spring day of showers and sunshine with a wind that buffeted the heads of daffodils and shook the blossom off the trees. Watching Emily approach, Clare thought how pretty she looked. Her wind-whipped cheeks were rosy, her eyes were bright and full of optimism, and her hair fell in becoming spirals about her face. *And I'm about to wipe that joy from her eyes*, Clare thought, and was sorely tempted to turn and run. But she knew she couldn't. Hattie's pregnancy was already the talk of the village and since there was no way of silencing the gossiping tongues, she had the baleful task of telling Emily before she heard the scandal from a stranger's lips.

Although only cousins, because she and Adam had been brought up together, they were more like brother and sister. But his years in America had weakened those close ties and the easy familiarity had gone. And of course, she had Christopher now, who was the most important person in her life. She had never quite forgiven Adam, either, for the heartless way in which he'd abandoned Emily to marry Isabelle. This affair with Hattie Bonner was beyond her comprehension, though, and the final straw. Their friendship could not survive this. But what had possessed him, and with a *maidservant?* Well, sex, she supposed.

Clare had guessed, by the regular trips Adam made into Leicester, and the abundance of food he took with him, that he had been trying to work his way back into favour with Emily again, and once the whole distasteful business had come to light, she'd begged Adam to

362

do the honest thing and tell Emily. But he'd just rolled himself up into a ball and sobbed that he couldn't, and it had been left to her to do his dirty work.

By now, Emily had seen her and she waved and quickened her steps. 'Are you waiting for me?' she asked, once they had embraced.

'Yes, I need to talk to you, dearest, on a matter of some importance.'

'But why here and not the shop?'

'I thought it would be better if we were alone. I'll walk with you to the centre.'

'You do make it sound serious,' Emily smiled.

Trying to prepare her, Clare didn't return her smile. 'It is, extremely serious. Look, shall we sit down for a minute?' she suggested, noticing a low wall.

'Why not? I've got half an hour to spare.'

Clare took Emily's hand, thinking to herself, *This is one of the worst things I'll ever be asked to do,* for no matter how carefully she chose them, there were no words that could spare Emily pain. Knowing she was prolonging the agony, she took a deep breath and said gravely, 'Emily, you are not going to like what I have to tell you, so I want you to prepare yourself and try to be strong.'

'It's about Adam, isn't it?'

'Yes.'

Emily clutched Clare's arm. 'Is he ill? Dying?'

'No, he's not dying, just very sick in his mind, at least that's the only excuse I can make for his behaviour. I'd give anything not to be the bearer of this news, but since I am I won't beat about the bush. There have been the most frightful goings-on in Halby. Terrible scandals.'

'What about?'

'First, Isabelle has disappeared, after Adam accused her of trying to poison him.'

'Accused her of *poisoning* him? That's a bit extreme, isn't it?'

'But that's not the worst of it. I'm afraid one of the maids at Trent Hall, Hattie Bonner, is pregnant.'

'So?' Emily queried sharply.

'Adam is the father.'

Emily stared at Clare with bleak, haunted eyes. 'No! Tell me it's not true.'

'I wish I could, but I'm afraid it is,' Clare said gently. 'Adam has admitted responsibility.'

Emily's head drooped on her slim neck like a broken flower. 'How could he do this to me?' she wailed, repeating the cry of so many women down the ages.

Clare put an arm round her shoulders and pulled her close. 'We've all asked the same question. Cry, let it all come out, you'll feel better then, my dear.'

'No! I will not waste my tears on a liar and cheat.' Emily pulled away, gripping the wall so fiercely her knuckles grazed against the hard stone. 'I've done with him.' And in her bitter denial of Adam, Emily wondered if she'd ever known his true character. How otherwise, could someone who professed to love her be so cruel as to woo her with honeyed words then go straight home to lie with a serving girl? It was a deliberate humiliation, but also his final betrayal. She'd purged her system of him and it was curiously liberating. There would be no more dithering and the direction of her life was now quite clear to her. She stood up. 'Clare, I must be going.'

'I think I should come with you,' answered Clare. She was amazed at Emily's self-control, but also worried that it was a front which would suddenly collapse.

'It isn't necessary, I'm fine, truly. And thank you for coming to tell me, it couldn't have been easy.' Emily tried a bright smile and it worked quite well. 'By the way, you and Christopher will be getting a wedding invitation soon. Rory has asked me to marry him, and I have accepted.'

Eaten up with self-pity, Adam spent his days in unproductive isolation, either riding aimlessly around the countryside or in the office with the door locked. He refused to communicate with anyone or deal with estate matters, which meant Matilda was forced to take up the reins again, even though she was bone weary.

The scandal reached Harry's ears even before he arrived in Leicester, and he'd rushed at once to Matilda's side. He'd imagined much of what he heard was an exaggeration, put around by rumour-mongers, but when he was given the true picture by Matilda it was even more dreadful than the gossip. He knew, too, that Matilda would be expecting him to take control of the situation, so when he asked, 'Do you want me to try and find Isabelle? A word in the right place might help,' he was surprised by her answer.

'No, leave it. She's gone and I'm glad of it. She was a minx.'

'But if she was poisoning Adam, she shouldn't be allowed to get off scot-free. It's the attempted murder of our son. He might have died, Matilda. If I ever got my hands on her ...'

'We have no proof beyond the arsenic, and she could have purchased it for her own use, as the superintendent pointed out. He seemed to think the case against her was slight.'

'Why did she run away then?'

'That's Adam's argument, and he's my main worry now. His mind is in such a fragile state, I fear for his sanity. But the worst thing is, I don't know how to help. He's legally tied to Isabelle, so he can never re-marry, which means there will be no grandchildren, and I hoped so much that this house would be full of them by now. Happy little feet running around.'

'There is Hattie Bonner's child,' Harry pointed out.

Matilda straightened in her chair. 'Don't talk to me about her! Or that bastard! She's already boasting that it's the heir to Trent Hall. The nerve of the girl.'

'Well, if that bastard is your only grandchild, it might well be. And let's be realistic about this, Matilda, half the blame for the situation lies at Adam's door, and that is something you will have to accept, no matter how difficult you find it.'

'Hattie has been provided with a cottage and the child will not go without, but neither will it get its hands on a groat of this estate. I'd rather give it to charity.'

'If Adam had been allowed to marry Emily, none of this would have happened.'

'That has already been pointed out to me, so don't rub it in, Harry. And they didn't, so there's an end to it. Anyway, the Fairfax girl is getting married tomorrow, which is another problem out of the way.'

Harry had never understood Matilda's hostility to Emily. There was the stupid, pointless feud between the families, of course, but she was a lovely girl—like her mother—and Harry remembered, with a whiff of nostalgia, that first time he'd set eyes on the delectable Rachel. 'Does Adam know about the marriage?' he asked.

'Certainly not, and don't mention it, please. I've got enough to cope with and I don't want to see him even more unhappy. I only know because Clare and Christopher have had an invitation, but Clare's hardly on speaking terms with Adam, so she won't let the cat out of the bag.'

'I won't say a word, either, I promise.'

'I hear she's moving to London directly after the wedding with her husband, a Rory Aherne. Do you know anything about him?'

'I certainly do. He's quite notorious in his way; Irish and a bit of rabble-rouser. He's deeply involved in the Chartist movement as well, and spent several months in jail.'

'More her type, wouldn't you agree, than our son? And keeping up the tradition of that family. Now, Adam's in the office, so can you please go and bang on the door and try to talk some sense into him, while I see Cook about luncheon?'

In spite of a deal of pleading by Harry, Adam refused to come into luncheon, and a short while later they saw him gallop off down the drive. After this Matilda pushed the food around on her plate and looked so miserable, Harry offered to go after him. 'Not that I can promise that he will come back with me,' he said at the door.

After Harry had gone, Matilda tried to settle down with a book. But she found it impossible to concentrate, so she took up a piece of embroidery instead. With each stitch, Matilda repeated to herself, *This nightmare will pass, Adam will return to his old self and life will get back to normal.* But she wasn't sleeping well, and gradually her fingers faltered, the posy of flowers she was stitching grew dim and her embroidery fell to her lap. She woke with a start to find the footman standing over her.

'Madam, there's a gentleman come to see Mr Adam,' he informed her, and held out a silver salver on which there lay a calling-card.

Matilda reached for the card, read out loud, 'Edgar P Randall, Exporter, New Orleans, Louisiana,' and sat up straight. 'Are you saying Mr Randall is here, in this house?'

'Yes, Madam, the gentleman's waiting in the hall.'

'Are you sure it's Mr Adam he's come to see and not his wife?'

'No, he was most definite. Mr Adam Bennett.'

How strange. But since Isabelle wasn't here, perhaps it was just as well. Explanations could prove awkward, Matilda reflected, patting her hair and laying her sewing aside. 'Show Mr Randall in please, Stokes, then bring us tea.'

The gentleman Matilda rose to meet was short, rotund, high-complexioned and several diamond rings flashed on his fingers. Money without taste, she judged, as he crossed the room with small fussy steps. 'How do you do, Mrs Bennett, and I must apologise for surprising you like this.' He spoke with the same deep-south inflections as Isabelle.

'Not at all, Mr Randall, do sit down. My son isn't here at present, but perhaps I can help. It must be a matter of some importance to bring you all the way from America to our small village.'

'It is indeed. And I suffered a great deal of sea-sickness to get here,' he complained.

'What a pity my daughter-in-law is away visiting. I'm sure she would have loved to have met you, coming as you do from the same part of America. Quite a coincidence, that.'

'Not too much of a coincidence.'

'You know her then?'

'I know Isabelle intimately; you see, she's my wife.'

Matilda rose from her chair and sat down again. 'Y ... your *wife?*' Wondering if her poor battered heart could take any more shocks, she closed her eyes.

'Are you all right, Mrs Bennett?' Mr Randall leaned over her, fanning her with a silk handkerchief that smelt strongly of eau-de-cologne.

Matilda opened her eyes. 'Well, I must admit to being somewhat startled by your news, since I thought Isabelle was married to my son.'

'I'm sorry, my dear lady, I should have broken it to you more gently.'

Through the window Matilda saw, with intense relief, Adam and Harry walking up the front steps together. 'Look, here is my son. I think if this matter is to be cleared up, you should speak to him,' she said and rushed to the door. 'Adam, Harry, could you both come in here, please? This is Mr Randall. He's come from America with some perplexing news. Now, will you repeat to my son what you have just told me?' Matilda requested.

Edgar Randall twisted a diamond ring around his finger, then cleared his throat apologetically. 'I'm afraid you might be rather upset by the information I have to impart, but you see, Isabelle is my lawful wife, not yours, and I have a marriage certificate to prove it.'

'Isabelle, your wife?' Adam's face was totally devoid of emotion. Only his flickering eyelids revealed his shock.

'Yes, it came to my ears that a Mr Clifford Bones was making enquiries about her on your behalf and I got in touch with him. I'd been searching for her myself and when I discovered she'd entered into a bigamous marriage with you, I was determined to expose her for the scheming little hussy that she is. You see, I took her out of a whorehouse—'

'Whorehouse?' gasped Matilda, 'But she told us her father had owned a plantation.'

'Her father was a dancing master, Mother, but continue, Mr Randall.'

'I married her, set her up in a fine establishment and she repaid me by running off.'

'Well, she's run off again, after trying to poison me.'

'Poison you? That's a bit extreme, even for Isabelle.'

'You might think so, but I don't. Anyway, if you can find her, you are most welcome to her, Mr Randall.'

'Thank you.'

Adam began to pace the room. 'But she should be made to pay for this, or there's no telling how many more men she might hoodwink.'

'You have a point there.'

'And bigamy is something we *can* prove and which she could go to prison for.'

'You have still got to find her, Adam,' said Harry, 'and it's easy to disappear. Being the sort of woman she is, my guess is that Isabelle would head for the bright lights, London or perhaps Paris. She speaks French well and it would be the ideal place for her to sell her wares.'

'In that case, while I'm in Europe I might as well avail myself of its pleasures,' said Mr Randall. 'So, I shall go to London first, look for her there and if I have no success, continue to Paris.'

'What will you do if you find her, Mr Randall?' asked Adam.

'I'm not sure. But she is my wife and I would be prepared to give her another chance.' Edgar Randall drew a watch from his waistcoat pocket. 'Well, it's time for me to be on my way. I want to catch the first train out of Leicester in the morning.'

'Will you keep me informed of any developments?' said Adam as the gentleman shook hands all round.

'I will indeed. And call me a silly old man if you like, but in spite of everything Isabelle's done, I'm afraid I still love her.'

Chapter Twenty-Seven

As soon as Mr Randall left, Adam went to bed and sank into a deep, dreamless sleep. He woke early the following morning and lay watching the patch between the curtains grow lighter, and listening to the triumphant swell of the dawn chorus. For months he'd been submerged under a great weight of misery, then suddenly a man he didn't know existed, arrived at the house with a bizarre story, and turned his life around. His problems weren't over, of course, but just to be rid of a hated wife was an alpha-plus in his book.

'I'm a free man, a bachelor,' Adam said out loud, testing the sweet words on his tongue. This was the first day of a new future and he could even risk feeling optimistic. But he had to settle with Emily first. He would grasp the nettle firmly and go and see her today, explain about Isabelle, and plead for her understanding over his lapse with Hattie. She would be tolerant he knew, because it was a woman's nature to forgive. Energised, Adam threw back the bedclothes and leapt out of bed. He washed, shaved and dressed, and bounded down the stairs whistling.

'Good morning, Mother.' Adam planted a kiss on the top of Matilda's head then went over to the sideboard and piled his plate high with bacon, eggs and mushrooms which, Matilda was delighted to see, he ate with gusto.

'Did you sleep well, Mother?' Adam asked, after he'd downed his second cup of coffee.

'Yes, for the first time in weeks, after I'd recovered from the shock. It's like having a death sentence repealed knowing that we need no longer concern ourselves with that ghastly woman. I dreaded a trial. I've been doing a bit of thinking as well. Presumably, this business makes your marriage to her void, as if it had never happened?'

'I imagine so, but I shall consult a lawyer. I need to know exactly what my position is legally, because I certainly don't want to find I'm responsible for her debts.'

'Do it as soon as possible. Once you've got your personal affairs sorted out, you can get on with your life. Poor Mr Randall, I do feel sorry for him, loving Isabelle. Do you think he'll ever find her?'

'I doubt it, she's too wily. I can't imagine what her paramour, Sir Austin, will make of it. He was really duped. By all accounts he gave her a diamond necklace, a family heirloom, which she has trotted off with. She'll sell it and live off the proceeds for a while, then her wits again I suppose, when the money runs out. And poor old Olivia's going to be hurt. My God, what a trail of destruction that woman has left in her wake.'

'And to think she gave herself such airs, when she was nothing but a common prostitute.' Matilda shuddered. 'Did you know she'd worked in a brothel?'

'Really, Mother!' Adam reproved.

Matilda shrugged. 'Just asking.'

'No, I was fooled like everyone else by Isabelle. Perhaps it's a trifle naïve, but I always assume people are telling me the truth. She gave me some cock-and-bull story about running away from an employer who was molesting her, and I married her because she was going to have a child, although whether it was mine or not I shall never know. Anyway, I expect she took one of her potions because she lost it coming over on the boat. It was when certain stories began not to add up that I started to become suspicious and employed Clifford Bones to investigate her. It was the best money I've ever spent.'

'Well, you're done with her now. And you'll be able to marry properly, a nice English girl from a sound family, whose background we know and who doesn't nurse any dark secrets.'

'Please, Mother, give me breathing space. Besides I'm not that good a prospect, and there is Hattie.'

'Hattie was your wild oats. A sensible girl will look at your fortune, not your mistresses. Men are allowed a few mistakes, unlike women. The Dower House is nearing completion, I'll be moving into it soon and you can't live here on your own.'

'You did.'

'I had you. Anyway, I've decided to have a party. We need to celebrate. Perhaps a mid-summer one. I'll let the dust settle a bit then send out invitations. What do you think?'

'Do as you wish, as long as you don't try and pair me off.' Adam finished his coffee and stood up. 'Well, there's no point in delaying it so I think I'll pop over to Loughborough and consult that lawyer.'

'What time will you be back?'

'Expect me when you see me,' Adam called, already on his way to order Jenkins to harness the prettiest horse, a bay mare, to the smartest gig. This done, he returned to his room. Humming to himself, Adam changed into light trousers, a double-breasted high-buttoned coat in dark blue wool, a black cravat and matching silk hat. He stood back to study himself. Although he'd grown thinner of late, Adam was aware of his good looks, the blue eyes and dark lashes that so many women found irresistible, his height. But only one woman's good opinion mattered and that was Emily's, and his mother could forget about her matchmaking.

Adam tapped on his hat, wished his reflection good luck and set off. Driving through the village he saw, with a tug of guilt, Hattie. She waved to him, but he ignored her and since she was heavier now and couldn't move fast, he flicked the mare across the rump and she picked up her polished hooves. In a few months the child would be born, grow, play on the Green and be a constant rebuke to him. He'd made so many mistakes, a whole chain, linked inexorably but today, finally, he was going to make recompense.

He would be absolutely truthful to Emily, make a plea for her understanding, then ask her to marry him. There was no impediment to their marriage now; they were both free, both over twenty-one and not a soul could do anything to prevent it.

Yesterday, the world had been mono-tone, today it was a licentious green. In fact, it dazzled and amazed him with its fecundity. The horse chestnut trees with their thrusting phallic blossoms, noisily copulating sparrows; everywhere Adam looked nature seemed to be burgeoning, reproducing, throwing down seeds carelessly.

When Adam reached the main road, instead of turning north to Loughborough, he headed south for Leicester. Leaving the gig at the Three Crowns he walked up through Horsefair Street into Friar Lane, where he called in on a lawyer and told him of his strange situation. The lawyer explained matters to his satisfaction and Adam left with an even lighter heart, making a leisurely detour round by Bath Lane to All Saints' Open. However, when Adam reached the hall he was disconcerted to discover it was closed, for he'd bargained on Emily being there. Neither was there the usual line of beggars. Trade had picked up with the return of the good weather, and there were less unemployed, but he'd heard nothing about the place closing down.

Without much hope, Adam hammered on the door, and called, 'Anyone in?'

'You won't find anyone there today, Mister, they're all over at the church for the wedding. Quite a big do it is,' commented a passer-by.

'What wedding?' Adam asked, but the man sped on round the corner and he found he was talking to himself. A stirring of unease in his gut propelled Adam into

High Cross Street, where he stopped and gaped at the sight that met his eyes. The normal dusty, dun-coloured thoroughfare had burst into life. Women, fluttering like brilliantly-hued butterflies, called and waved to friends. Men, stiff in their best clothes, greeted each other more formally as they all filed into the church. Then, his chest tightening with dread, further down the road he saw Emily, slim and pretty, walking arm in arm with her father. She was wearing a love-in-the mist blue dress, and on her head, a garland of blue and and white flowers which were repeated in the small posy she carried. Worse, she looked radiant, as a bride who is marrying the man she loves, should.

Suddenly, Adam's cravat was choking him and he tore at it compulsively. No, she couldn't marry someone else, not Emily. She was *his*.

Father and daughter paused at the door of the church, Jed patted her hand and gave her a quick kiss, then they moved inside. Adam slipped in behind them and saw, with a stricken heart, Rory Aherne turn and smile as Emily glided up the aisle towards him.

He must stop this!

But the white surpliced priest had already begun. 'Dearly beloved, we are gathered together here in the sight of God and in the face of this congregation, to join together this man and this woman in holy Matri—'

Half mad with love, Adam shot out into the aisle. 'No!' he shouted, and the whole congregation turned in mute astonishment as Adam, both hands extended, walked slowly towards the bride. 'Emily, you can't marry him, not when it's me you love. And I'm free now, and it's not too late, so come away with me while you still have the chance,' he pleaded.

Emily stared with an uncertain expression, first at Adam then Rory and went as if to move away. But Rory clutched her hand, pulling her back. 'No, don't Emily,' he said quietly. 'He's always let you down, now he's trying to ruin our life. Don't allow it.'

Adam continued to move forward but suddenly Jed stepped out, arms spread and barring his way. 'Go, before you put a further curse on the family, Bennett,' he thundered, pointing to the door.

At the harsh authority in Jed's voice Adam's head jerked up. 'You're to blame, not me,' he accused. 'I love Emily. I *love* Emily,' he chanted relentlessly, swinging round and round in a mad spiral.

There was a movement in the silent watchful crowd, a quiet, 'Excuse me,' as Clare pushed her way along the pews.

Moving to her cousin's side, she said in a firm voice, 'I think it's time to go, Adam,' and led him from the church.

He went obediently, head down, defeated; his feet shuffling like an old man's. There was a clatter of metal as the heavy door swung open, a strip of sunshine shone briefly on the stone floor, then it closed again with a thud.

The priest held up his hand. 'Shall we continue?' But no one was listening. Struggling to quieten the buzzing congregation and bring the day back to some sort of normality, he smiled encouragingly at the bride and groom. 'Are you ready to take your vows?'

Emily put her hand to her head. 'I don't know.'

'She's had a shock, I think she needs to sit down,' Rory said, and led her to the front pew.

Rachel, stunned by it all, came and sat by her daughter. She said nothing, offered no advice, just held Emily's hand. But her mind drifted back to the start of it all and she felt more than a passing sympathy for Adam. He was reckless, of course he was, but out of love, and if any two people were made for each other, it was Emily and Adam. But a cruel fate continued to deny them their rightful love.

Aware of Emily tugging away from her

382

and standing up, Rachel watched her with concern. The smile she gave Rory was a bit tremulous but she appeared to be bearing up well.

'I'm ready,' she said.

'Are you sure?' Rory asked quietly. 'If you have any doubts ...'

She reached up and kissed her husband-to-be. 'I have no doubts. Not one.'

'Good.' They moved to the altar together, the priest found his place in the Solemnisation of Matrimony and started again. Emily made her responses without a tremor of doubt.

Outside, Adam lifted his ravaged face to Clare. 'I've lost her finally, haven't I?'

Too overcome with pity to speak, Clare nodded.

'I thought so,' Adam answered then, his heart scoured with sorrow, his head fell onto his chest and he wept, while inside the church, Emily's voice rang out firm and clear:

'I WILL.'

This Large Print Book for the Partially sighted, who cannot read normal print, is published under the auspices of

THE ULVERSCROFT FOUNDATION

1.